If you don't have any triggers, skip this page to prevent spoilers.

If you do have triggers, read the list below. Although I make every attempt to list them all, I make no guarantees as what may be triggering for one person is not for another. Listed below are the obvious.

Warning

This book contains the following topics and mentions that may be triggering:

Difficult childbirth resulting in loss of mother and/or infant.
Murder
Seizure disorder
Suicide
Domestic violence
References to death and dying.
Child neglect/abuse
Natural disasters (all)
Bullying
Kidnapping
Animal sacrifice (Rat)
Cult
Child cancer
Miscarriage
Rioting
Mass shooting
Infertility

Libitina
by
M. A. Savino

Cover art
by
Frina Art
&
Internal images
by
Etheric Tales

Can you see me?
I'm right here, waiting for you to notice me. I'm the glimpse of something in the corner of your eye. The presence you feel when goosebumps plaster your skin. I raise your fine hairs like frigid winter air, chilling your bones.

I am death, and I am tired of waiting…
I bet you think I am a man, but you are mistaken. I am what you make me. I am your fear, pain, hatred, and regrets, all twisted into a creature of your own design.
No one has ever seen me.
No one until now…

Chapter One
When I Come for Her

Newborns are easy. They come into this world with nothing. No memories, no shame, nothing to lose, no regrets. It's the only time I am a blank slate. I can't sense anything from them, but the waiting is daunting.

The birth canal of this mother is not cooperating. I hover over her as the doctor makes an incision across her lower abdomen and rips open her body. The unresponsive, blue baby girl dangles before the doctor's eyes.

I grasp her tiny hand as a nurse clears her airway, trying to get her to breathe. The little ones always fade away with me when I come for them.

Not this time.

She pops open her eyes, and peers past the doctor. As her face changes from ashen blue to peach, the infant smiles at me. Not a reflex as some would say. It catches me off guard, and I let go. She saw me. No, it's not possible. No one can.

The infant belts out a scream unlike any other. Not from pain, not from fear, but from anger. My presence angered her. As though to say, 'How dare you try and take me in the hour of my birth?' The noise pierces through my frame, deafening me with its sound.

I've been doing this for centuries and nothing has changed until this moment. In cases like this, I take the child every time when the choice is either the mother or the baby. They're easier. But this one is special. For this one, I'll make an exception, something I have never done before. But there is a price.

I take her mother's arm and pull her into the void above her bed. The doctors work fast, but it's too late. The mother is mine now. Blood drips onto the floor creating a small puddle, as a nurse hangs another bag of 'O' negative.

Her husband pleads into her ear. "Please don't leave me. Come back to me."

No amount of experience or expertise can save her. Monitors fall silent as the doctor calls her time of death. A nurse swaddles the little one and extends her to her father. He places his palm against the baby's blanket and pushes her back. "I don't want to see her right now."

"Sir, it isn't her fault. These things happen. You are her father, and she needs you."

"And I need my wife," he scoffs as he exits the room.

The mother gazes at me with solemn eyes and disappears through the wall. My job is to remove their souls from their bodies. Where they go after isn't up to me. She may choose to stay and haunt him, or she may go with her loved ones taken before her.

I float down the hall toward a room where a woman with chest pains moans. The nursery bells chime over the intercom announcing to the entire hospital a new baby has joined this world. What should be a joyous occasion has turned tragic.

When I gravitate to the older woman's bed, her eyes flutter open, but she doesn't turn her head.

"I know you're there," she says to the empty room. "I am ready. Take me home."

It doesn't work that way, but she doesn't know. Her death will come as she sleeps, silent and peaceful. A young woman enters the room, passes through me, and sits in a black leather chair.

"Brrrr…Mom, are you cold?"

"No." She turns and pulls on her daughter's sleeve. "I'm going to be with the Lord, Jeanie. It's time. The angels have come for me. They are in the room right now," she whispers.

"Mom, stop talking like that. Everything is fine. You're coming home with me tomorrow, remember?"

"No, dear. I'm not."

Jeanie taps her mother's knee and turns her attention to the television. A storm is rolling in this evening, bringing dangerous lightning and a severe weather threat. I love these storms. They keep me busy.

Infant shrieks echo through the hallway and grow with every second that passes.

It's her.

The wailing takes me to the nursery. The staff is bathing her, and she hates it. The sound boils my insides, and I need to make it stop. The light above them flickers as I dive inside the fixture. They look up but continue washing her while she hollers. The bulb bursts, darkening the room, and the nurses stare at each other. The baby stops crying. They dry her dark brown head full of hair, slip on a diaper, and swaddle her in a warm blanket.

"Has her father come back?" the head nurse asks as she looks up at the broken light and shuffles out of the room.

"No. I don't think so," the other nurse murmurs. She carries the baby out of the washroom and sets her under a Bili light.

"If he doesn't return by morning, we'll have to call Child Services."

"She's a beautiful baby," the head nurse says, running her fingers through the infant's fine locks.

"Yes, she is." The nurse's eyes water. "I would take her if the hospital would let me."

"You'll make a great mom someday."

They leave the infant as she falls asleep, and I glide to her side. What is her story? Why does she cause me pain?

A tall young nurse strolls in and rolls the baby away.

I follow.

She steers her into a private room where her father awaits her arrival. Tears stream down his face as he bites his thumbnail with his front teeth. He paces from one side of the room to the other as the nurse lifts the baby from her bassinet. She raises her brow, and he stops walking. His arms tremble as the nurse transfers the baby to him. The father clears the liquid from his bloodshot eyes with the back of his hand. He folds back the blanket covering part of his baby's face.

The nurse steps out, giving them some privacy. A mistake she'll never realize as the man presses the fabric over his daughter's mouth and nose.

A painting of white roses, a framed canvas, dislodges from the wall, tumbles onto the tile, and lands by his feet. He stops and uncovers her face. She takes a deep breath.

The nurse returns and grabs the art by its corner.

"What happened here?"

"The painting fell," he says, wiping his cheek and pointing to the wall. "My wife loved white roses."

"Perhaps it's a sign." The nurse smiles as she hangs it back up on its nail. "Have you named her yet?"

"I haven't thought about it."

"Well, you have until tomorrow when we discharge her."

"Tomorrow? I'm not ready. I don't have a clue what I am doing."

"There are resources and case workers who can help you. Right now, everything is hard, but it does get easier." She grins as she places her hand on his and squeezes. "The main things to remember are to feed her, change her diaper, and keep her safe."

"I don't want to do this by myself."

"Do you have any family who can come help you?"

"No one lives close."

Unsaid words hang in the air, but the father stays silent. A pit develops in the nurse's gut.

He's not ready. She thinks to herself.

"We have people here who can teach you how to do diaper changes, burp her after you feed her, and help you create a schedule. Her sleep will most likely be a mess at first; awake at night and asleep during the day. But there are ways to make slow and steady adjustments to make her schedule come closer to yours. We have people who will make home visits if you're interested. I can call them."

"No. It's not necessary. My house is in the woods and would be too hard for anyone to get to. If someone can show me the basics today that will be fine."

"Suit yourself. I will give you the person's card with her discharge information."

"Okay."

The nurse leaves a bottle on a wooden stand by a rocking chair. "If she wakes up, you can give this to her."

"Wait. You're leaving?"

"I'm calling the caseworker to come and meet you. He will talk you through the process and give you some pamphlets with all the instructions you'll need."

"But what if she poops or something?"

"Inside this table are diapers and wipes. The tabs go under her back, and make sure you wipe front to back," she says as she slides the drawer open.

"I don't think I can do this."

"Believe it or not, I have seen many fathers come through here, some with significant others and some without. I have never seen anyone who doesn't figure things out. Some are better parents than the child's mother could ever be. Things may be difficult at first, but we are here to help you if you have questions or need someone to talk to. Everything will be fine. I promise."

The nurse scurries out of the room, leaving him alone with her once more. He glares down at his baby girl as though she is an abomination.

"Murderer."

The words of hate flow so easily from him. As though they have always been there, waiting for the opportunity to use them.

"You killed my wife. We are supposed to be doing this together, and you killed her," he says as he plops her back into the bassinet and begins pacing once more. He pauses, curls his fingers around the rim of her bed, and shakes it. The infant stirs and starts to fuss. It's quiet, and less painful at first, but as the speed and intensity of the rocking increase, the baby begins to scream.

I take the wings of a crow outside and steer it into the hospital window, cracking the glass. The loud thump redirects the father away from the child and brings the nurse back.

"What the hell just happened?"

"A bird flew into the window," the father says over his shoulder as he stares at the black and bloodied body on the roof.

The nurse slides the curtain aside and touches the textured glass with her pointer finger. "Great. I'll have to tape this," she huffs as she hoists the baby into her arms and puts the bottle to her fussing lips. "When she cries, nudge her bottom lip like this. It tells her where the nipple is, and she'll open her mouth. See?"

The crying has stopped, and the discomfort has ceased. I need to escape from this place and away from this child who shreds my insides like a blender, but I'm intrigued.

The father still stands at the window as fierce clouds burst outside. The rain bangs on the rooftop bouncing droplets of water back upward. A deafening crack of thunder startles the child who begins crying once more. The nurse places her over her shoulder and pats her back.

"Libitina," the father says as his gaze follows a lightning bolt from the heavens to the earth.

"Excuse me?"

"Her name. I've chosen it. Libitina Rose Yarrow."

"That's a cute name. You can call her Libby for short," she grins showing her pearly teeth.

"No. It will be Libitina, not Libby, Libs, Tina, or Rosey," he says as he approaches the staff member with fierce dark eyes. "Libitina. It means death. That's what she is. That's what she brings. So, that is what she shall be called. Period."

Chapter Two
Red Flag

The nurse backs away from Libitina's father and clutches her tight. "Mr. Yarrow, I understand you are grieving the loss of your wife, but to take it out on her isn't right on so many levels. She's a beautiful gift from God."

"You take her then," he chuckles.

"Believe me when I say, if I could, I would. To have a child is a blessing," the nurse says, brushing Libitina's cheek. "I'm taking her for now and having a grief counselor come and speak with you."

"I don't need counseling."

"Oh, but Mr. Yarrow, you do," she insists as she turns her back on him and takes her away.

It's quiet.

Libitina is asleep, and the pain she brings subsides. The emergency room double doors crash open beside me. A gurney, covered in blood and stained gauze, rolls past me. The man lying on top is as white as the sheet beneath him. A blade protrudes from his chest. The paramedic holds it steady as they head straight for the operating room. It's not a large blade, but it penetrated the right ventricle, nonetheless.

The staff prepares him for surgery after the doctor reviews his X-rays. I pass through the doctor, raising the hairs on his arm as he grips the handle of the knife. Without warning, the patient sits up, wide-eyed, and grabs the surgeon's hand. They try to stop him, but the man is determined to remove the impaled object. Blood gushes from the gaping wound, and the man appears beside me as his heart monitor flatlines.

His hand glides through me as he stares at the worst of himself. Everything he did wrong in his life flashes before his eyes. His regrets, his crimes, and the people he's killed, all dance between us like a home movie playing on a projector. A prelude for what's to come.

A dark hole swirls open in the floor tiles and smoke billows out. The man's eyes turn to saucers as black-clawed hands reach through the abyss, seize him by the ankles, and drag him to hell. This doesn't happen to everyone. Most people move on to the light or stay and wander until they resolve their unfinished business. This man is a chronic sinner and has done too many unforgivable things, murder being one of them.

Screams burn through me as Libitina hurts me from afar. As I close in on the nursery, the intensity increases.

I have no flesh, but if I did, it would be on fire right now. Libitina is upset. A nurse removes a needle from her thigh and places it in a sharps disposal container.

A man wearing a suit and tie enters the room and rests a briefcase on a side table as the nurse rocks the baby in her arms. "I understand you have a difficult case for me?"

"Yes. This baby's mother passed away giving birth, and the father blames the child."

"It's not uncommon," the counselor points out as he slides his pudgy hands into his pockets. "What room?"

"346."

"I'll come back and speak to you after we talk."

"Okay."

The counselor strolls to the elevators and punches the button. We stand together and wait. The fluorescent bulb flickers and the counselor gazes up at it. He turns his head to the side as he senses my presence. As the doors clank open, he shakes his head, rubs his temples, and steps inside.

I float through the ceiling and meet him in Libitina's room where her father waits.

"Mr. Yarrow, my name is Jack. I'm a caseworker for the hospital."

"I told the nurse I don't need you."

"Mr. Yarrow, losing someone is never easy. Now, I'm not saying I can take your pain away, but what I can do is listen and supply some tools to help you cope during this difficult time."

"I wish the baby died instead."

"Sir, it is natural to feel that way, but I'm sure if your wife had a choice, she would choose her child."

"Well, she's not here. Besides, it's not like we couldn't have more children."

"And if things ended the same?" Jack asks.

"I would choose my wife every time."

"Do you think that is fair?"

Mr. Yarrow turns away from the window and stalks toward him. "I don't care about what's fair. I want my wife back. She is who I love, not that thing in the other room."

"That thing is your daughter, and she is helpless and afraid. She knows nothing of your pain," the counselor huffs as he removes brochures from his briefcase. "I think it is in your best interest for you to have daily visits for the first week you are home."

"And if I leave, and don't take her with me?"

"Well, you have every right to do so according to the law, but you may regret it later if you change your mind."

"I won't change my mind," Mr. Yarrow announces as he bumps past him.

Mr. Yarrow stops at the nursery viewing window, presses his forehead against the glass, and fogs it with his breath. Libitina's locks curl around her crochet hat as she twitches in her sleep. His cell rings, and he lets it go to voicemail. He glances down at his phone as he begins walking away and listens to the message. The hair on his neck stands to attention as I slip inside him so I can listen.

'Mr. Yarrow, this is Marcia from the Social Security office returning your call about your wife's benefits. First, I am sorry for your loss. Second, your monthly survivor benefit amount will be one thousand eight hundred dollars, and your daughter's benefit, once you supply her birth certificate and her social security card processes through the system, will be an added seven hundred and fifty dollars per month. Please return my call when you can so we can schedule an appointment to fill out the paperwork.'

Money changes everything. For most, it is an opportunity to buy something they always wanted or catch up on bills. For Mr. Yarrow, it is a reason to keep his child despite how he feels about her. He leans his palms against the glass and smiles for the first time. Not because he loves his daughter and can't wait to hold her, but because she is his cash cow. Between his wife's benefit and Libitina's, he can afford to pay all his bills without working overtime.

"Beautiful. Is she yours?" A young blonde in blue scrubs asks, stopping beside him.

"Yes, she is."

"Congratulations. I am sure you and your wife are excited to get her home," she smiles as she glances at the gold on his ring finger.

"We sure are," he says through clenched teeth as the girl shuffles into the elevator when it pops open.

Mr. Yarrow returns his attention to Libitina as she stirs under her receiving blanket. "Looks like you're coming with me after all."

Jack is heading down the hallway, so he flags him down. "I changed my mind. Can someone please show me how to care for her when I get home?"

"Glad to hear it. I'll have a nurse meet you back in the room we spoke in previously."

The counselor moseys back to the nurse's station to relay the information to Libitina's primary nurse.

"Something's not right," she says when he explains the plan. "He just said he didn't want her, and now, out of nowhere, he does."

"Well, I guess she touched his heart when she looked at him."

"You guess? No offense, Jack, but guessing isn't an indicator of whether a man can take care of his child or not. I'm telling you, this is a bad idea."

"Well, Regina, I'm the caseworker and you're a float nurse, so the decision is mine. I will note your concerns in the file. Besides, he agreed to home visits for now until things settle down. Can someone show him the basics before discharge tomorrow?"

"Yes," Regina utters, crossing her arms. "This is a mistake. You'll see."

"I don't make mistakes," Jack insists as he turns on his heels, scoops up his briefcase from the counter, and walks away.

"You did this time," she murmurs as she peers at Mr. Yarrow in the distance.

A bald young boy, wearing a gown, stands in the doorway of his room. I grip his hand and lead him to another door filled with light. Another child who appears to be his twin, and dressed the same, comes through the illuminated door, and pulls him through. His mother bursts from his room, bawling as her crying husband clutches her in his arms. To lose both children to the same disease is disheartening but more common than you think.

As I wander past them, the pain starts slowly and grows with intensity. An older nurse, with a tight gray bun, is showing Mr. Yarrow how to change Libitina's diaper, and it isn't going well. He's vomiting in a lined trash can as the nurse rolls her eyes, and Libitina screams when I enter the room.

Feces drip down the front of his red flannel when he stands and wipes his lips of puke. "Jesus. How can something so small shoot poop out of her butt like that?"

"It happens sometimes. The key is to be prepared for it."

"By what, wearing body armor and goggles? It's disgusting," he snaps as he takes off his soiled top.

"Mr. Yarrow, getting upset will make her cry more. She can sense your stress and frustration. Try and remain calm."

"Calm? I have shit on my shirt."

"I'm aware. I can get that cleaned for you and find you something to put on in the meantime. Right now, we need to finish getting her cleaned up."

Mr. Yarrow wipes Libitina front to back as instructed. With every swipe of the cold cloth, she screams a little louder.

The nurse is right. Letting him take her is a bad idea. I'll never have peace if she is with him. At home, she is unprotected. He won't kill her, because he needs her, but it won't stop him from causing her pain, and her pain is mine. So, I have no choice. I'm following them home.

Chapter Three
Reportable

The screaming is endless as he continues to ignore her. The abuse starts on day one. It's day five of treacherous pain. No one from the hospital ever came. Somehow, she slipped through the cracks and has gone unchecked.

Mr. Yarrow stuffs protective foam meant for his factory job farther into his ears and places a pillow over his head.

Libitina is hungry, but her father is trying to nap before going to work. The case manager set him up with a reliable babysitter, but when Libitina is home, he pays little mind to her.

I flick a framed photo of his wife above his head, knocking it off the wall, and striking him in the face with it.

"Son of a bitch," he hollers, pressing the bridge of his nose to stop the flow of blood as he gazes at the fractured glass littering his wife's face.

He lifts the picture and brushes off the shards. A scratch runs diagonally across the center of her face as a tear rolls over his stubbled cheekbone. He pinches the noise suppressors from his ears and crushes the image of his beloved in his grasp as his daughter bellows down the hall.

Libitina screams in her crib as he enters with her bottle and cotton sticking out of his nostrils. He stuffs the nipple between her lips and props the bottle up with blankets. The stench of a dirty diaper wrinkles his face. He leaves the room, changes for work, and packs his lunch.

The bottle falls away from her mouth as she spits up, cocks her head to the side, and smiles at me. I don't know why she does this. Perhaps to let me know she sees me. Her father reenters, places a diaper in her bag, and holds her at arm's length to his pickup truck.

The foul odor overwhelms the vehicle, and he rolls down the window. The spring air is chilly, and Libitina shivers in her car seat as he turns into the driveway of the sitters. A woman around forty, with bleach blonde hair and long manicured fingernails meets him at the door.

"Someone's ripe," she says, waving her hand in front of her face.

"She pooped in the car," Mr. Yarrow insists as he turns his back on her and climbs back in his vehicle.

Every day it's the same, and every day, she complains to herself but not to him about the condition Libitina comes to her in—soiled diaper, rash, wearing the same outfit as the day before. Erin is a good person, and I am thankful when Libitina is with her.

She strips her clothes and diaper off and places her in a bath. She hums to her as she massages lavender shampoo into her silky hair.

"Beautiful girl," she smiles as Libitina yawns.

She hoists her from the water and wraps her in a towel. The rash is worse than last time. Erin takes ointment and dabs it on. Libitina pouts her lips right before she erupts into a blood-curdling scream.

This daily occurrence frustrates me. I have yet to discover why she causes me such pain. The spirit of her mother and my presence can only do so much. The sitter is doing nothing wrong. This is her father's fault. I insert myself inside Erin and be the voice inside her head.

'*Take her to the hospital.*'

Erin shakes as I exit and stands at once.

"That's it. I'm taking you to the hospital. I don't care what your father says."

Erin places Libitina on her lap and pulls onto the road leading to the highway. Driving without a car seat is dangerous, but Mr. Yarrow refuses to leave her one.

The air smells of floral gardens as she circles the roundabout in the parking lot. Red and pink daylilies alternate in color as she passes the Heart and Cancer Institute. The hospital specializes in the top two killers of women. It's too bad they didn't have treatment for child abusers. *Perhaps a lobotomy to Mr. Yarrow's head would straighten him out.* Erin thinks to herself.

She loops around a third time, but there is no available space in the lot, so she parks at the curb and feeds the meter. The drive from Lebanon to Fairfax takes less time than finding a place to park. Erin sits with Libitina, while I float down to the emergency room to take a patient.

The battered woman's brain swells as they snap the first X-ray. She is motionless as they lift her eyelids with no response. Her spirit slips in and out of her body as she fights to stay alive.

"Die, you stupid bitch. Die," a bloodied-faced man screams as officers fight to restrain him. "You shouldn't have left. I warned you what would happen. Didn't I?"

As much as she wants me to take her, it's not her fate. It's his. I have never been so excited. He grasps his chest and falls to the tile as the officers struggle to hold him erect. His fight with them is over as he slithers away from his corpse and appears before me. The abuser gawks at his distorted mirror image as a portal opens beneath him. He reaches for his former self, as the monsters of the deep yank him into the hollow.

A single tear slides down the woman's face as her eyes peel open, and the nurse beside her grips her arm. "He can never hurt you again. Keep fighting."

She's crying harder now. Refusing to believe it's over. Goosebumps flood the nurse's flesh as I hop inside.

'Show her.'

I direct her hand into her pocket where her cell phone waits and lead her to the man's body on the tile. She snaps a photo as the police object, returns to the woman, and shows her.

The abused nods as they roll her away to an unknown room, and I vacate the nurse's frame as Libitina calls to me.

She screams as a nurse examines her rash. I levitate around the bed and peer inside. The blistering skin bleeds as the nurse shifts it with her gloved finger.

"This is awful. How long has it been like this?"

"It's grown worse over the last several days," Erin grimaces.

"As her mother, you should know neglecting to change her diaper in a timely fashion can cause this."

"I'm not her mother. Her mother died in childbirth."

"Do you have permission to treat from the custodial parent?"

"He won't let me take her out of the house when I am watching her. Mr. Yarrow is not a loving father."

"Did you say, Yarrow?" The nurse stops her exam.

"Yes. Why?"

"Excuse me. I will be right back."

The nurse hustles out of the room and disappears. Erin lifts Libitina and places her over her shoulder. A loud burp brings a smile to Erin's face.

A different nurse, the one who expressed concerns for Libitina's safety to Jack, barrels into the room. "I knew it. I told Jack allowing Mr. Yarrow to take his daughter home was a mistake."

"I know Regina. That's why I came and got you," the original nurse says.

"What is going on?" Erin asks, holding her tighter. "Who's Jack?"

"I didn't want Mr. Yarrow leaving the hospital with Libitina. He is not in the right frame of mind to care for an infant so soon after the loss of his wife," Regina sighs as she takes the baby from Erin's arms and rests her back down. "Let me look."

The Velcro crinkles as the nurse removes the diaper and places her hand across her mouth to stifle her cursing. "Unbelievable. Does he change her at all?"

"I don't think so," Erin says putting her head down. "I have her when he's working. I bathe her, change her, and leave her naked sometimes so she can air out, but then she goes home with him and comes back a mess."

"Is he aware you brought her here?"

"No. I didn't dare to ask. If I am being honest, he scares me," Erin admits as she strokes Libitina's hair. "He treats her like an object instead of a person."

"We have to call him," the original nurse says flubbing her lips.

"Please don't. I'm afraid he'll take my choice to bring her here out on her. Can't you just give me something to put on the rash?"

"It's hospital policy to obtain parental consent," Regina says placing her hands on her hips. "What I can do is contact child protective services and have them speak to him."

"That's fine, but I don't want him to think I turned him in for abuse."

"I will make it clear to him that you don't have anything to do with them being called."

Erin nods as she steadies her shaking hands.

An hour later, Mr. Yarrow, dressed in a navy jumpsuit, covered in bits of shaved metal, storms into the room. "What the hell is Libitina doing here?"

"Mr. Yarrow, this rash is severe and needs treatment. Your babysitter is seeking medication to help ease her pain. Don't you want that?" Regina asks.

"Of course, I want that," he insists dropping his balled-up fists.

"Perfect. Sign this consent to treat, and we can call down to the pharmacy and have them send up some cream."

Mr. Yarrow's dark eyes are set on Erin when the nurse disappears around the corner.

"How fucking dare you?" He backs her into a corner as she squeezes Libitina to her breast. "Give her to me."

He seizes the infant and places her on his shoulder. "Don't you ever do anything like this again without my permission, understand?"

"Yes, Mr. Yarrow," she cries as her tremoring hands wipe the tears from her cheeks. "I just wanted to help."

"Well, don't," he orders as the nurse returns with papers.

"Change her as soon as she soils herself. Bathe her daily and allow a few minutes of naked time. Apply the prescription ointment with every diaper change after cleaning. Use a clean, warm washcloth to cleanse the area of feces," the nurse reads aloud. "Mr. Yarrow, do you understand these instructions?"

"Yes, of course. Thank you for taking such great care of her," he smiles with his teeth and turns his attention to Erin. "And thank you for bringing her here. I appreciate it."

It's for show. His smile, his demeanor, and the way he's holding Libitina is all an act. If I could kill him, I would, but it's not his time.

He scoops his keys from the bedside table and heads for the door.

"Mr. Yarrow, we are not finished yet," the nurse states as another woman enters the room. "This is Janet Pulser. She is our Child Services advocate."

"Child Services? I'm not abusing my daughter. She's fine. It's a rash, for crying out loud."

"No one is accusing you of anything, Mr. Yarrow. I am just here to speak with you about basic care of your daughter when she is home with you and not at the sitters," Janet explains.

"What did you say?" Mr. Yarrow asks advancing towards Erin. "Did you tell them I am hurting my child?"

"No, sir. I…"

"Mr. Yarrow, it's hospital protocol when a child shows possible signs of neglect for us to get involved. A diaper rash this severe, and of this magnitude, is cause for concern, but does not necessarily indicate neglect."

"I'm not neglecting her."

As the lie spills out of his mouth, I roll a pen, at a slow and calculated pace, across the child advocates' paperwork, and point the tip to the words 'unannounced visits.'

The advocate turns the page to read it and says, "At this time, I recommend changing Libitina at once when she's voided or defecated and bathing her daily to ensure a rash this size doesn't come back." She lifts the white sheet from the wooden top. "Sometime in the next week or so, I will stop by and check in on how things are going."

"When? I work. I can't just come when you show up. I need a date and time so I can request off."

"Don't worry, Mr. Yarrow, you can give me your schedule, and I can work around it. There is no need to miss time," Janet smiles as she nods for the nurse to join her in the hall.

Libitina fusses in his arms. "I can't lose her. I need your help," he pleads.

"Help with what?"

"Come to my house on the weekends. Clean, change her, and bathe her."

"Sir, when I took this job, I told you I work Monday through Friday. Weekends are my time for myself. I am not a maid or a nanny."

"I'll pay you double for weekends. Please."

"Triple," she insists, crossing her arms.

"Listen here, you greedy little bitch," he steams.

The nurse plows into the room as a code blue in the emergency room echoes through the intercom.

Erin's face pales as the nurse hands her a bag. "Are you alright?"

"I think I am coming down with something," she proclaims, peering at Mr. Yarrow.

He needs her. She lives the closest and charges the least to watch Libitina. If he doesn't give her what she wants, she may quit.

The nurse presses her palm on Erin's forehead. "You don't have a fever so try getting some rest. If you aren't well by morning, you shouldn't care for Libitina."

"Oh, I wouldn't dream of getting her sick, ever," Erin glares at Mr. Yarrow. "Her welfare is my top priority when she's with me."

"Mine as well," Mr. Yarrow jeers through clenched teeth.

"Good. We are all on the same page. Here are her discharge instructions as well as a follow-up appointment we set with her primary doctor."

"Primary doctor? I don't have a primary doctor," he says.

"You do now. The first year of a child's life is full of doctor's appointments, developmental testing, and immunizations," the nurse smirks. "Get used to it, Mr. Yarrow. Life is not about you anymore. It's about her," she utters as she tickles Libitina's palm with her finger.

Amen.

Chapter Four
For Show

As soon as they exit the hospital, Mr. Yarrow passes Libitina to Erin.

"Where are you going? "Erin asks, as he opens the door to his truck.

"Back to work. You want to play mommy, now is your chance."

Erin furrows her brows as he drives away from them and disappears around a corner.

"And he still didn't give me your car seat," Erin murmurs to herself. "I guess you're driving."

Libitina stares behind her and coos at me. She's happy and content with Erin. It's too bad she couldn't stay with her forever.

An ambulance screams into the parking lot, startling Libitina. Erin pops her bottle in between her lips, calming her as the paramedic unloads a patient.

A dangling arm, with irregular shaped, dark liver spots swings forward and backward as the gurney lands hard on the blacktop. The emergency room staff directs the paramedics to an available bay. A woman, around eighty years old, stands beside me.

She's waiting for him.

The physician rests paddles on his chest right before a nurse runs into the room. "Stop! We have a do not resuscitate on file."

Everyone backs away as the man flatlines and appears before his wife. The woman smiles as she cups his cheek with her palm, and he does the same as they ascend into the rays of light shining from the ceiling.

I can't say I mind when people go on their own or have a lifelong partner who is waiting to do my job for me. They are easy. The hardest are the sinners. They spend their whole lives taking from everyone without fear of the repercussions. But when it's their time to go, now they are afraid.

I don't blame them; the dark ones scare me too. When those sinister hands breach the surface and reach for them, I step away. If I don't, they try and drag me to hell with them.

Libitina calls to me with her raging temper. She's resting on Erin's shoulder as she exits her vehicle and crosses her well-manicured lawn.

"Ouch," Erin cries out as she touches her bare upper arm.

A tiny, crescent moon bleeds as Libitina digs her unmanicured nails into her flesh. Her little fingers whiten as she curls them into Erin's unprotected skin over and over.

Erin rests Libitina in her bassinet and unzips her diaper bag. One diaper, one bottle, and no wipes are all Mr. Yarrow sent her. When he sends more, she takes them out for days like this, creating a stockpile.

"Come here. How about some naked time, little one?" Erin sighs as Libitina continues to holler.

She lifts her from her bed, rests her on her thighs, and unsnaps her pajamas. After taking the diaper off and cleaning her angry bottom with a warm washcloth, she lays her on a plush tie-dyed pastel blanket and applies her medicated cream. Within minutes, Libitina stops bawling. She kicks her little bare legs and stares at the light on the ceiling as I make it flicker.

Erin looks up at the blinking annoyance. "Is your mom here? Is that what you are looking at?"

No, she is not.

Mrs. Yarrow is standing beside her husband as he gulps another shot of whiskey at the bar. Mr. Yarrow lost his job today. He forgot to finish locking out a machine before he left for the hospital, a dangerous oversight, and grounds for immediate dismissal.

The bartender drops an ice-cold beer in front of Mr. Yarrow. "On the house. Sorry about your job."

"It's that little bitch's fault," he steams.

"Who?"

"No one. Bring me another drink."

The stool snaps without warning under Mr. Yarrow, and he crashes to the floor in a heap. I'd be lying if I said I didn't smile a little. He flails his arms as he staggers to a standing position. A bolt from his seat rotates in a circle as Mr. Yarrow stares at it. Round and round it goes before he puts a stop to it with his steel-toed boot. He lifts his sole and it rolls toward the front door with the help of his wife.

She wants him to leave, but instead, he sinks into a corner booth and leans against the wall.

"You, okay?" The bartender asks as he rests his glass on the table.

"Are you fucking kidding me? Am I okay?" Mr. Yarrow says as he slides off the bench and comes face to face with the bartender. "I have lost my wife, my job, and my freedom all in the same week. What the fuck do you think?"

"You haven't lost everything, Mr. Yarrow. You still have a beautiful baby girl at home from what I hear."

"What have you heard, and from whom?" Mr. Yarrow asks with balled-up fists.

"Perhaps you should leave," the bartender says as he steps back.

"Not until you tell me who is discussing my private business with everyone like the town crier!"

"I'm sorry. I don't want any trouble. Please, go."

Mr. Yarrow seizes the bartender by his collar and shakes him. "Tell me!"

Two construction workers snatch him by the arms and yank him away from the bartender. They drag him to the door and use his head like a battering ram to open it. Blood gushes from his forehead as they launch him onto the crumbling blacktop as it begins raining.

A puddle surrounds him as he pushes himself onto his hands and knees, turns his face to the heavens, and screams. Pain, anger, loss, and frustration flood through him all at once as he topples over and cries on his side alone in the dark.

Erin gazes up at the clock on the wall. Mr. Yarrow is hours late picking up Libitina. She tries calling him for the third time, and he still doesn't answer, so she leaves him a message.

'Mr. Yarrow, it's Erin. Libitina is asleep at this point, so don't bother coming to get her. I don't know where you are, or what you are trying to pull, but I don't appreciate it.'

Midnight rolls around, so Erin turns off all the lights and flops onto her mattress. Libitina stirs as I hover above her. I peer over at Erin across the room and then return my attention to Libitina. Her eyes are now open, startling me. Even in the dark, I can see her smiling. Perhaps someday she will be old enough to tell me why she does this. Pain envelopes me as she belts out a scream. Erin jumps out of bed, and runs through me, giving her chills as she lifts Libitina.

"What's the matter, baby girl? Did you have a bad dream?"

Erin bounces her in her arms as she warms her formula in a saucer on the stovetop. Erin giggles as Libitina passes an audible fart.

An overwhelming stench filters through Erin's nostrils within seconds. She uses metal tongs to take the bottle from the steaming water, sets it on the counter, and shuffles to her green suede sofa to change her. Libitina's nails fold over as she digs the fabric beneath her and kicks.

Erin glances at the wall clock. It's been over four hours. Libitina sleeps well for a newborn. She feeds her, burps her, places her back to bed with a pacifier, and climbs beneath her comforter.

Mr. Yarrow should be thankful. Erin thinks as she pulls the covers under her chin.

The sunrise came fast and so did Libitina's appetite. Erin rolls out of bed, wipes the goop from her eyes, and saunters to the bathroom, taking her cell with her. No messages or missed calls from Mr. Yarrow.

After changing Libitina's clothes and feeding her, she slides behind the wheel of her car with Libitina sitting on her lap and drives the short distance to his house.

The front door is open when she arrives. She places Libitina over her shoulder and bounces her as she calls his name. "Mr. Yarrow? Are you here?"

No answer.

Erin moves from room to room and stops at his closed bedroom door. It creaks open when she turns the knob and pushes. Air sticks in her lungs as she gasps. Mr. Yarrow is on the floor, resting on his side, and facing away from her. The dank aroma of vomit overwhelms the space and stains the carpet. Erin takes Libitina to her crib across the hall and returns to his side. She exhales when he shifts under her touch.

"Mr. Yarrow?"

Tears erupt from his face when he opens his eyes and gazes at Erin. He grips her around the waist and sobs. "I miss her so much."

"I know," Erin says placing her palm on his unruly hair. "I'm sorry."

He's grieving. His sorrow brings with it neglect. Mr. Yarrow is in no condition to raise his daughter. Someone needs to intervene.

I made my way to the hospital and found the nurse who cared for Libitina. As I enter her body, she loses her train of thought. She rubs the fabric of her purple scrubs between her fingers as she struggles to remember what medication she needs from the locked cabinet, but her mind is blank. I manifest images of Libitina's rash into her head and her brows furrow. Tingling floods over her as I steer her toward the child protective services office. She stops shy of the entrance as I hop out, and she remembers the medicine she went to retrieve.

"Where's Jack?" she asks the secretary at the desk.

"Lunch, as usual, Regina. I swear all he does is eat and shit."

"Did he send anyone to the Yarrow residence?"

"I don't think so. Every time I bring it to his attention, he sets the folder aside and continues playing solitaire on his computer."

"Give it to me," Regina insists.

The secretary passes the file to her and answers her ringing phone. The nurse finds his address and writes it down on a pink memo pad.

"What are you planning?" The secretary asks as she hangs up.

"I'm going there on my lunch. If that idiot can't do his job, I will. I need to make sure he's taking care of her."

"It's not your responsibility."

"Is that what your excuse will be when she winds up dead?"

The secretary pushes her glasses up on her nose and grimaces. "I am just saying you could be fired for taking it and going off on your own. I'm not lying for you if he comes looking."

"Somehow I doubt he'll notice," Regina says as she hustles out and heads to the breakroom to punch out.

I place images of Erin inside the nurse's head as she cruises down the highway. If Erin took her for a little while, I would be able to continue my work pain-free.

When Regina arrives at the Yarrows, she is surprised to find two vehicles in the driveway. She hesitates when she realizes it's a weekday and Mr. Yarrow should be working. The glovebox slams open as she takes out a handgun and shoves it into her purse. Her brother makes her keep it with her for protection. The nurse cups her hands around her face as she peeks in the front window. Erin is on the couch asleep with Libitina on her chest. Mr. Yarrow is nowhere in sight.

Her hand prickles as I control her mindless movements. She draws in a deep breath and taps the door with her pointer and middle fingers.

Chapter Five
Take a Break

Erin's eyes pop open when she senses Regina's presence. She peers at the front door. "How did you get in here?"

"The door is unlocked," Regina says taking a seat in the recliner across from her. "Where is Mr. Yarrow?"

"Asleep," Erin whispers as she pulls herself upright. "He's not doing well."

"That's why I am here. The idiot controlling her case is too lazy to do his job." Regina rubs her palms together softly as she finds the words, and the courage, to ask Erin to care for Libitina. "Erin, I know this is a big ask, but do you think you could take her, just temporarily, until we can get him some help?"

"Listen, lady…"

"It's Regina."

"Sorry, Regina. Don't get me wrong, I love Libitina, but I'm not her mother. Besides, Mr. Yarrow would flip if he thought we were trying to take her from him."

I dive inside Erin. No is not an acceptable answer, so I overwhelm her with guilt for not giving things a chance. Erin's expression shifts from defiant and red to one of sorrow as a single tear slides down her paling face. That's enough sadness for her for one day. I don't want to break the poor woman.

"Erin? Are you alright?" Regina asks as she waves her hand before her eyes. "Hello?"

"Okay. I'll take her for a couple of weeks," she says smiling down at Libitina who's now awake. "Only because I know he needs help and won't get it if he has her."

"Perfect. Go home and take her with you. I'll talk to Mr. Yarrow."

"Oh, I don't think that's a good idea. If he wakes up and she's gone and you're here, he will flip out."

"It's better that he does when she is not here. Understand?"

"Yes."

Regina helps Erin pack diapers, wipes, and several outfits with the tags still hanging from them in a bag. She then follows her to Mr. Yarrow's truck and removes the car seat to place into Erin's sedan. They buckle Libitina in as she gazes past them and coos at me. Erin and Regina exchange glances and peer over their shoulders at no one behind them.

Erin exhales through her nostrils. "I don't think we should do this."

"Look at me, Erin," Regina insists taking her by the forearms. "This isn't about what or how we feel; this is about doing what's best for Libitina."

Regina steers her into the driver's seat and closes the door. "Give me your address and I can stop over after and let you know how things went."

Erin scribbles her home location and phone number on an old, wrinkled receipt with a leaky pen and passes it to her.

The front door crashes open. "Where the fuck are you going?" Mr. Yarrow screams.

"Go, Erin. Right now," Regina hollers as she slaps the roof and stuffs the smeared paper in her scrubs. "Go!"

Erin stomps on the gas, and the car hops into motion as she peels out of the driveway and disappears out of sight.

Mr. Yarrow strikes Regina in the side of her face with his palm, knocking her to the damp earth. He straddles her frame and seizes her by the wrists, pinning her down. "Where is she going with my daughter," he sneers.

"Mr. Yarrow, please. We are trying to help you."

"By taking my child away?"

"We are just giving you a break."

"I don't need one. Call her back. Right now!"

His face is so close to hers that she can smell the booze from the night before. She pushes back with her body and knees him in the balls. He tips over like a glass of milk spilling onto the ground. Mr. Yarrow rolls back and forth, holding his angry testicles in his grasp. Regina struggles to her feet, unzips her purse, and pulls out her Glock.

"Listen, Mr. Yarrow. I am not planning to press charges for you striking me, but if you don't seek counseling and I mean today, I will."

"Do you even know how to use that?"

Regina removes the safety and aims it at his head. "Don't test me, sir. Self-defense is easy to prove in this case, and this is a stand-your-ground state."

Mr. Yarrow nods and puts his hands up in surrender. "Fine. How long do I have, and what do you want me to do?"

"I asked Erin to give you a few weeks. You must go to grief counseling or seek out a support group for others who have lost their loved ones. I have a form in my car. It requires a signature each time you go."

"How often?"

"At least twice a week."

"Jesus."

"Mr. Yarrow, your daughter needs you. Not this version of you, but the one that existed before your wife passed," she says lowering the gun. "I'm not taking her. I'm trying to keep you from losing her."

"Fine. I get it. Give me the information and the forms."

Regina reaches into her SUV without turning her back on him. She removes a manilla envelope and hands it to him. "Everything you need is right here. You can drop off the signature page on Friday."

He takes it from her and hangs his head, refusing to make eye contact as she climbs into her vehicle.

She keeps her eyes on him in the rearview mirror as she drives away. He falls to his knees and places his face in his palms. Regina almost feels sorry for him.

Almost.

I float into her oversized ride and step inside to listen to her thoughts. She wishes, like me, Erin would take Libitina forever. She switches on her heated seat to warm her chilled bones as I plant ideas. There are resources available to Erin if she takes her, including financial support.

Regina makes a sharp left into Erin's driveway, just missing her white mailbox with daisies painted on it. Erin is rocking Libitina as she feeds her on the covered, front porch. She stands and hustles to Regina. "Oh, my God. Your face. What happened?"

"I'm fine. He has agreed to do counseling in some form at least two days per week and must bring me proof. Now this isn't official, and there are no courts involved. So, if he comes over here and wants to take her, he can."

"I don't want any trouble."

"Erin, I don't think he will try anything," Regina says pulling out her weapon. "But just in case he does, take this."

"I don't know how to use a gun. Are you crazy?"

"No. I want to know you two are safe. It's loaded, and a round is ready in the chamber. See this right here? This is the safety. Click it, aim, and fire. That is all there is to it."

"What if I miss?"

"Keep shooting. Squeeze the trigger, don't pull."

"Squeeze, don't pull. I got it," Erin stutters as her lips quiver. "Regina…I'm scared."

"Me too," Regina admits. "I have paperwork for you to read. Libitina needs someone who is safe and cares for her. I think you are that person. At least, that is what my gut is telling me. There are financial benefits to being a foster parent. You should consider it."

"I know that's what would be best, but giving up my freedom for a stranger's child is not how I pictured my future."

"I understand. I'm not saying he won't change, but I have my doubts. I just want you to consider it, that's all."

"I'll read the paperwork when I have time. Thank you for checking in. Please let me know if he goes through with counseling."

"Will do," Regina says as she strolls back to her car.

I drift passed Mr. Yarrow's house, as I follow Regina back to the hospital. He is sitting on the porch reading the information she gave him. A positive sign. Perhaps there is hope for him after all.

Screaming comes from the emergency room as I glide through its doors. An arsonist misjudged his chemicals, and their reaction, leaving him with severe, third-degree burns over nearly fifty percent of his body. A nurse vomits in a trash can as she runs out of the room. The nauseating smell of melted flesh meat is too much for her weak stomach. Doctors work to remove any loose clothing from the victim, as a nurse hangs an IV bag of morphine. The man bounces between life and death.

Despite the efforts of the staff, the damage is too extensive, and the man appears beside me. I show him his mistakes, those he has hurt, and the lives he has taken. In the end, most of them still don't understand when the black claws of Hades' demons come to take them away. The man's face twists as he trades one hell for another and disappears beneath the tile.

The doctor covers his charred remains and notifies the police of his passing. He burned all his bridges a long time ago.

How ironic.

No family waits for him in the lobby. No one has called to check his status. No one cares.

They roll his body to the morgue, where he will stay until a funeral home, willing to bury him at little to no cost, comes to retrieve him.

Yelling echoes through the halls as Regina and Jack engage in a heated argument.

"You crossed the line, Regina, and you know it."

"Well, if you did your job instead of playing card games on your computer, I wouldn't have needed to."

"What I do in my free time is none of your business," he snaps.

"Seems like all you have is 'free time,' Jack," Regina says, making air quotes. "I did what I did on my lunch break which is more than you will ever do being paid."

"I'm reporting you to HR," he barks, wagging his finger at her.

"Good luck with that," she shouts at his back as he storms out.

The secretary shrugs her shoulders and fixates on her computer screen.

Regina goes back to her office and flops in her chair. She shifts the pile of paperwork on her desk and flutters her lips. Her laptop dings as a new email appears.

'This message is to inform you of a recent referral who has joined the Gatherers of Grief support group. Thaddeus Yarrow has scheduled an in-person appointment for tomorrow and Friday. We look forward to helping Mr. Yarrow in his time of need.'

Tessa Payne, Certified Grief Counselor.

The papers on Regina's desk shift as she blows out a forceful breath. She picks up her cell and sends Erin a message informing her that Mr. Yarrow has made his first two appointments and hits send.

Three dots appear in a bubble as Erin types her reply.

'Making appointments and showing up are two different things.'
'Indeed. I guess we shall see. It's a waiting game at this point.'
'For her sake, I hope he follows through.'
'Me too.'

Me three.

appearions of whatever pieces road I don't even remember
how I used to look before I turned naked and sit this solemn

Chapter Six
Too Quiet

After hundreds of years of removing souls, I have seen it
all. Today is no different than any other time. A woman,
driving drunk for the third time, has wrapped her vehicle
around a tree, killing herself, and her passenger. I wonder
what makes people think that running will save them. Can't
you see yourself lying on the hood with your face ripped
apart thanks to the shattering windshield?
Denial.
It is the only thing that would explain these attempts. She
runs to a church and smiles.
I'll give her an 'E' for effort.
Her body floats through the door and returns just as fast.
The spirit of a pastor who lives inside drags her out by the
arm. "Sinner," he hollers as he releases her to the streets
from which she came.
Instead of accepting the inevitable, she continues
running. Multiple portals appear before her, stopping her in
her tracks. She turns around and more appear behind her.
Most of the time, I only see the claws of the dark ones, but
on these rare occasions, I see all of them. Sometimes they
have the faces of people the recently deceased knew, and
other times their faces don't exist, just eyes in black
shadows.
Her friend stands beside me, watching the fiasco. If we
could eat popcorn, we would, but alas we are merely

apparitions of who we once were. I don't even remember how I used to look before I became tasked with this solemn job.

Four demons breach the pavement and creep towards her from all directions. She screams as two take her by the arms, and the others follow. They descend into a wormhole, and it closes within seconds. The woman beside me grins as she turns to the beam shining from the heavens and steps inside its halo. I steer clear of these windows. Years ago, my shoulder shifted into the illuminated space, just a smidge, and it burned like fire. Perhaps we reapers are like vampires, sucking the life from people instead of blood.

Libitina is doing well with Erin. It has been almost two weeks, with her having only a few meltdowns, so I have kept my distance. Mr. Yarrow has attended more group sessions than recommended, which surprises me and seems suspicious. He has not contacted Erin to check in, nor has he come to visit.

My curiosity gets the best of me, and I glide to his house. An extra car sits in the driveway, but it's not Erin's or Nurse Regina's. I pass through the wall and find Mr. Yarrow snuggling on the furniture with a woman. His wife sulks across from him in the rocker with her arms crossed. He's moving on. His thoughts of her are fading, and so is she. Her unfinished business is nearing its end, but her concerns for Libitina, and her husband's mental health, delay her departure.

On the coffee table are his signed attendance documents. The signature matches the woman who is stroking his thigh now. Tessa. The grief counselor from the group and the same person who sent the email informing Regina that Mr.

Yarrow signed up for the sessions. Did he even go? I slip inside him to read his thoughts.

He did go. If he hadn't met Tessa, he would have stopped after reaching his four-session limit. Turns out, they began flirting on day one, prompting him to return daily for every meeting, Monday through Friday, for the last two weeks. This is their first time alone together, and he can't wait to have sex with her.

I pull away from him and slide into her. She is head over heels for him and wants to get married and have children. Talk about love at first sight. She too is eager to do dirty deeds.

The heavy petting starts slow but heats up fast, so I vacate her body. I stand behind the wife who cries in the chair, watching their exchange of bodily fluids. The air reeks of their sweaty bodies and hot breaths, prompting us to float to another room. That's when reality strikes us both.

All the images of his wife and himself are gone. Only square stains, where the frames once were, remained. We enter Libitina's room, and it's empty of all things baby. Is this all for show? Did he not tell her he has a child? We search every room for signs of Libitina's existence, but there is nothing, not even a binky. He's abandoning her, which I am fine with, but what about Erin? If she's not up for the task of taking her, she may end up in foster care with some careless family. Don't panic. Not all people are assholes, just Mr. Yarrow.

I leave Mrs. Yarrow behind to deal with her grief in private.

Regina sips black coffee and rubs her temples as she reads a patient's chart at her desk. When I enter her body, she shivers and peers around the room. I push an image of

Mr. Yarrow into her head with Tessa beside him on the sofa. Regina shakes the thought out of her mind and continues working.

An empty hallway, bare of any photographs, flashes before her eyes. She tosses her reading glasses onto a pile of medical journals, walks her fingers through her filing cabinet, and removes Libitina's folder. Inside are images of the Yarrow residence, Libitina's medical records, and the signed grief counseling paperwork. She inspects the dates. The next session is this evening. Perhaps a road trip is in order. She dials Mr. Yarrow's cell phone.

No answer.

She's not surprised. He never answers. She scans the page with her fingertip and finds Erin's number.

She picks up on the first ring. "Hello?"

"Erin, it's Regina. Have you heard from Thaddeus?"

"Mr. Yarrow? Yeah right. He hasn't come to see her or even called since I have had her."

"Interesting. He hasn't contacted me either, and on Monday she is supposed to go back to him."

"I know. I have a vacation coming up that's already paid for. I mean I'd take her with me if I could, but it's a singles cruise."

"Oh, I don't blame you. There is a grief session tonight, and I am attending."

"Let me know what you find out."

"I will. How is Libitina?"

"She is amazing. Last night she slept six hours in a row. I freaked out when I woke up and realized how long it had been. I ran to her bassinet to make sure she was okay."

"I'm glad she is sleeping well for you. I'll call you after group."

After hanging up with Erin, Regina leaves to find Jack. She needs a plan in place if Mr. Yarrow doesn't want Libitina back and Erin isn't able to take her. Jack isn't at his desk when she arrives. His secretary points across the hallway to the restroom.

"How long has he been in there?"

The secretary glances at the clock. "Twenty minutes."

"Jesus."

Regina pushes the door open and peers under the stalls. Snoring echoes from the one closest to the far wall. She bangs on the partition with her fist. "Jack, get out here."

"What the hell, Regina? This is the men's room," he snaps as he zips up his fly and exits.

"No shit. Save your naps for lunchtime and weekends. There is a pile of work sitting on your desk unfinished. If you don't straighten up, I'll turn you in to HR."

"Regina let's not forget, you went to a patient's house and had someone take their child away on your own time. I too, can contact Human Resources."

"Listen, Jack. There is a problem that neither one of us may be able to fix."

"What? Your little plan backfire?"

"Not in the way you would think. He's going to the classes, but won't take my calls, and Erin hasn't heard a peep out of him."

"So?"

"So, it is possible he doesn't want her back, and if that's the case, I need to have the paperwork ready and a place for her to go."

"Well, she'll have to go into foster care of course."

"Can I have access to the foster parent files to vet them out?"

"Absolutely not. I'm not letting you dive into my foster family's lives because you fucked up. Libitina will go wherever she goes, and you will not interfere or try and sway the outcome," Jack shouts as he points his unwashed finger at her. "You did this. Now you can accept the consequences. End of discussion."

He yanks the door open, storms across the hall, and slams his office door.

What a douche.

Regina stays in the room well after Jack leaves. A man in a gray suit opens the door and stops short of entering. He checks the sign says, 'Men' and closes it again. When he shifts his blazer to place his hands on his hips, a shiny badge sparkles under the fluorescent lights.

"Ugh, I think you're in the wrong room."

"I know."

"So, can I get passed, and use the urinal?"

"Sure," Regina says raising her eyebrows and stepping aside.

"Are you planning on staying?"

"I'm thinking," Regina murmurs as she stares at the peeling, mint-green wallpaper.

"Thinking about if you want to leave or thinking in general?"

"Both," Regina says, facing him. "Can I ask you something?"

The man makes no move to hide himself as his urine stream starts flowing. "Sure."

"If a man neglects his child, then refuses to pick her up after taking her to a babysitter, can't you arrest him for abandonment?"

"No. The most we would do is call Child Protective Services and place that child with another member of the family or foster care if there is no family. Do you have that problem now?"

"I think so, but I won't know for sure until later."

"What's later?"

"The guy is attending his last grief counseling session. Want to join me?"

He finishes washing his hands and dries them with a towel. "Do you feel you need police protection?" he asks, glancing down at her name tag. "Regina."

"He can be violent."

"I'm on duty this evening. Here's my card. If you need me, call this number," the detective points. "It's my cell."

"Thank you, Detective Gerard."

"Please. Call me Will," he insists, opening the door for her.

"Thank you, Will. I'm hoping I won't need you."

"I'm hoping you will," he smiles as he scans her body, making her blush.

"Get out of here," she says, smacking him on the shoulder.

How cute. Regina and the detective are flirting. Mr. Yarrow isn't the only one feeling Cupid's arrow. The emergency room is quiet at this time of day. Not too many deaths during the daytime hours on a Friday. Tonight, on the other hand, is another story. Weekends are the busiest. With shootings, stabbings, drunk drivers, and drug overdoses, it becomes so chaotic that other reapers sometimes appear. I don't mind the help. We don't challenge each other and keep score.

When the time of the grief session nears, I plan on slipping away. The others can handle whatever comes their way. I need to hear what Mr. Yarrow is thinking when he lays eyes on Regina.

Another reaper appears beside me. Then another, and another. Something big is coming. The doors slam open as a gurney carrying a child rolls by. Outside another ambulance pulls under the overhang and unloads a second one. A school bus crashed on the highway and reports are flooding in of a multiple casualty event.

I float to the roof where a helicopter landed moments ago. The driver, a seventy-year-old woman, is in critical condition. She doesn't want to live anymore. She is tired of working for nothing. Her social security didn't cover much beyond her bills, so she became a bus driver to pay for food and other household needs. Who knew retirement would suck so bad?

The paramedic pumps her chest up and down as she stares at him. She gazes up at me, grins, and hops back inside. Then hops back out, and back in again. She's toying with them. A last laugh on the people who screwed her over on her pension. She used to work here. All these people were her coworkers, and when she asked them to join her and help press the union for new policies regarding pensions, no one stood with her.

She received half of what she expected. Now she is forcing them to fight to save her, despite knowing the results. Only this time, they will lose. I place my arm around her shoulders as she joins me one last time, and I steer her to the golden circle waiting for her. She's led an amazing life and took care of many people, bringing them joy, laughter, and advice. In the end, they fought for her. They just didn't do it when it mattered the most. When she was still alive.

Chapter Seven
Tension

The grief counseling sessions are inside the basement of an aging Baptist church. Every Thursday they have a farmers' market. They place leftover produce and baked goods on white folding tables in the lobby so anyone who arrives over the weekend may help themselves.

Regina shakes out a paper bag and selects two apples, a squash, and some overripe bananas. She loves baking pies and bread in her spare time.

"Hi," a familiar voice says.

"Detective Gerard? What are you doing here?"

"I didn't like the idea of you coming here alone with a potentially dangerous person. So, I thought I would swing through and see what the fuss is about."

"That's sweet of you, Will," she smiles as her cheeks redden. "Nice outfit."

"I stopped at the gym and changed my clothes. I thought wearing a suit and badge would make people uneasy. Love your dress."

"Thanks. The triple stripes on those blue track pants are a nice touch."

"Hey, they don't make them like these anymore," he grins as he slides his hands in the pockets and fans them. "There are holes inside too."

"In case you need to scratch."

"You betcha," he winks.

He is her type, and she is his, but now is not the time for distractions and flirting. They need to stay on task. I force myself inside his head and leave just as fast. The things he is planning to do to her are playing on repeat. I climb in her head instead. She is interested but nervous. Her last relationship ended poorly, and she doesn't want to jump right into another. I planted an image of Libitina in her head before leaving.

Remember why you are here.

"Hey, you, okay?" Will asks as he caresses her upper arm with his fingertips. "Your face is white as a ghost."

Regina rubs her forehead and sighs. "Just worried, that's all."

"I'm here. Come on. Let's get this over with."

They enter the meeting room. Eight other people are milling about, sampling cookies and cake, and drinking coffee.

"Who are we checking out?" Will asks.

"See the guy with the dark blue jeans and black polo top? That's Mr. Thaddeus Yarrow. His wife passed away a few weeks ago, and he's been neglecting his newborn daughter ever since. He hasn't called or made any contact with the sitter who currently is taking care of his child while he attends these classes. The funny thing is, he never wanted to do them. He only had to attend four."

"And how many has he done?"

"Nine."

"Interesting. Perhaps he realized it was helping and decided to keep going."

"No. That is not it. He is not the type."

"What type is he?'

"Mr. Yarrow is the kind of person who hits someone if he doesn't get what he wants. He was so upset that his wife died, and his daughter lived, he almost left her at the hospital."

"He hit his wife?"

"I don't know," Regina grimaces. "But he walloped me, and if he can hit a stranger, without even flinching, I am sure he struck her too."

"He hit you?" Will asks as he pulls her back by her upper arm. "Why didn't you report it?"

"Because he's grieving, and his emotions are all over the place."

"Doesn't matter. You should have reported it."

"Well, it's too late now. So, divide and conquer?" she asks, offering him her fist.

"Divide and conquer," he agrees, bumping her fist with his.

A large circle of chairs rests in the center of the room. Will and Regina take a seat across from each other. Regina's in plain clothes, with hair and makeup done, so when Mr. Yarrow eyes her, he doesn't recognize her right away. A woman, with medium-length brown hair, twisted into a bun enters and sits beside the detective. She adjusts her floral maxi dress, shifting her long tan legs to the outside of her clothing. Mr. Yarrow smirks, leans forward, and rubs his palms together.

This is her. This is Tessa.

Now that all the players have arrived, let the games begin.

The detective has a spiral notebook on his lap. I float to his side of the room. He is sketching a headshot of Regina. If my eyes were human, I would roll them. I send a piercing jolt through his right temple, making him stop at once. He flips the page and rests his pen.

One by one the participants spill their angst to the group, releasing the weight on their shoulders. Then it gets to Mr. Yarrow.

This ought to be interesting.

He talks about his wife in detail. How long they were together, and even their desire to have children. Then, the lie spills from his lips with little effort as though he had done it a thousand times before.

"Losing my wife and unborn daughter was the hardest thing I have ever been through," he cries. "Sometimes I get so overwhelmed. I had to take down all the photos of her in the house. Looking at them became too much. I feel so numb."

"Thank you for sharing, Thaddeus," Tess says as she dabs her watering eyes. "Let's take a five-minute break."

Everyone disperses to different locations inside and outside the room. The detective meets Regina at the exterior entrance. "I thought the baby lived?"

"She did!" Regina shouts. "That slime didn't tell anyone he has a child. I don't think he intends to take her back."

"Then why bother going to the sessions? What is the motive?"

"To keep up appearances, I guess, or buy some time."

"Time for what?"

"I don't know. You're the detective. Figure it out."

"Listen, I know you are upset, but I'm a homicide detective, not a private one," he murmurs. "But from what I saw, he has the hots for that Tessa chick."

"The lady running the sessions? How do you know?"

"Body language. The feeling appears mutual judging by her reaction to his attention."

"We need to know for sure. I'm going back in."

They ascend the steps in unison. Tessa and Mr. Yarrow are not in the room when they enter. The detective strolls toward the restrooms, while Regina wanders down a long dark hallway.

Heavy breathing comes from a private office with the door cracked. She peers through the slot. Mr. Yarrow has Tessa bent over the pastor's desk ramming her from behind with Jesus on the cross bouncing on the wall above their heads.

Blasphemy.

Regina stalks away to find Will. She nods to the exit, and he hustles after her as she storms down the steps and into the parking lot. If thoughts and feelings were visible, hers would be flames and smoke shooting from her head and eyes.

"That son of a bitch," she huffs.

"Calm down. What did you see?"

"Calm down? That dirtbag is drilling the grief counselor doggy style on the Lord's desk. I have every right to be upset."

"Wow. That's got to be a sin, right?"

"If it isn't, it should be." Regina paces back and forth. "I'm going in there, and I am calling him out in front of everyone."

"Oh, no you are not," he says, seizing her around the waist. "I know you are angry, but announcing their indiscretion and his lie in front of a room full of grieving widows and widowers is not the time or the place. Set up a meeting with him later. You need to cool down."

"Fine. I will call him Monday and see him Tuesday."

"Perfect. Now, want to go grab a drink with me?"

"Aren't you on duty?"

"Not as of five minutes ago," he smiles, staring at his watch.

"Fine, I could use a stiff drink after my day."

"Oh, I've got something stiff for you," Will chuckles as he opens her car door.

"You're kind of a pervert. Do you know that?"

"Yeah, but only when I like someone."

"Well, Will, I am not that easy. So, let's get something straight. You're buying the drinks and when the evening comes to an end, I am going home, alone. Got it?"

"Yes, ma'am. I'll be on my best behavior," he says as she turns the ignition.

"Somehow, I doubt that."

Regina drives away staring at Will in the reflection. He's a handsome guy, with dirty blonde crew-cut hair, a lean frame, and a sleeve of tattoos on his right arm. She is excited to have drinks but distracted by thoughts of Libitina. Telling Erin what she has discovered is not going to go over well.

On a positive note, if he doesn't want her back, then my pain and troubles may be over. But, if the agency places her with the wrong family, things may be worse. Much worse.

I drift down the dark streets under the light of the moon and arrive at Erin's. She is in the tub. Her eyes are bloodshot, and her hair is disheveled. I enter her body, chilling her naked skin.

Caring for Libitina is taking a toll on her mentally. She's exhausted and wishes Mr. Yarrow would get his act together so she can have some time to herself.

It's understandable. Caring for your own child is difficult enough, but assuming responsibility for someone else's is harder. She can make no choices for her medically, or spiritually. Erin's not allowed to take her out of state, open a bank account for her, or collect her mother's social security. Right now, she pays for everything out of pocket as she decides to forego becoming a foster parent. She is not ready to make that commitment.

I pull away from her and venture across the hall to her bedroom where Libitina rests in her bassinet. I gaze over the edge, and her eyes are like bright circles. She fixates on mine. Most babies blink at some point, but she does not waver. I levitate above her and try to enter her thoughts, but a force blocks me. I tried a second time and once again, I'm unable to penetrate her peach-fuzzed flesh.

What sweet madness is this? Another anomaly, another riddle. Not only can she see me, but she is also impenetrable. Another first in my soul-sucking career. I reach for her, hell-bent on making entry.

She blinks for the first time since our staring contest began. Her mouth opens wider than humanly possible and screams.

Erin passes through me in a towel as I cringe. The agonizing scream drives me from the room. I pause in the doorway as Erin slings Libitina over her shoulder. She lifts her unsteady infant head, glares at me, and smiles.

Chapter Eight
Poor Choices

After a long and entertaining weekend of drinking and brunch with the detective, Regina returns to work. Finding the courage to call Erin and making an appointment with Mr. Yarrow are her first two orders of business. She rifles through Mr. Yarrow's file and finds his number.

It's growing thicker by the day. At this rate, he will need his own cabinet. Inside is a photo taken of Libitina when she was born. She has a tiny smile tugging at the corner of her mouth.

"What makes you smile, Libitina?"

Me. I make her smile. For some reason, my pain amuses her. Once she is old enough to talk, I expect some answers. But for now, I wait.

Regina lifts the receiver and calls Mr. Yarrow. No answer. She leaves him a message telling him she will be stopping by for a visit the following day but doesn't give a time. Her fingers drum her desk as she stares at Erin's crinkled receipt paper. She reaches for the phone but stops when her cell vibrates. It's the detective.

'Lunch?'
'My break is at 11:30.'
'Pick you up at the front entrance.'

'K.'

She rests her knuckles on her mouth to hide her blushing smile. Her finger slides Erin's note under her smiley face painted rock paperweight to remember to call after lunch. All her distractions have caused her cases to pile up on her desk. She flips through them one by one until lunch.

The detective is leaning on his black Dodge Charger when she exits. He opens the back door for her.

"Why can't I ride in the front?"

"Against the rules, Regina," he smiles slamming the door. "You're my prisoner now."

"Funny," she chuckles. "So, where are we going?"

"There's a burger place all us guys go to for our lunches. I thought I'd show you off a bit to the boys."

"Me? Why? It's not like we are dating."

"Sure, we are. First, I bought you drinks. Then, we had a meal together at a fancy restaurant. Date two. Now this is three. Any more than two is dating."

"Oh really? And what if I say no, walk away, and disappear before three begins?"

"Well, I'll come to the hospital, find your office, and force you to have lunch with me by candlelight in front of all your peers."

"You wouldn't."

"Try me," he smiles with his eyes in the rearview mirror. "On a serious note, I want to discuss something with you." He pulls the car to the curb, shifts it into park, and twists his body to face her. "I did a background check on Mr. Thaddeus Yarrow. You were right. He hit his wife. Only once. The police showed up at their house, and she wouldn't press charges. Called it an accident."

"Accident, my ass."

"Regina, this guy has a violent past, even before he smacked his wife. Promise me you won't go visit him alone."

"I need to go tomorrow, and we are short-staffed."

"Cancel."

"I can't. I mean, I guess I can ask Jack, the technical case manager to come with me, but he's a lazy prick. I doubt he'd peel away from his desk to lift a finger for me. Then there's Erin."

"The babysitter?"

"Yeah, but she has Libitina, and if things go sideways, I don't want her present."

"Understandable. If you can't find someone to come with you, call for a police escort. They can keep the peace while you have a conversation with him."

"I can do that."

"Please do. Now come on. I'm starving."

Regina returned from lunch an hour ago and hasn't called Erin. I touch her hand, making it tremor. She gazes down at her shaking appendage and steadies it with the other. After wiggling her fingers, she yanks the receipt from under the stone, dials Erin's number, and places her on speaker.

"Hey, Erin. It's Regina. I have some news."

"From your tone, I'm guessing it's bad."

"Mr. Yarrow is seeing a woman from the group, and she doesn't know he has a baby."

"How could she not know?" Erin raises her voice. "Don't they discuss these things in their sessions?"

"Yes. The problem is, he told everyone his wife and child died."

"What!" she shouts. "That fucking asshole. Here I am, we are, trying to help him, and give him time to get himself straight so he can get his daughter back only for him to tell people she's dead. No, fuck that. I am going over there right now and giving him a piece of my mind or my fist, whichever comes first."

"No, please don't. I am going tomorrow."

"Someone needs to kick his ass."

"I know you're upset, but we can handle it. I have a detective who is helping me, and he said not to go alone."

"And what about Libitina? I have a cruise next week. I'm exhausted and need my vacation."

"Once we find out his intentions, we will find a suitable family for her."

"Okay, but I still want to hurt him."

"Me too, Erin."

Regina leaves her office and walks the short distance to Jack's. "I want to review some families for Libitina Yarrow."

"We have had this discussion, Regina. I'm not letting you pick and choose families."

"Jack, I'm not asking to hand-pick one from the dozens you have available. I'm just asking to take a few off the table and narrow down the pool."

"Fine. I'll give you ten folders. Of those options, remove five. Then I decide from the remaining five. Will that get you off my back?"

"Yes. Thank you."

"Yeah, whatever," Jack says, reaching behind him to a bookshelf.

He thumbs through the stack, removes the upper layer, and passes them to her. "This is it. Understand? Even if you don't like any of them, you're not getting more."

"Understood."

"You can show yourself out."

Regina hustles to her desk, eager to explore her options. After reviewing every folder, she came to the same conclusion. They all suck. Jack tricked her. He must have taken the crappiest ones and set them on top of the pile predicting her return.

I enter her mind, as she reviews them all, one more time.

Choice one is up to seven foster children living with them. They are not new to fostering, but unless the children are all from the same family, which they are not, they shouldn't have so many children crammed into a three-bedroom thousand-square-foot ranch. They're collectors.

Option two is more promising than the last. An elderly couple who has been working with children for over sixty years. They have two teenagers in senior high school and one in the eleventh grade. Per the husband's response to taking in an infant.

'Although we open our homes to all children, the ones with us at this time will reach their eighteenth birthday soon. If it were up to my wife, we would take an infant in a heartbeat. I, however, am looking forward to traveling, and alone time with my wife.'

She wants Libitina, but he doesn't. The odds of them fighting are high if she manages to convince him to take her in.

Option three has never been a foster before. Everyone must start somewhere, right? The issue is, this one is too eager. There is page after page of daily records of phone calls and conversations as to why no one has called her back about fostering. A fine line exists between having the desire to help a child and being obsessed with the idea. Jack would love for her to choose this one just to make her stop calling.

The next seven folders have multiple red flags. She closes the final folder and shoves the pile away from her. Jack passes her office doorway heading home for the evening.

She scurries down the hall to his office, hoping to sneak a different family's folder, but his secretary hasn't left for the day.

"What are you still doing here?" Regina asks.

"Jack didn't want anyone to see his desk a mess, so he asked me to clean it. Not sure why I bother. He's going to dirty it up again in less than five minutes." The secretary stands erect. "Regina, what are you up to?"

"Okay, fine. The families Jack offered me are horrible. Please, give me one worth a damn."

"No. Are you trying to get me fired?"

"You don't have to tell him you gave it to me. I can say it somehow slid inside another."

"I know you care about this baby, Regina, but don't you think you are a little too invested in this?"

"You don't understand. Libitina will have a hard enough time growing up knowing her father didn't want her because he thinks she killed her mother. Do you want to stick her with a family who won't give her the life she deserves?"

The secretary vibrates her lips, removes her glasses, and sighs. "Regina, there is one family I know who would love to have her, but Jack refuses to put her with them."

"Why?"

"Here," she pulls a folder out from inside a drawer. "I keep this one with me because every time a newborn comes up for fostering, I slap it back on the pile. I think you'll understand why he won't place her with them."

Regina opens it with her pointer finger. The photo gives her the answer. The family is Hispanic, and their second language is English.

"Seriously. Jack won't pick them because of a potential language barrier. Does he not realize the benefits?"

"I tried telling him raising a child in a bilingual household increases brain power and cultural understanding. Not to mention, the endless opportunities when she starts job hunting. Besides that, they put in their application that they primarily speak English and will only teach the baby Spanish if she wants to learn when she is older."

"He's ridiculous. Thank you for this," Regina says, wiggling the folder over her head as she exits.

Regina jogs to her desk and sinks into her chair. The Alvarez family lives in a large ranch near the edge of town. They have a three-year-old daughter, Fabiola, who would love to have a little brother or sister. The husband is in real estate and the wife works from home. They have three bedrooms and two bathrooms, so Libitina would have her own room. Their credit is spot on, and their criminal background check came back clean.

They're perfect.

The problem is Jack. Regina takes the elevator to Human Resources on the second floor. If she wants this family to take in Libitina, she will need them on her side. Margaret Cook, the Human Resources Manager, stands behind her desk, reaching for her purse when Regina knocks.

"Margaret, I have to tell you something."

"My husband is downstairs waiting for me," she says, turning off the light and entering the hall. "Can't it wait?"

"I'm afraid not. I can give you the quick version, and if you want to fire me for what I have done, can you do it after I place Libitina with this family."

Margaret stops and glares at her. "What do you mean, what you have done?"

Regina inhales a deep breath and spills it all as she exhales. From start to finish, she explains how she used hospital resources, what she did on her own time, and everything in between.

Chapter Nine
Crumble

"Regina, have you lost your mind? I could fire you right now," Margaret says waving her hands in the air as she continues walking. "Don't get me wrong, I understand why, but you should have come to me if Jack wasn't doing his job."

"Come on, Margaret, you and I both know the last person who crossed Jack ended up getting fired when he went out of his way to dig up dirt on them."

"Listen, come to my office tomorrow, and we can figure this out. Right now, I need to eat," Margaret insists as she opens her car door. "And Regina, stay away from the Yarrows."

"But I made an appointment to speak with him tomorrow."

"Regina, if you go there tomorrow, I will have no choice but to terminate you. Talk to Jack and see if you can get him to go instead."

"He won't. I know him," Regina murmurs as she crosses her arms.

"Come see me then. I will handle Jack."

Regina shakes her head as she drives away. Streetlights flicker above her as the darkness of an incoming storm triggers them hours early. She returns to her office and calls Erin.

No answer.

That's strange. Erin should be home. Perhaps she shut off her ringer to avoid waking Libitina. As long as she is not crying, it pleases me.

I float through the floor down to the intensive care unit of the hospital. Another child from the earlier car accident crawls away from his physical frame and gazes up at me.

"Am I dead?"

I nod my head, and the boy peers across the room as his grief-stricken father holds his inert frame. Light emanates through the door. An old man, wearing blue jean trousers emerges from the illuminated space.

"Grandpa!" the young boy hollers as he grips him around the waist. "Are you taking me with you?"

The elderly man strokes the boy's hair and steers him to the entrance where an angel waits to take them home.

A sharpness stabs through my immortal frame. Since the day she was born, Libitina has never caused so much pain. Something is wrong. I disappear and then reappear at Erin's house, but no one is home. Libitina is nearby. I can feel her anger, her rage, her anguish. It's tearing me apart. The closer I come to Mr. Yarrow's residence, the worse I become. I fight the urge to leave as distance makes no difference. The only thing that stops the hurt, is to make Libitina stop.

Erin's, Mr. Yarrow's, and Tessa's vehicles are all parked outside. The front door whips open, and a single gunshot drops Tessa to her knees as Mr. Yarrow stands over her and fires a second round into her head. His eyes are dazed and solemn. Erin runs through a side door and disappears into the trees with Libitina screaming in her arms. A dark creature appears from the black puddle beside Tessa's corpse and drags her confused spirit beneath the earth. Mr. Yarrow enters the tree line, pursuing Erin and Libitina.

Erin's feet fumble across the dark, uneven terrain until she reaches the road. She zig-zags across the pavement as Mr. Yarrow fires several rounds in her direction. Libitina screams as Erin presses her hard against her bosom. She almost makes it home.

Almost.

A bullet hits Erin's leg dropping her at once. "Please, Mr. Yarrow. Don't do this," she begs.

"Why did you have to tell Tessa I had a baby? We were happy. You ruined everything. Why couldn't you just take Libitina and let me live my life?"

"She's your daughter, Mr. Yarrow. She needs you. We were just trying to help. You're grieving."

"I was moving on with Tessa, but you had to go and ruin it by telling her about that abomination."

"She is your child."

"No, she is the devil and deserves to be in hell," he yells as he points the gun and fires.

Erin falls to the side and drops Libitina as the bullet pierces her heart. Mr. Yarrow towers over Libitina's tiny distraught body and squeezes the trigger.

Nothing.

He tries again.

Nothing.

Erin's spirit separates from her skin and vanishes into the sky above us. The screaming needs to stop, but if he's here, there is no resolution. Mr. Yarrow startles when he catches a glimpse of me in the corner of his eye. His head rotates the opposite way as I appear there too. I whisper his name, and it echoes around him.

"Who are you?" he screams into the dense forest. "Come out. I know you are there."

I dive inside him, and his face and mind go blank. The only way to keep Libitina safe was to steer him far away so he couldn't find her. If her screams bring me pain, what would her death cause?

We move over boulders, dead tree trunks, and litter as I lead him across the road and into another set of trees. Up ahead is a waterfall. Don't get me wrong, the temptation to kill him is there, but it isn't allowed. I exit him after two miles of walking in a straight line.

Mr. Yarrow blinks multiple times. His eyes dart around him as he searches for Libitina and Erin's body. Leaves crunch under his heavy steps as he stomps through the brush and then stops to listen. A truck horn gives the location of the road away, and Mr. Yarrow jogs in the direction of the sound. He pauses one more time at the edge of the asphalt.

There she is. In between the tweeting birds, and the rustling of leaves, Libitina's faint cries are audible. Before Mr. Yarrow has a chance to react, I flood him to his core with shaking anxiety. His teeth chatter as he holds his body around the waist with both arms. Adrenaline rushes through his pounding heart as he gasps for air through his tightening chest. His will is strong, but I am stronger. I dart in and out of his field of vision as he stumbles in the middle of the road. A driver blares his horn as Mr. Yarrow drops to his knees on the double yellow line.

"Stop, please," he cries to the empty air around him.

"Get out of the road, asshole," the driver yells as they pass him.

"Fuck you," Mr. Yarrow shouts as he fires a round, striking the rear windshield of the driver's hunter-green SUV.

The driver slams on his brakes, launches his door aside, and hops out carrying a Ruger semiautomatic hunting rifle. Mr. Yarrow's eyes turn to saucers. He takes off into the woods, as the driver fires a round, and chases after him.

How's it feel to be hunted, Mr. Yarrow?

They plow through the woods in the direction of Libitina. The driver closes in on Mr. Yarrow as they round a set of joined trees. Mr. Yarrow scoops Libitina in his arms and points the handgun at her. She shrieks at the top of her lungs as enormous tears flood her raging red cheeks. The hunter points his rifle at him. "Put the baby down."

"I'll shoot her," Mr. Yarrow stutters as he shifts his weight from one foot to the other. "Get back."

The hunter gazes at Erin's empty eyes but keeps the muzzle pointed at Mr. Yarrow. "Mister, I don't care what you did, but if you don't put that baby down and walk away, I will blow the back of your head off and splatter it against the tree behind you."

Mr. Yarrow glances behind him. The gun shakes in his unsteady hand as he slowly kneels to the ground. "Back away," he orders the hunter.

The hunter takes a few steps back as Mr. Yarrow rests Libitina in a pile of wet leaves, then bolts through the bushes and out of sight. The man rests his rifle on the mossy earth and places Libitina over his blue plaid-laden shoulder. "I got you little one. You're safe now. John won't let him hurt you," he murmurs as he removes his cell phone from his breast pocket.

I cringe as she continues to wail.

The hunter crouches to Erin and removes a bottle from her blue cardigan. He props it against his chest and presses it between Libitina's starving lips. Using his left arm and the side of his face, he flips his phone open and dials 9-1-1.

'9-1-1 what's your emergency?'

"Yes, I have a baby here and a dead woman and there's a guy in the woods with a gun, and I think he's the killer. Please, send the police," the hunter says breathing heavily.

'Sir, remain calm. What is your name?'

"John."

'Okay, John. Can you tell me where you are?'

"The county road just off the highway. I think it's eighty-three."

'I have your location narrowed down the police are on their way. Are you still in the woods?'

"Yes."

'John, I want you to head toward the road and meet the trooper there. But don't hang up until he arrives, alright?'

"I understand. Walking there now."

'Is the baby injured?'

"No. I don't think so."

'I'm dispatching an ambulance. Did you say there's a woman dead?'

"Yes."

'Did you check her pulse to be sure?'

"Didn't need to. She took a hit to the center of her chest and her eyes are open and empty."

'I'm sorry you had to see that. Officers and an ambulance are less than a mile out. Are you on the road yet?'

"Just got here. I see them."

'John, you can hang up now. They will take care of you from here.'

"Thank you."

John closes his phone and stuffs it in his back pocket. The first trooper to arrive exits his vehicle with his gun drawn. "Put your gun on the ground," he hollers as he points his weapon at the hunter.

The hunter lets the rifle drop to the asphalt. "I'm the one who called. There's a guy in the woods. He shot at my vehicle and pointed his gun at this baby," John explains.

The trooper glances at John's missing window and lowers his weapon. "Where is the gunman?"

"I chased him away."

Two more officers roll towards them with an ambulance bringing up the rear. "Sir, take the baby to the paramedics. We will take it from here."

"There's a woman's body about a mile in by two trees that grew together straight that way," John raises his left arm and points to the trampled path he created.

"Can you give me a description of the man you saw?"

"He's a white guy, with brown short hair and he had on blue jeans and a white t-shirt," John says as he passes Libitina to a paramedic.

The trooper nods and jogs to the other officers to give them a description. A fourth vehicle barrels toward them and comes to a stop. An officer steps out and unloads a Belgian Malinois from the back seat.

Mr. Yarrow doesn't stand a chance.

Libitina cries as the female paramedic removes her blood-stained clothing and diaper and checks her over. She wraps her in a warm blanket after cleaning her up but leaves her naked. John sits across from them with his head in his hands. "Is she okay?"

"She's perfect. We are taking her to the hospital for observation. Are you injured?"

"No. That lunatic pointed a gun at her head," John says as he grips his knees and rocks back and forth. "How can someone do that to a child?"

"Some people are cowards," she says handing Libitina back to him. "She seems to like you, so you're coming with us."

John nods as he bounces Libitina on his shoulder.

Barking, followed by screams, breaches the silence of the forest. The K-9 found Mr. Yarrow. A smile spreads across the hunter's face as the doors to the ambulance swing shut.

Chapter Ten
Terminated

All eyes are on Regina when she steps inside the hospital. No one says a word, but she can tell something is wrong. Inaudible whispers come from everyone as she punches the up button on the elevator. The squeaking wheels of the pully system unnerves her. The doors slam shut behind her as she steps off and focuses on the speckled tile.

Margaret waits outside the doorway of the Human Resources office. Her crossed arms and wide-open stance create a pit in Regina's stomach as she closes in on her.

"Morning, Regina. Come inside and sit down," Margaret sighs.

Regina scoots her chair forward and sinks into its brown leather. "What's wrong?"

"Regina, I have been working here for over ten years, almost as long as you have been employed here. Never in all that time has any nurse ever put me in this position."

"Listen, Margaret, if this is about what I did, I'm sorry. I'm trying to do what's best for Libitina. Erin is at her wit's end, and Mr. Yarrow has no intention of taking her back. That's why I found her a suitable family."

"You mean this family?" Margaret slides the folder to Regina.

"Well, yes. Jack didn't want Libitina with them because he worried about the language barrier, but I think…"

"No, Regina. See that's the problem. You didn't think. Now, I am happy to contact this family for Libitina, but as of this moment, you're fired."

"Margaret, please. I'm sorry. Can I at least finish out the week and oversee the transfer of custody from Erin to the Alvarez family?"

"Oh, my. You haven't heard, have you?"

"Heard what?"

"Erin is dead. Mr. Yarrow shot her and his grief counselor last night. If it weren't for a jammed gun, and a disgruntled motorist, Libitina would be too."

"What? Oh, my God," Regina stutters as her eyes begin to water.

"I'm sorry, Regina," Margaret says as she comes out from behind her desk. "I will place Libitina with the Alvarez's. It may be the only positive thing that comes of this tragedy."

She isn't wrong. Though the death of Erin is unfortunate, Libitina will be happy with her new family. And if she is happy, I am happy. I float beside Regina. She keeps her head down, ignoring the judgmental eyes of her coworkers as she returns to her office to pack her belongings.

The door creaks on its hinges as Will peeks inside. Regina storms to him and slams her fists on his chest. "You should have called me," she sobs.

"I'm sorry," Will says as he draws her into his arms.

"Tell me what happened."

"Regina, I can't. It's an ongoing investigation," he says holding her at arm's length.

The detective's phone rings in his pocket, and he walks away from her to answer. His pinkie and thumb squeeze his temples as his face pales. "Jesus."

"What?" Regina asks, stopping in front of him.

"Mr. Yarrow tried hanging himself with his sheets. The corrections officers saw him on camera and got there in time. He's in the hospital under suicide watch."

"What a coward," Regina says wiping her running nostrils.

"I'll call you later, okay?" Will says as he smudges the tears from her skin with his fingertips.

Regina nods her head and throws her tissue into the trash as someone from security leans against the wall by her door. Will pecks her forehead and leaves as she drops her peace lily into a box. She presses her head on the wooden top of her desk.

Someone clears their throat making her look up.

"I told you this would backfire," Jack smirks as he stuffs his hands in his wrinkled khakis. "Now two people are dead, and you've lost your job. Tell me Regina, was it worth it?"

She dives across the furniture between them, snatches him by his tie, and shouts in his face. "Fuck you, you lazy son of a bitch. None of this would have happened if you did your fucking job."

Jack drags her over the desk the rest of the way and seizes her wrists. "Remember whose fault this is Regina," Jack hisses as he pulls her off him and pushes her aside.

"That's enough," the guard demands entering the room.

Libitina cries out from the nursery, drawing me away from the drama unfolding in Regina's office. She hates her baths, but the nurse must wash blood from her hair. Regina comes down the hall with security. She pauses before the viewing window. "I'm sorry little one," she whispers.

The guard ushers Regina away as the nurse scrubs Libitina's scalp. Her face reddens with anger but stops when she looks at me. The nurse glances over her shoulder. "What are you staring at? Is someone behind me?"

Not someone. Something. I wait for Libitina to blink but it doesn't happen. Her eyes are stuck as though she's somewhere else. Anywhere but here.

The nurse snaps her fingers, and Libitina turns away from me. "Where did you go baby girl?"

Libitina's lip pouts when she slips a onesie over her head. "Oh, no. Don't cry," the nurse says lifting her from her bed and sitting in a chair.

I stand behind the rocker as the nurse pats her back. "Ouch," the nurse snaps as Libitina digs into her skin. "We need to cut those nails."

The nurse crosses the room and rifles through a drawer. She takes her tiny fingers and trims them one by one. Libitina curls her fingers, gripping the sharp edge of the scissors, cutting herself open.

"Shit," the nurse murmurs and sets her in the crib while she grabs a sterile gauze pad.

I tilt my head as Libitina stuffs her bleeding fingers in her mouth and sucks them.

The nurse passes through me and shudders. "No, that's yucky," she yells taking Libitina's appendages away from her.

Libitina blows up like an atomic bomb, flooding the room with a raging scream and destroying anyone's ears nearby.

"What did you do?" Another nurse runs into the room.

"I nicked her finger by accident, and she was sucking on it, and I made her stop."

"Well give it back to her."

"No. That's gross. I need to clean it."

The nurse grabs Libitina's bottle to calm her but she refuses to take it.

Margaret enters the room with a Hispanic woman and a little girl. "This is Mrs. Alvarez and her daughter Fabiola. They are here to meet Libitina," Margaret yells over the crying.

Mrs. Alvarez opens her arms and takes Libitina from the nurse. She sings a Spanish lullaby to Libitina as she rocks in the chair, and Fabiola strokes her fine hair. She's quiet now and fixates on the mouth of Mrs. Alvarez. The nurse reaches for Libitina's hand to dab the blood from her finger.

"Let her be," Mrs. Alvarez insists resting her palm on the nurse's hand. "She is content."

The nurse steps back and glances at Margaret.

Jack barrels into the room and slams a folder on the end table beside them, startling Libitina. "What is the meaning of this, Margaret?"

"Jack, let's step into the hallway."

He storms out behind her, and she closes the nursery door. "Jack, I don't want to hear it."

"Don't want to hear it? That family is not the right fit for the Yarrow baby. I have a whole pile of people waiting for me to call them back and let them know whether they can foster her or not."

"Jack if you had done your job to begin with, we wouldn't be here right now. Call the other families and tell them she is no longer available for fostering."

"Placement is my decision, not yours."

The stale odor of this morning's donut escapes his breath as Margaret leans in and hovers an inch from his face. "If you spent less time stuffing your face and playing solitaire, I wouldn't have needed to go over your head. The only reason I haven't fired you is because the hospital president is your uncle. Now get out of my sight."

Margaret storms away from him. He peers through the window as Mrs. Alvarez stands and pats Libitina's back. We gaze at them together as Libitina raises her head and smiles.

"This isn't over," Jack says stalking away.

He's going to be a problem. I continue watching the Alvarez family for a few more minutes before returning to my post in the emergency room. It's quiet for now, and fate calls me elsewhere, so I leave.

I appear in a pregnant woman's bedroom while she sleeps, reach inside her abdomen, and take her unborn baby. This isn't the first time I've been here. She and her husband keep trying, but the result is always the same. Her eyes pop open when the cramping starts. She cries silently to herself, afraid to wake her husband and tell him it's happening again.

This will be the last time they try. He told her the last time they wouldn't bother anymore after this. It's too hard. You would think being a soothsayer she would expect it, but she never does. Perhaps her gift is the reason for her barren state. Their next step is adoption.

Her husband leans over her, wipes her tears, and pulls her into him. "It's okay. I love you."

"I'm sorry," she cries.

"Don't be sorry. This isn't our path. God has a plan. He always does."

He helps her out of bed, and into a pair of pants. The quiet ride to the hospital speaks volumes about their feelings. Guilt overwhelms the wife. She thought the third time would be a charm, but her body rejected new life once again. Three died because of her selfishness and determination to keep trying. These are her personal feelings not the beliefs of the masses. Some people never give up, but she and her husband agreed to stop at three.

As they pull into the medical center parking lot, the Alvarez family exits with Libitina. One family gains a child while they lose one again. As the wife passes Mrs. Alvarez an image flashes in her head stopping her from moving forward. Her husband whispers in her ear. "What did you see?"

The wife turns to Mrs. Alvarez as she places Libitina on her shoulder. Her face goes blank as she moves without trying and stops within a foot of Mrs. Alvarez. "Can I touch her?"

"Excuse me," Mrs. Alvarez says raising an eyebrow.

"I just want to hold her hand," the wife smiles.

"What is your name?"

"Sara."

"Well, Sara this little girl has been through a lot, and I'd rather not have a stranger touch her."

"Sara let's go inside," her husband insists.

"She's special," Sara says smiling at Libitina as she reaches for her.

Mr. Alvarez rounds the front of the car and steps in between them. "Get away from them," he huffs in a thick accent.

Mr. Alvarez opens the passenger side's back door, takes Libitina from his wife, kisses her head, and sits her in her car seat. After strapping her in, he turns to Sara. "Of course, she's special. All children are, but she's not some animal at a zoo you can pet. Now move away from our car."

"I'm sorry, sir. Sara didn't mean to upset your family."

Mr. Alvarez ignores the husband as he follows him to the driver's side of the car. "You don't understand. My wife sees things, but she has to touch her to catch a glimpse into her future."

"Get away from us," Mr. Alvarez yells as he shifts the car into drive. "You and your wife are loco."

The family rolls away as Sara collapses to the concrete doubled over with severe cramping. Her husband hoists her off the ground and carries her inside.

Mr. Alavarez gazes into his rearview. Mrs. Alvarez sits in the middle of the back seat between Libitina and Fabiola. They smile at each other with their eyes as Libitina holds her pointer finger, and smiles.

Chapter Eleven
No Ordinary Baby

Fabiola grips the crib bars and peeks in at Libitina. "Baby."

"Yes, that's Libitina. Can you say Libitina?"

Fabiola shakes her head and runs out of the room. Mrs. Alvarez hoists Libitina from her crib and lays her on the changing table. The light above her head flickers behind them. Libitina cranks her head up and gazes at the corner where I hover.

Mrs. Alvarez puts her face beside Libitina's to match her line of sight. "What is so interesting in that corner?"

She carries Libitina to where the two walls meet after she changes her diaper and stands inside me. Chills encapsulate every bit of her skin, and she moves away from me at once.

"Well, well, well. It appears we have company, but you already knew that didn't you Libitina?"

Libitina coos as Mrs. Alvarez holds her up to the ceiling. "You are special, aren't you?"

My presence does not rattle Mrs. Alvarez. A rare occurrence indeed. She brings Libitina close and kisses her silky locks as Fabiola sprints into the room in her pink footie pajamas. She swipes her long, straight black strands from her face and passes Libitina's bottle to Mrs. Alvarez. "Here, Mama."

"Thank you, sweetheart. Did Papa make this?"

Fabiola sticks her fingers in her mouth as she nods then runs around the corner and disappears. Mr. Alvarez stands in the doorway, watching Mrs. Alvarez rock Libitina. "How is she?"

"She's perfect, Hector." She sits Libitina on her lap and pats her back. "You couldn't ask for a better baby."

The family feline, a long-haired Siamese, strolls into the room and rubs Mrs. Alvarez's leg.

"I think Luna wants to meet Libitina," Hector says, kneeling in front of Mrs. Alvarez. "Let me take her."

Hector brings Libitina down to floor level. Luna crouches, sniffs Libitina, and growls as she backs away slowly. Hector and his wife exchange looks as the cat retreats to the corner where I am standing, leaps straight up in the air as though it sat on a tack, and darts from the room.

"Your cat is loco," Hector chuckles. "Why do you love it so much?"

"She sleeps with me at night and makes me feel safe." Mrs. Alavarez smiles as she takes Libitina back from him.

"Keeping you safe is my job," Hector says, kissing her on the cheek.

"Well, Luna is my backup. If anyone breaks in, I'll throw her at them."

They both laugh as they walk down the hallway to the living room where Fabiola sits in front of the television. Mrs. Alvarez places Libitina beside her in a bouncer, and heads to the kitchen.

The television station switches to a disaster documentary. Fabiola runs from the room and returns dragging her father by the pant leg.

"Cartoons."

"If you want cartoons, don't change the channel, Fabby," Hector insists as he turns it back.

He strolls back to the kitchen to help Mrs. Alvarez make breakfast as they do every Sunday. The screen flickers multiple times and changes to the national weather channel where anchors are discussing the bizarre weather patterns.

I gawk at Libitina as Fabiola stomps out of the room.

Can it be? Is she changing the channels?

"Cartoons, cartoons, cartoons," Fabiola chants from the other room.

Mrs. Alvarez enters the room drying her hands with a black and white checkered towel. She pauses with her finger on the remote and listens to the weatherman discuss the possibility of a tornado forming in a line of thunderstorms coming through this evening.

"Cartoons!" Fabiola screams startling her mother, and Libitina.

"Okay, Fabby. Don't shout. You scared the baby."

"I'm sorry, baby," Fabiola says as she hugs Libitina.

"Ouchy," Fabiola cries out as she holds the side of her neck.

"Let me see," Mrs. Alvarez says.

Fabiola moves her palm away from her throat. A long scratch bleeds onto her shirt. Mrs. Alvarez grasps Libitina's fingers and examines her nails. "We need to cut those."

"Mama, baby mean."

"She didn't do it on purpose."

Libitina's eyes widen as past reports of tornado damage flash across the screen. A list pops up recommending viewers be prepared to shelter in place and have enough food and supplies on hand for several days as well as first aid kits.

"Hector, a storm is coming. Do we have everything?" Lola yells to the kitchen.

"No, but we can go after breakfast."

Lola furrows her eyebrows and turns her attention back to the weather.

"Don't worry. We bought this place because it has a cellar, remember?" Hector points out as he stops beside her and reads the banner flowing across the screen.

Fabiola yanks the remote from her mother and passes it to her father. "Cartoons, Papa."

"Okay, okay cartoons."

After eating, the entire family climbs into the car and drives a few miles down the road to the local food mart. The packed lot leaves no close spaces to park in.

"I'll drop you girls in front and go park," Hector says rolling to a stop at the entrance.

Lola exits first, grabs a shopping cart, straps Fabiola in the front, and places Libitina's seat in the back. The checkout lines run to the back of the store as people stock up on supplies. Lola turns down the baby aisle in search of formula. A woman, in her twenties, removes all ten of the canisters of formula Lola needs from the shelf and puts them in her cart.

"Excuse me. Can I have a couple of those?"

"No."

"Well, the news says you only need enough for a few days and that's more than a month. Please, I only ask for a couple."

"You want some? Meet me outside and I'll sell them to you for twice the price," the girl sneers as she vanishes around the corner.

Lola hustles after her, determined to take at least one when she isn't looking. A six-foot endcap with shelves full of glass jars of spaghetti sauce collapses on the greedy woman and crashes to the floor. Red liquid and broken shards surround her as Lola reaches down, picks up two cans, and smiles. "Karma."

Fabiola giggles as her mother steers around the woman, careful to avoid the mess, as Hector approaches with a gallon of milk. "I got the last one. What happened here?"

"She wouldn't share the formula."

"So, you what? Threw a fit?"

"Not me. The universe spoke for me," she says patting his cheek. "And it doesn't care for selfish and greedy people."

They finish shopping and stand in line. The fluorescent bulbs on the ceiling flicker and buzz, and everyone peers up. Heavy rain bangs on the metal roof as darkness envelopes the parking lot. Emergency alerts flash across multiple cell phone screens. A county-wide tornado watch is in effect until eleven p.m. with a severe thunderstorm warning from two-thirty this afternoon until ten in the evening.

Hector glances at his watch as many others in line do the same. It's already two. "This is taking too long. We should go."

Hector is right. The longer they wait, the greater the risk. I touch the bulb of the light in the lane the manager is standing in front of with his clipboard. Lola swerves to his lane at once and begins unloading.

"I'm not open," the manager insists as he unplugs the faulty fixture, and a new line forms behind Lola.

She looks behind her, and back to him. "You are now."

"No, I'm not. Go back in the open lane."

Loud moaning comes from the crowd, followed by an eruption of bickering about what order in line people were in. Libitina starts crying. It begins as a whimper, but as voices grow, so does her anger. It sails above the noise and pierces the manager's ears.

"The sooner you ring us out, the faster we will be out of here," Lola grins unaffected by the infant shrieking.

Fabiola covers her ears and screams beside Libitina. They bellow their displeasure in unison as the fighting amongst the customers intensifies. The manager shakes his arms in the air, and Hector places their remaining items on the conveyor belt. A bagger comes to the rescue and loads their groceries back into the cart.

"Thank you. Have a great day," Hector hollers over the chorus of emotions.

The wind rips the cart out of Lola's hands and launches it in the direction of the road as they exit the sanctity of the building. It rolls fast into traffic before Hector has a chance to stop it. Cars swerve around it one by one as it circles the center line. A horn blares as Hector grasps the handle of the cart and covers the girls with his frame as a dump truck barrels toward them.

I take the wheel of the frozen driver, yank it to the right, and send him into a ditch. Lola stops short of the blacktop, as Hector removes Fabiola from her seat with one hand and picks up Libitina's car seat with the other.

"Oh, my God. My babies, are you alright?" Lola says as she embraces Fabiola and checks every inch of smiling Libitina.

"That was close," Hector says as he shields them from the wind. "Come. We must go."

He jogs to the car and loads Libitina in the backseat. As the belt snaps closed, he pauses when Libitina winks at him. Shaking it off as a reflex, he says nothing to Lola as she finishes belting in Fabiola. Flashing blue and red lights flood the street as fire and police arrive to help the truck driver in the ditch. Hector and Lola make the sign of the cross and kiss their thumbs as they whisper a silent prayer to make it back safely.

Hector drops his hand on Lola's tremoring floral leggings and squeezes her thigh. "It's okay. We will be home soon."

A single tear speeds down her face, and he catches it with his finger. She grips his hand and kisses the back of it. "I don't know what I would do if I lost you and our babies," she whimpers.

"I'll protect them with my life. All of you."

"I know, but I'm scared."

Hector makes a right turn into their driveway as lightning flashes above them. He turns to Lola, seizes both her hands, and holds them against his heart. "Nothing will ever happen to you or the girls when I am here. You don't have to be afraid."

"Papa, baby stinks," Fabiola whines as she wrinkles her nose.

A foul odor stifles the air inside the car, forcing them to vacate.

"Phew. You stink little girl," Hector announces as he unbuckles Libitina from her seat. "Take Fabiola to the basement. I'll change her and meet you there."

Lola passes a light bag to Fabiola and strings the remaining four on both arms leaving her hands free to open the exterior metal door. A massive piece of hail bounces off the metallic surface as Fabiola and Lola disappear beneath the ground.

Chapter Twelve
EF4

The wind howls through the house as Hector lays Libitina on her changing table. Through the window, hail strikes the pavement. The bulb above them blows out like a candle and so does every light in the house across the street as the storm takes out the power.

Lola yells from the basement beneath his feet to hurry. His phone flashes as a tornado warning banner plasters his screen. The windows rattle and thunder booms outside.

There is no time. He scoops Libitina up in the black of the room, dives to the floor between the inner wall and bed, and pulls the mattress over them. Snapping wood, breaking glass, and a deafening freight train-like sound pierces Hector's eardrums.

Libitina is quiet. Too quiet.

Hector stares at her, wide-eyed when a bolt of lightning lights up the room illuminating her grin. Most babies would be afraid, screaming, and distraught, but not Libitina. She fears nothing.

Hector holds her tiny palm and prays as she squeezes his finger. The storm ends, and an eerie silence takes its place. Warm liquid wets Hector's clothes as Libitina relieves herself. He moves the partition above them and surveys the flawless room. Outside, debris covers the road, and the house opposite them no longer exists. Hector lays Libitina on the bed, puts on her diaper, and pinches the snaps on her onesie.

"Hector!" Lola cries as she enters the room with Fabiola and embraces them both. "It's a miracle. Come see."

She snatches Hector's hand and pulls him into the front yard as the sun breaches the clouds and shines on the only house left standing on the street. Theirs.

Neighbors come from their cellars and walk dazed toward them.

"Unbelievable," the neighbor beside them says shaking his head. "Do you have a forcefield around your house or what?"

Hector and Lola glance at Libitina as she glances at the sky.

She's protecting herself and therefore, protecting them. Interesting.

Pressure leads me down the block where a woman struggles to breathe between the roof of her house and her kitchen floor. She didn't make it to the cellar either, but the result wasn't the same. Nothing protected her as the ceiling caved in. She's suffocating. If she wanted to scream for help, she couldn't. The weight of her home is too much. I sit beside her and wait.

"Mommy," a little voice calls from the barricaded basement below.

A tear races to her temple as her eyes fall empty. She saved her children and has always been a good Christian earning her a place amongst the stars. I pull her to me and show her the worst of herself, which amounts to nothing more than losing her temper a few times. She is as close to a perfect person as you could get. A rarity these days. A bright light envelops her and leads her through the rubble.

If everyone were like her, perhaps there wouldn't be so much hatred and violence in the world, but that's not who the species has become. A bunch of greedy, self-centered, earth-polluting evil beings who prefer war over peace to dominate the planet.

Jokes on them.

When faced with death, they all say or think the same way, 'I wish I knew this was coming. I would have done things differently.'

Would you though? I doubt it. Even the ones who come back from the lights of death carry on in the same manner despite having a second chance. They author books about their experience and talk of their mortality, but go home, and continue the same behavior as before. Their notoriety is all that has changed.

I float to the sky where multiple beams of light shine down throughout the city as angels do God's bidding. Another reaper floats miles away assessing the damage as well. The EF4 tornado ripped a path of destruction through the city. The last one to strike Ohio happened almost a century ago in Lorain.

Shadows move in and out of homes and buildings as reapers work to remove the souls of the deceased. A teenage boy runs from the dark ones. A serial killer in the making, his death is no loss to society and puts an end to the missing cats and small dogs from the neighborhood. When they come for him, he wails for his mommy as they drag him down below. If she died too, she would join him for she knew what he was and refused to seek help. Ignoring the bleached skulls hanging on his bedroom wall, she is no better than the rest of the parents who allow their children to commit crimes and go unpunished.

Even now, in this hour of destruction, people choose themselves. They loot for goods, food, jewelry, televisions, luxury clothing, and anything they can steal while the police are busy.

But not everyone is like them. The Alvarez family opens folding tables in their front yard. They do not keep what they have to themselves. They open their arms and welcome those in need into their home. Lola stirs a large kettle of noodles, while Hector brings all the first aid supplies they have to the sidewalk. Fabiola sits in her highchair and Libitina vibrates in her seat as Lola hums them a lullaby surrounded by candlelight.

The generator runs the electric stove and refrigerator as well as an extension cord running outside for a torchiere shining beside a white cloth-covered table. Lola hauls a steaming metallic pan loaded with her famous spaghetti as Mr. Alvarez sets melamine bowls and forks beside it.

Neighbors line up and help themselves to a hot meal as they wait for the sun to rise so they may salvage what's left of their lives.

Hector leans on the bumper of his undamaged car and smiles as the neighbor from down the street shakes his hand. "God bless your family, son," the elderly man says.

Hector peers over at Lola as she rocks Fabiola on her knee. His eyes fixate on Libitina in her bouncer as her hand opens and closes around the fabric, bending her nails back. A tiny smile lingers on her face as she looks at something in front of her. He strolls over to her, squats, and rubs her clenched fist. She stares behind him, and I move as Hector spots me in the corner of his eye, startling him.

He crab-walks away from her as his wife giggles. "Hector, what are you doing?"

"I saw something."

Lola removes Fabiola from her lap and murmurs to her husband. "So did she."

She pats his shoulder and stands as the last of the spaghetti scrapes from the aluminum. "Time to make more food," Lola says extending her hand to him. "Have you seen my cat?"

He glances at Libitina one last time before taking the hand his wife offers him. "Not since the storm."

Fabiola kneels and kisses Libitina's forehead. "She ran away."

"What do you mean, Luna ran away?" Lola asks.

"She doesn't like my sister."

"I'm sure she'll come back," Hector insists picking Fabiola up.

"No, she won't," she says hugging Hector around his neck.

"I can keep an eye on them while you cook," a familiar woman dressed in black offers as Hector and Lola turn to go inside.

"Thank you," Lola says turning around.

"No problem," the woman smiles as she boops Fabiola's nose and grins. "It's the least I can do."

Hector and Lola hustle into the house and begin making more food. They used all the spaghetti pasta, so they opened a box of macaroni and added canned diced tomatoes, garlic, corn, chopped peppers, and onions. Lola's eyes water as the vapors from the onion reach them. She dabs her eyes with a hand towel and drops the vegetables into the saucer with the other ingredients.

"Hi, Mama," Fabiola says tugging her top. "I'm hungry."

"Almost done. Where's Libitina?"

"I don't know."

"Is she outside with the lady?" Hector asks, turning away from the stove.

Fabiola shakes her head, and Lola runs to the porch followed by Hector.

"Where's the baby?" Hector asks all the neighbors sitting on the curb.

As they each shrug, Lola's heart breaks. The woman in black took Libitina.

"Call the police," Lola shouts behind her as she sprints down the street, looking for them.

Hector takes his phone out and dials 9-1-1, but it doesn't go through. "Please someone my phone doesn't go through. I need the police," Hector yells to his neighbors.

The old man who shook his hand before piped up. "I have a landline if it's still intact. You can try it," he offers.

The man leads Hector to a house several hundred feet away. The tornado turned it on its side and its walls are now the ceiling.

"The kitchen is through that doorway. Do you see the fridge? It was on the wall right there. If the line is still in one piece, it should work."

Hector grips the man's shoulder and disappears through the shattered window. The phone is off its receiver, and he hangs it up and then listens for a dial tone. He gives the man watching through the pane a thumbs up as he dials 9-1-1 then slams the phone back down.

"It's busy."

"Keep trying. You're bound to make it through," the old man says as he climbs inside.

After three more tries, Hector makes it through.

'9-1-1 what's your emergency?'

"My daughter is missing. Please send the police."

'Sir, a lot of people are missing. We will dispatch someone to your location as soon as they are available.'

"No. You don't understand someone took her. She's a baby."

'Are you saying someone kidnapped your child?'

"Yes, now please hurry."

'Sir, I have your location, but finding you may be difficult for the officer as most reports coming from that area say the neighborhood has been leveled.'

"My house is the only one left standing, so we stick out."

'I will notify the officer. Do you have a description of the person and the baby?'

"The woman is skinny and wears all black clothes and my baby is in her seat and wearing a pink onesie and diaper."

'I have someone heading your way, but it may take some time.'

"Thank you. My wife and I will keep looking."

"Libitina!" Lola screams as she heads toward the house Hector is climbing from.

"Lola, think about the woman. Where did she live?" Hector asks, grabbing her by the shoulders.

"I don't know. She looked familiar, but I don't remember from where."

"Mama," Fabiola says yanking her shirt.

"Not now, Fabby."

They take Libitina's hospital photo and show everyone up and down the street the image, but no one remembers her or the woman in black. Blue and red lights flash down the street as an officer approaches and stops by a pile of debris. He exits his car and climbs around the mess.

"Someone call about a missing baby?" he asks, adjusting his bodycam.

"Yes, here," Lola and Hector shout and wave to him.

"Mama," Fabiola cries as Lola drags her behind them.

The officer removes a notepad and pen from his pocket. "Describe the person who took your child."

"She's white, dressed in black clothing, and skinny with blonde hair," Hector says.

"Mama!" Fabiola screams at the top of her lungs making them all jump.

"Fabiola Marie, do not yell."

"But I have to tell you a secret," she whimpers.

The officer sticks his pad in his pocket, pulls out a 'kid sheriff' badge, and lowers himself to Fabiola's level. "Now that you are a sheriff you can tell me any secret you want," he says pinning the shiny plastic shield to her pajamas.

Fabiola smiles and peers up at her father. Hector nods, giving her permission to speak to a stranger. She leans in close, cups her hands around her mouth, and whispers in the officer's ear. "Sara has my sister."

Chapter Thirteen
Sara

Sara can't help herself. Her desperate need for answers outweighs the crime. There is something about Libitina that is special, and she takes her to find out what it is. I penetrate her front door as she sets Libitina down in her living room. The bright and cheery decor is not what I expected.

Most Mediums I encounter decorate their houses in spiritual decor, but not Sara. Her walls are neutral with bright large open windows, colorful vases, paintings, and family portraits. One of the images is a generational photo with Sara standing beside a woman who appears to be her mother. A much older woman stands behind them both holding the handles of a wheelchair while a frail, gray-haired woman with sunken orbs for eyes grins in the background. Around her neck hangs a large triskele medallion.

Interesting.

The next portrait is of Sara, her mother, and grandmother, and the next is just her and her mother. Their lineage shrinks with time, and Sara has yet to produce a child. Perhaps this is the end of her family tree.

Sara's husband will be home from work soon so there is little time. She unbuckles the infant from her seat and wraps her hands around her waist. That is as far as she can go. Flashes of images rush through her mind. Something is wrong. Her insides shake violently as she releases Libitina and collapses to the Berber carpet. I enter her, but only find flames burning through her memory. It is as though Libitina let her see the future and then lit it on fire, erasing all knowledge of its existence.

Sara's eyes roll as her husband enters the house and rushes to her side. "Sara, what have you done?"

He steadies her with one hand and pushes the coffee table away from her with the other giving her a safe space to have her seizure. This isn't the first one of this kind. The last time this occurred, Sara had a stomach bug causing a dangerous drop in blood sugar.

Her husband rests his palm on her forehead as she begins to cry. "You're burning up, Sara," he says gazing at Libitina who's watching them. "Is this the baby from the hospital?"

"I'm sorry, Tom."

"Well, I hope it was worth it," Tom says wiping sweat from her face. "We need to return her to her parents."

"No. I need to try again."

"Try again? Didn't you already?"

"Yes, but I don't remember what I saw."

"Well, whatever you envisioned, caused a seizure, so you're not touching her again."

Sara sinks into her favorite antique white armchair and rubs her temples. "I wish I could remember."

"Perhaps you weren't meant to."

"Or there is something she doesn't want me to know."

"Sara you are being ridiculous. She's a child, not some devious adult trying to hide their dirty deeds."

"This is different."

"No, Sara. The difference this time is you kidnapped a baby. Now I need to find you a lawyer who can help get you out of this."

"Let me talk to her parents. If they understood, perhaps they won't press charges."

"Wouldn't you if you were them?"

"Yes."

"There is your answer, Sara," Tom scoffs, raising his voice. "I have to go. Stay here and don't do anything stupid."

Tom straps Libitina in her car seat and drives to the nearest police station. The tornado spared their city but destroyed whole neighborhoods a few miles down the road. They were lucky.

Multiple vehicles line the streets near the police station. Tom circles the block several times, waiting for someone to pull away. A man, wearing a green polo and driving a red pickup truck waves him over. "I'm leaving now if you want to wait for this space."

"Thanks."

The man nods on his way by as Tom parallel parks. He carries Libitina through the front doors and sighs. The packed lobby leaves nowhere for him to sit, so he leans against an open wall and slides to the floor. Libitina grunts and a loud fart echoes through the room. The desk sergeant chuckles and comes around his elevated platform.

"Who do we have here?"

"I found her sitting on the sidewalk," Tom lies.

"What? That's insane. Let me see if we have any missing children reports."

The sergeant thumbs through the paperwork in his folder, and eyes Tom when one catches his attention. "Sir, she was kidnapped early this morning."

"Oh," Tom whispers.

"You don't seem surprised," the officer points out. "Do you know someone named Sara?"

"Yes," Tom murmurs refusing to make eye contact. "She's my wife."

"Stand up," the officer orders, removing his cuffs from the holder on his belt. "You're under arrest."

"You don't understand. My wife, she…"

"I don't want to hear excuses. Where's your wife now?"

"Home."

The sergeant hands Tom off to another officer and removes Libitina from her seat. She grins at me and the officer peers behind him. "What's back there, huh? You see something funny?"

He sniffs the air and furrows his brow. "Hey, Torrence. Do we have any diapers in Property?"

"I don't know Sarge."

"Find out for me. This little one needs a diaper change."

The officer disappears through a secure door. A few minutes later, he returns with a diaper bag with pink quilt patches. The sergeant carries Libitina to the ladies' restroom and props the door open. Such a common issue. A ton of businesses only place changing stations in the women's restrooms as if men don't have diaper duty. Lucky for Libitina, the sergeant has four girls at home, so he's done this hundreds of times. He removes her soiled diaper and wipes her tiny bottom.

Heels clank on the tile floor, making the sergeant look up. "I'll be out of here in a moment," he says to the woman wearing a designer suit as warm liquid fills his palm.

"Oh gross."

The woman giggles and covers her nose. "Is she yours?"

"No. Some idiot's wife kidnapped her, and he brought her back."

"That's awful," she frowns. "Need some help?"

"That'd be amazing."

The woman takes over as the sergeant washes his hands in the porcelain sink.

"Thank you for helping."

"No problem," the woman says, kicking the door stop aside, and closing the door.

The sergeant returns to his desk and calls the phone number on the missing child report. Lola answers at once. "Hello?"

"This is Sergeant Tomas of the third precinct. I have your daughter."

"Oh, thank God. Can you bring her to us?"

"Yes, ma'am. We have arrested the husband of the woman who took your child, and an officer is on her way to pick up the wife. Are you at the address on file?"

"Yes."

"The closed roads and debris may slow me down, but I'll be there as soon as I can."

"Thank you, sir."

The sergeant hangs up and carries Libitina out to his car. They weave through traffic with lights, but no sirens to keep from scaring her. People mill about, dragging downed branches to the edge of the road and cleaning up trash and broken pieces of their lives from their yards. The closer he came to the Alvarez family's neighborhood, the worse the damage. He parks a block down and walks the rest of the way.

A paramedic covers a body with a white sheet as a reaper steers the deceased to the halo beside them. Red "X's" marks the homes rescuers have searched and deemed unsafe. The sergeant strolls by a Red Cross tent with accountability forms and vouchers for local hotels. The officer gawks from afar at the only house left standing with a massive crowd sitting on the curb across the street. A woman sprints toward him balancing a toddler on her hip.

"Libitina," she cries out setting her other child down. "Is she okay?"

"She's perfect."

Hector wraps his arms around Lola and his girls and holds them tight as the sergeant glances at a neighbor's bowl.

"Is that goulash?" the sergeant asks.

"Yes. Please come eat," Lola insists.

Hector scoops a large helping of steaming goulash into the sergeant's bowl while Lola places a bottle of water beside his chair. The sergeant thanks Lola as she cups Libitina's fine locks in her palm, and Hector kisses her head. A happy ending indeed. Fabiola skips to the officer and shoves a paper towel into his chest. "Here's a napkin for your face."

"I'm saving it for later," the sergeant smiles as Fabiola runs away.

Whispers carry from one person to the next as the entire neighborhood discusses the Alvarez's hospitality and good fortune. Some roll their eyes when others say how blessed the family is. Their lives are their blessing, but jealousy keeps them from seeing that. Libitina whimpers as Lola backs into her yard, keeping her eyes on the slow-approaching woman.

"Get away from us," Lola yells startling the sergeant as he leaps to his feet.

Sara approaches the family with her arms raised. "I remember what she showed me," she sobs.

"Ma'am put your hands in the air," the sergeant shouts pointing his weapon at her.

"My flesh burned when I touched her," Sara cries staring at her open palms. "Don't you get it? It's over. We are all going to die."

"Lady, everyone dies eventually," the sergeant says placing her in handcuffs.

Sara drops to the pavement and screams, "The fire burns us, and the smoke will suffocate us all."

Neighbors and search and rescue surround the distraught woman, cranking their necks to listen.

The sergeant hoists Sara upright. "What the hell are you talking about?"

Sara's hot breath fogs the sergeant's glasses as she hisses in his face. "A war is coming."

The crowd giggles as a nun wedges her way to the front, rolling a rosary between her fingers. Her lips move, but the words aren't audible. I slip inside to eavesdrop on her thoughts. She's praying for Sara and asking God to bring her peace.

How sweet, but sometimes you can't fix crazy. If I can't penetrate Libitina's head, Sara can't either. It's impossible. I slide out of the nun and into the officer.

Ask her more.

"Oh yeah. A war huh," he frowns holding Sara at arm's length. "Where and with whom?"

"Everywhere," she murmurs and gazes at Libitina. "With everyone."

Chapter Fourteen
Blessings

The staggering sound of beads hitting the blacktop breaks the silence. Fabiola snatches the nun's rosary and swirls them on her wrist. Lola takes them from her and passes them to the woman wearing a black veil.

"I'm sorry," Lola grimaces.

"Don't be," the nun smiles. "I'm Sister Mary Beth."

"I'm Lola. This is my husband Hector, and our two children, Fabiola, and Libitina."

"Libitina? The Earth or Death Goddess."

"Excuse me?" Hector asks moving Lola and the girls aside. "What did you call my daughter?"

"I didn't mean to upset you. The Latin translation of Libitina is Death or the goddess of funerals and burial. Didn't you research the name before giving it to her?"

"We are her foster parents. Her mother passed away in childbirth, and her father didn't want her. He is the one who named her."

"Such a beautiful child. May God bless you and protect you, Libitina," Sister Mary Beth says resting her palm on the infant's forehead and closing her eyes.

Everyone around them bows their heads and prays. Libitina turns her head from side to side trying to remove the hand pressing on her. Her cries begin as a silent whimper but grow into a screeching howl of anger, but the nun does not waver from her prayer.

Libitina claws into the back of her hand, drawing blood and making her let go.

"Oh my," she says staring at the crimson liquid draining from her skin.

Libitina smirks as she pushes her stained fingers into her mouth and sucks them. The nun scrunches her nose, and opens her mouth to speak, but decides to remain silent.

I enter Sister Mary Beth and listen to her thoughts.

This child needs the house of God. Something evil lurks behind her smile. We must baptize her and turn her to the Lord.

Lola snaps her fingers in the nun's face. "Sister, are you alright?"

"Yes, of course. Has this infant been baptized?" the nun inquires rubbing the goosebumps on her arm.

"I don't think so," Hector replies as he takes Libitina and cradles her in his arms.

"Sister, Libitina has been through a lot, and we appreciate your prayers, but right now, we would like to focus on helping our neighbors," Lola insists.

"Your neighbors can be witnesses to her baptism. We can put water in the small pool resting by your house, and…"

"No," Hector shouts, startling the nun and Libitina. "Now is not the time for this. We have work to do."

"Let me help. I can cook or serve."

"We have everything covered, but you are welcome to stay," Lola offers as Hector furrows his brow.

Lola shrugs and heads for the kitchen as Hector sits in a folding chair and feeds Libitina.

Fabiola sprints to Sister Mary Beth's side and tugs her clothing. "Can you fill the pool for me?"

"If your mom and dad say it's okay."

Fabiola dances to Hector and whispers in his ear. He nods his head, and she runs to the small blue plastic pool by the house and pulls it flat. The nun unwinds the hose and begins filling it as Lola steps off the porch with a pot of macaroni and cheese. All the neighborhood children run to the clothed table and hold out their paper plates.

Lola makes this meal for the annual block party at Christmas time, and everyone loves it. The whole block decorates their houses. Not one is dark or void of lights for the holiday. They barricade the streets and set up games, and food tables. A local band supplies music as well. Looking at the current state of their street, there will be no party this year.

A member of the emergency management team stands in the middle of the road and gawks at the Alvarez residence. "Excuse me. Do you live here?" he asks Hector.

"Yes."

"I need to check it for damage."

"My wife is inside. You can go in."

The inspector strolls down the walkway, examines the exterior, and strolls around the entire house. He stops in front again, shakes his head, and ascends the front steps. After several minutes inside, he appears with Lola and a piping-hot bowl of macaroni in hand.

"It's unbelievable," he says to Lola as she stops beside Hector. "Not even a cracked window. It was as though the tornado reached your house, took a sharp turn, and kept going."

"Yes. We are lucky," Hector smiles.

"Lucky and generous. Thank you for the food. It's a relief seeing neighbors helping each other for once."

"You're welcome," Lola blushes as he shakes her hand.

A utility and tree service truck roll towards them. They stop beside a massive oak and begin shredding the smaller branches. Libitina needs a nap, but between the noise of the woodchipper, and the hum of the chainsaw, it isn't happening. Hector carries her inside, places her in her crib, and goes to use the bathroom.

The nun peeks around the corner and sneaks into the nursery. She grips the side rail, gazes at the entrance, and picks up Libitina. Her hand digs around inside her pocket. She removes a small cork-sealed vial and pops its lid with her thumb. The holy water moistens her fingers as she tips it on its side and makes the sign of the cross on Libitina's head. The nun bounces Libitina in her arms as she starts to cry.

I penetrate the nun, sending chills down her spine. A wave of regret comes over the woman, and she lowers the infant onto the mattress with shaking hands. I shift out and hover beside her.

Libitina smiles at me, making the nun freeze as she senses my presence. Her fingers curl around the cross dangling from her neck as she turns her eyes to the right without moving her head. I move at once darting out of her line of sight. She runs out of the room crying as Hector exits the bathroom. He glances in on Libitina whose eyes are heavy and almost closed before chasing down the nun.

"Hey, Sister" he hollers after her. "What were you doing in my daughter's bedroom?"

She doesn't respond as she speed-walks down the road.

"Answer me," Hector insists grabbing her by the forearm and spinning her around.

"I blessed her, but I don't think it will make a difference."

"You did what? I told you no."

"You're missing the point, Mr. Alvarez. Something is with her. It's not inside her, it's just there, waiting."

"Waiting for what?"

"I'm not sure but be careful. If it's evil, it may be waiting until she's old enough to do its bidding," she says removing his hand from her arm. "The woman who took your daughter and made a scene on the street mentioned fire and war. Now her message is either coming from the spirit world or Libitina."

"Libitina is a baby, and that woman is crazy. You need to go."

"Please, Mr. Alvarez, listen to me."

"No, you listen. Stay away from my family and stay away from Libitina," he hisses as he turns his back on her.

"Your family could be in danger."

"Look at our house. God protects us and Libitina. Goodbye Sister Mary Beth."

The nun stalks down the road and stops at her car. She clicks her fob, but nothing happens, so she unhooks the physical key and lets herself in. She stuffs the key in the ignition and turns it.

Nothing.

The wrinkles on her face deepen as she tries again.

Nothing.

A finger taps the glass, and she rolls down her window.

"Need a jump," one of the workers asks.

"Guess so. I must have left a light on or something."

"I got you. Pop the front."

She does as he asks, and the worker pulls his vehicle around to face hers. He removes the red and black jumpers from the bed of his truck and hooks them on her car battery. His vehicle springs to life as he charges her battery for a few minutes.

"Try and start it," he yells to her.

She slides behind the wheel, presses the brake, and twists the key. Sparks fly under the hood and ignite a small fire as the sister's eyes turn to saucers. The tree service worker grabs her and yanks her out a second before the sedan bursts into flames. The heat penetrates their skin, making them sweat as they struggle to stand. Neighbors from down the street jog in their direction as the utility worker takes out his phone and dials 9-1-1.

Sister Mary Beth glares at Hector as he walks down the sidewalk with Libitina on his shoulder. Even from a distance, she can see the smile spread across Libitina's face, angering her. She storms away, screaming at the sky.

What an unexpected response from such a godly woman.

The emergency room summons me, so I float there without hesitation. Multiple critical patients crowd the hospital bays and operating rooms. The overwhelmed staff wipe salty liquid from their brows as they rush from one room to the next, trying to save lives. As rescuers search homes and find trapped people, they take them to the medical center.

Patients wear wristbands in yellow, red, or green signaling their order in line like a bizarre amusement park. A nurse changes a red band to black.

Someone is getting a ride sooner than they expected.

I hitch along and take the man's soul. I'm not sure how they planned to save him. His brain hangs out of his skull like a swollen sponge. The man wanders away from me and slips in and out of patient rooms. He's looking for someone.

Another reaper walks a woman into the hallway where she joins hands with the wandering man. A circle of light shines above him and a black hole swirls below her. The man tries to pull her into the illuminated space, but the demons have her by the legs and refuse to release them. They yank her back and forth like a game of tug of war except there is only one winner here. The angel wraps her wings around the man as he accepts his wife's fate and flies him to heaven.

Everyone has a story, and no one is perfect. Not anymore. Anyone who says they are perfect is lying, plain and simple.

Chapter Fifteen
Shakey Ground

Over the last half-century, twice as many people have ventured below the earth as before. Every year, the number of souls traveling up decreases a little more as people lose faith.

The Alvarez family is the exception. Despite what they've seen and the presence existing around Libitina, they treat her the same as Fabiola. They attend church, give to their community, and pray every day with their children.

In between taking souls, I visit Libitina. The last several months have been uneventful. But now that insurance claims have begun paying, the neighborhood is noisy. Some people chose to rebuild, while others put their lots up for sale after the removal of debris from their former homes.

Libitina cries as a construction worker jackhammers the old sidewalk across the street. Her bedroom faces the street, so when the hammering began at seven in the morning, she woke up screaming.

Lola is an attentive parent and races into the nursery at once to console the frightened infant. She carries her to the living room, but the racket penetrates the walls, nonetheless.

I cross the road and shake the man from the inside out. He tosses the jackhammer aside and turns to his coworker. "Did you feel that?"

"What?" The man asks biting into his ham and cheese on white.

"A tremor. Almost like an earthquake."

"Nope," he says wiping mayonnaise from his yap. "Want me to take over?"

"Nah, I need a break though. I think all the vibrating is giving me aftershocks or something."

I return to Libitina's side as Lola spoons apples into her mouth. She spits it out at once and scrunches her face. "Don't like apples little one? Let's try corn."

She twists the top of another jar of purée and presses it in between Libitina's lips, but the result is the same.

"Well, we are wasting food here young lady."

Six months old and already a food critic.

Lola reaches for the squash, takes off the lid, and dabs a bit on Libitina's lips with her pinkie.

Success.

The infant licks her lips and opens for the orange-colored mush. After eating the entire container and changing her, Lola puts her on the floor near me.

I expected her to gaze up and smile as usual, but not this time. She crawls over, and touches me, burning my flesh with her tiny appendages.

I can feel her, and she can feel me.

What sweet madness is this?

Not only can she produce pain with her infernal hollering, but she can also cause it physically as well. I move away from her, but she pursues me, and giggles. Fabiola leaps onto her hands and knees and crawls beside

Libitina. They both laugh without control. Libitina at me, and Fabiola at Libitina. I vanish through the exterior door, stopping their forward advance.

Brat.

"What are you girls doing?" Hector asks entering the room.

"We are crawling on the floor Papa."

He grins at Fabiola but grows concerned with Libitina's behavior. She's stationary and staring at the front door. He stoops to her level, and a shadow moves in the light beneath it. He seizes Libitina and stands as knuckles thump on the door.

"Who is it?"

"Regina. I used to work at the hospital where Libitina was born."

Hector opens the door and furrows his brow.

"Wow. She's growing so fast," Regina says raising her eyebrows.

"Yes, she is. What do you want?"

"I came to see Libitina and update you on a few things."

"I thought you didn't work for the hospital anymore."

"I don't. I'm employed by social services as a nurse case manager. Mr. Alvarez, I'm here to inform you about Libitina's father."

Mr. Alvarez raises his palm. "Wait. Let me get my wife. She needs to listen too."

He exits the room and comes back with Lola. She sits across from Regina, and Hector gives her Libitina.

"Mr. Yarrow received a twenty-to-life sentence today. He'll be eligible for parole after fifteen years."

"They shouldn't let him go. Not after what he did," Hector huffs as he stands and paces.

"I agree. But they are taking into consideration the loss of his wife and his mental health," Regina murmurs and lowers her head. "There's more. I've spoken with his brother and his wife, and they would like to meet Libitina."

"They want her?"

"They may."

Lola and Hector exchange glances and respond in unison. "No."

"I understand you love her, but any judge in the world would prefer she is placed with family over strangers."

"Why now? It's been months and nothing."

"Jack. The man who didn't want you to have her. The one I went over his head to place her with you guys. He is trying to make it happen. All but convinced them it's their responsibility to take her."

"No. Can we adopt her?" Lola inquires as she burps Libitina.

"You can file the paperwork and try, but they might fight you. My advice is to let them visit so they have a chance to meet you and see how happy she is. Perhaps they'll change their minds."

"When?"

"They are driving into town tomorrow."

"Tomorrow? We have no time to prepare," Hector says raising his eyebrows.

"Mr. Alvarez, I know you're upset, but this is the reality of things. If you'd like, I can be here for the visit."

"If you think you could help us," Lola sniffles as she embraces Libitina.

"I'll call you later and let you know what time."

"Thank you," Hector says shaking her hand as she walks out the door.

Lola releases a staggered breath as she and Hector's eyes follow Regina as she drives away. Losing Libitina would devastate their family. The last thing I need is for them to thrust her into an uncertain future with people railroaded into taking her.

It can't happen. I won't allow it.

A lightning bolt electrocutes me as Libitina seizes the lower part of my apparition. She refuses to release me, despite my attempts to launch myself through the ceiling. The tighter she squeezes, the worse the pain, but there is more.

Crying. That's what it sounds like. Libitina is distraught but trapped in a body that's not ready for verbal communication. She's trying to tell me something.

Hector dives onto the carpet and turns Libitina over as the tremors begin. Her eyes roll as her head arches back and her arms and legs stiffen into straight rods.

"Hector, what's happening?" Lola yells as she runs to their side.

"I think a seizure. My nephew had them when he was little."

"What's the matter with my sister," Fabiola sobs.

"She will be okay. Fabby, go to Libby's room and grab her bag. Lola, start the car," Hector says.

Fabiola darts down the hallway as Hector lifts Libitina from the floor. As her body relaxes, that's when the real punishment begins.

The shrieking, violent outburst of furious screams tears me apart like paper in a shredder. If the demons from hell opened their portal before me, I would take the chance and jump right in. Anything would be better than listening to and feeling Libitina's frustration over what happened. I'm unsure if it came about because I couldn't understand her, or from her attempt to communicate with me non-verbally.

"I got you, baby girl," Hector insists as he wraps Libitina in a fuzzy blanket, turns her body horizontally, and places her against his abdomen.

Fabiola races out the door and passes the bag to Lola as Hector carries Libitina to the car. He climbs in the passenger seat and rests the infant on his thighs.

"Shouldn't we put her in the seat?" Lola asks.

"No. I need to keep her airway open," he says taking Lola's hand and squeezing it. "Drive."

She nods her head and backs out of the driveway.

I try and follow, but the tantrum weakens me like Kryptonite, trapping me behind the walls of the Alvarez home. How can something so small be so powerful? Perhaps this is punishment. We all have bosses to answer to. The demons to Satan, the angels to God, and we reapers to God or the devil depending on who we defy or anger. So, who does Libitina answer to?

Once I can penetrate solid objects again, I head to the hospital.

A doctor shines a light in Libitina's eyes as she sucks the bottle Lola feeds her. "A technician will be in to hook her up to an EEG. Once the results are in, I'll let you know where we go from here."

"What caused this?" Lola asks.

"Sometimes it's something simple like vitamin B deficiency or infection, but other times it can be a genetic abnormality or injury at birth. We won't have a definitive answer until her results come back. Try not to worry," the physician insists as he draws the white curtain aside and moves on to the next patient.

"Try not to worry. Is this guy for real?" Hector asks, wiping his face with his palm. "I think we should take her somewhere else."

"We're already here. Let's see if they find anything," Lola says patting his bouncing knee.

A young girl dressed in purple scrubs with little brown teddy bears rolls a machine into their room. She removes several leads and sticks them to Libitina's head one by one.

"Can I try?" Fabiola asks as she grips the cart and jumps up and down.

"Fabby, sit down," Hector snaps.

Lola glares at him, and he raises his hand. "I'm sorry. I didn't mean to yell, Fabiola. Come sit on Papa's lap."

Fabiola rubs her tear-stained eyes, scales his legs, and lays her head on his maroon-pocketed t-shirt. He strokes her shiny dark hair and kisses her scalp.

"She's a robot, Papa," Fabiola giggles.

She isn't wrong. Libitina has more wires sticking out of her than the sound equipment at a rock concert, but she doesn't seem to mind. After several hours of waiting, the physician returns with unexpected news.

"All her tests are normal."

"How can that be? She had a seizure," Lola asks glancing at Hector.

"Sometimes these things happen, and we don't understand why. It's called an idiopathic neonatal seizure, or another possibility is idiopathic epilepsy. Either way, one presents itself within the first few days after birth, and the other doesn't occur until around school age. So, for her to have one now is rare, and likely an isolated incident."

"Should we take her to a neurologist or something?" Hector asks.

"I wouldn't do that yet. If it happens again or more often, then yes," the doctor says as he texts on his phone. "I'll have the nurse bring in your discharge papers."

The physician strolls out of the room and slides the partition closed behind him.

Hector's face reddens as he clenches his fists. "I think that doctor is idiopathic."

"There are so many patients, Hector. Everything is normal. Let's go home."

"Ice cream," Fabiola sings as she pulls Lola's top.

"You haven't eaten dinner," Hector says.

"Ice cream, ice cream, ice cream," Fabiola chants as she dances in a circle.

Fabiola gazes up at him with a pouting lip. "Oh, okay. You've been good. We can go," Hector sighs.

"Yay."

They load the kids back into the car and travel to the ice cream store a few blocks away. The bug-eyed frog out front holds a cone in its grasp while its long tongue wraps around a pink frozen dessert. Lola picks a table as Hector and Fabiola head to the counter.

Libitina is quiet. Too quiet.

How odd.

I coast around the table and hover beside her. She cranks her head, and scowls, as loud air escapes her nostrils like a bull ready to charge.

She is mad at me for not understanding. I get it. She's trapped inside her body without the ability to communicate, and I imagine it's frustrating.

Chapter Sixteen
Family Meeting

Last night after ice cream, the Alvarez's hatched a plan to deter Mr. Yarrow's brother and wife from wanting to take custody of Libitina. Telling them about her odd behavior and the presence they sense nearby might be enough.

It's not like they've ever seen me, but they are aware of my lurking presence. I don't like it when someone uses me, but under the circumstances, I'll make an exception.

Around the world, people portray me as some terrible entity, blaming me for taking their loved one's souls. Listen, people, I'm just doing my job. Besides, I only remove souls. The angels and demons take care of the rest. Pray all you want, it's not up to you where the departed go. If I didn't exist, dead people would all end up under the earth's surface. No souls would go to heaven, or hell for that matter. They'd be stuck inside their physical form with no way out. Is that what you want? Of course not. Who would want to be beneath the grass all claustrophobic and dark like some magician in a box trying to escape his own trick? Granted the ones pulled below don't care to be there. It's not exactly prime real estate, but at least they have plenty of room to move around.

Lola rocks Libitina on the front porch as Regina pulls into the driveway and another vehicle, a black Chevy Tahoe, parks at the curb.

"Hector," Lola calls out. "They're here."

It's showtime. All I need now is some spiritual nachos, a fat cup of iced tea, and a bucket of buttery popcorn. I wonder how they plan to bring up my existence. I'm not helping. I can't interfere in human lives any more than I can select the location of where people go when they die. The only exception is Libitina. She has an unexplainable hold on me.

Hector steps out onto the porch with Fabiola on his hip. The couple on the street don't leave their SUV right away. They're waiting for Regina. She climbs out of her sedan, shoots the Alvarez family a soft smile, and inflates her cheeks as she walks over to the Yarrow's car.

A blonde woman, with hair cut into a neat shoulder-length bob, exits the passenger seat, and shakes Regina's hand as a tall, dark brown-haired, tan gentleman with huge shoulders comes around the bumper. He nods at Regina, and they stroll toward Hector and Lola.

"Hector, Lola, and Fabiola, this is Gerald Yarrow and his wife Nadine."

Gerald? What an awful name. Who names their sons Gerald and Thaddeus? Their dad must have hated them. No wonder Thaddeus Yarrow became an asshole as an adult. Let's see how Gerald turned out.

"Hello," Nadine says forcing a smile at Libitina as Gerald shakes Hector's hand. "Pleasure to meet you, Lola. Do you mind if I hold Libitina?"

Lola peers behind Nadine at Regina who nods her head. After several seconds of hesitation, Lola passes the infant to Nadine.

Nadine holds Libitina before her face, "Beautiful baby girl. I am your Aunt Nadine."

If ever there were a more perfect moment to vomit, it was now. Formula shoots out of Libitina's mouth like water from a fire hose and splashes inside Nadine's partially open lips. Gerald holds his balled-up fist against his mouth, trying to hold back his lunch as a tiny smile creeps across Libitina's face.

Gerald gags, folds over the bushes beside the front steps, and yacks into their dense vegetation. Nadine yanks the hand towel Lola offers her as Regina takes Libitina.

"Well, that was unexpected," Nadine says shaking her head.

Inside her intestines are boiling like hot noodles. She's anxious and now angry. Her designer blouse has a stain.

Oh no. The horror.

"So, what can you tell us about Libitina?" Nadine asks without looking up.

"How much do you want to know?" Hector replies as he glances at Lola.

"Everything," Gerald utters as he rinses his mouth with water and spits on the walkway.

Lola grimaces at his smug face as she stands, whips her screened door aside, and storms into the house. Gerald, Nadine, and Regina stare at Hector waiting for him to say something, but he stays silent.

The door crashes open as Lola comes out with a blue bucket full of hot, soapy liquid and slips it into Gerald's grasp. "Clean your spit water off my property, Mr. Yarrow.

I keep a neat home, inside and out, and I don't appreciate you spitting your dirty mouth fluids on my walkway."

Libitina breaks the awkward silence with a burst of laughter. Fabiola joins in, and now they are both laughing.

Hector and Lola smile at their outward display of tomfoolery at the expense of the Yarrows' uncomfortable position. Gerald tosses the watery substance across the concrete, ridding it of his bodily fluid. He rests the bucket on a step and scales the remaining steps to face Lola. "I apologize for disrespecting your home. I didn't intend to. I don't know what I was thinking."

"Apology accepted."

I guess the anger gene didn't transfer to Gerald. Then again, a lot of people act one way in public and another behind closed doors. Perhaps this is all for show.

Nadine finishes wiping her top with tight lips and reaches for Libitina.

"My turn," Gerald says blocking Nadine with his arm.

She rolls her eyes and moves aside as he lifts Libitina under her armpits and places her against his black button-up dress shirt. Libitina stirs beneath his touch and begins crying. He bounces her up and down to calm her, but it doesn't make a difference as her cries escalate into a blood-curdling scream. Gerald raises his shoulders high as he cringes. Hector takes the infant from him, turns her on her side, and rocks her in his arms. The shrilling ceases as Libitina drifts off to sleep.

"Well, that's unfortunate. I guess we have some work to do," Gerald says rubbing his palms together. "Now, where were we?"

He wants her. Despite how poorly things are going, he's staying the course. Nadine, however, is hesitant. I drift inside her trim, athletic frame, to read her.

She doesn't want children. Never has. Her body, routine, and life are perfect the way they are, and a baby would ruin everything.

How vain.

I exit her as she rubs the raised hair on her arms and enter Gerald. His thinking is the opposite. He wants a child of his own, but Libitina may be the closest he ever comes to getting one. He loves his wife, but having children has been a source of tension between them for years. Perhaps she will accept this compromise.

No.

Gerald's head bobbles as I leave him too fast. Nadine grips his forearm. "Are you okay?"

"Yeah, just a bit light-headed, that's all."

Hector passes Libitina to Lola so she can carry her to bed. "Libitina is no ordinary baby," Hector blurts as he stands in the Yarrow's airspace. "Something follows her wherever she goes."

"What the hell do you mean follows?"

"Angels, her mother's ghost, demons, or something else. We aren't sure."

"So, you're saying she's haunted," Nadine says elevating her voice.

"Protected. There is a difference."

"And you believe this, why?" Gerald asks, lifting his eyebrows.

"We sense it every day," Lola says through the screen. "Look around Mr. Yarrow. Our house still stands because of her."

"You got lucky. Libitina has nothing to do with it."

"She should be dead. Your brother pointed a loaded handgun at her and pulled the trigger and not just once, but each time, the gun wouldn't fire. The police say it was a miracle it didn't go off. They found nothing wrong with the weapon itself when they test-fired it. Before the storm, the wind took my girls into the street and Hector ran to save them. A dump truck would have crushed them to death, but it swerved away, saving their lives. Believe it or not, God or something else is with her, keeping her safe from harm."

"Unbelievable," Nadine scoffs. "You don't want us to have her, do you?"

"Absolutely not," Hector says as he steps within inches of Gerald. "Libitina is our daughter, and we will fight for her with every penny we have."

"They are petitioning to adopt Libitina," Regina chimes in. "She's happy here with them and to take her away now, well, it's not ideal for a child's development."

"Why did you bring us here if they didn't want to give her up?" Gerald asks.

"Because I needed you to see your niece is safe and with a family that loves her."

"Safe? They think she has an imaginary spirit and talk about her like she's a rabbit's foot or something. Not to mention, they didn't even invite us in. What are they hiding?" Nadine questions Regina as she crosses her arms.

"If you wanted to come in, all you had to do was ask," Lola insists as she holds the screen door ajar.

Nadine stops before Lola and huffs through her nose. "I don't care for the way you are treating us."

"Mrs. Yarrow once you enter our home, we are not responsible for what happens after."

"Are you threatening me, Mrs. Alvarez?"

"No. I'm warning you."

Nadine stomps through the doorway like a spoiled child as Hector leads Gerald down the hall to Libitina's nursery. Her naps are never long. Libitina kicks her legs as the Yarrows peer over the railing of her crib. I hover in the corner, as I always do, to keep anyone from passing through me on accident. Gerald gazes into Nadine's eyes and smiles as Libitina peers between them to stare at me. Her focus stays on the corner of the room despite Gerald snapping his fingers in her face. She doesn't blink or stir.

"Why is she doing that?" Nadine asks.

"Pick her up," Lola insists. "She sees something."

Nadine hoists Libitina from the mattress and her eyes stay on me. "What is she staring at?" Nadine inquires. "Is something the matter with her?"

"Libitina has had one seizure, but her tests are normal. So, no she has nothing medically wrong with her," Hector murmurs.

"Stand in the corner," Lola says with an outstretched hand.

Well, this ought to be interesting.

Nadine shakes her head and laughs. "This is ridiculous. You want me to stand in the corner like a scolded child so I can feel something?"

"Yes," Lola and Hector say in unison.

The Yarrows erupt in laughter. "This is silly," Nadine chuckles. "But I will do as you say."

Gerald wipes tears from his eyes as Nadine strolls to the corner, turns around, and backs into me.

Nadine's face changes from happy to sad like the sock and buskin masks at a theater. Her body shakes violently as Libitina erupts like a long-dormant volcano. Everyone in the room covers their ears. Everyone except Nadine. A tear slides down her face as I plant images of Erin and Tessa's bodies and the moment the gun did not discharge when Thaddeus pointed it at Libitina's head.

But that isn't all.

A scene plays for Nadine like a trailer for an upcoming movie, but I didn't put it there, so this is the first time I have seen it as well. The forest is on fire. The flames rise high above the earth and blacken the moon with their smoke as screaming comes from everywhere and nowhere at the same time.

Gerald yanks his wife from the corner, but she doesn't respond when he asks her if she's okay. Hector smiles with his arms crossed as he gazes at Regina's concerned face.

"What is going on?" Regina asks.

"We are leaving," Nadine says after blinking several times.

She places Libitina in Lola's arms and shuffles from the room.

Gerald goes after her and spins her around in the living room. "What are you doing? We agreed we'd give this a try."

"It doesn't matter anymore," Nadine whispers as she rests her palm on his chiseled face. "Nothing does."

She drops her hand away from him and walks out the front door.

Hopelessness.

That's what Nadine felt. I know because I felt it too.

Chapter Seventeen
Message

"What the hell was that?" Regina asks as Hector closes the door behind the Yarrows.

"As we mentioned before, Libitina is special," Lola says slipping her thumbs into the pockets of her dress. "We won't let her go. Not now, or ever. Libitina's ours now, and we will protect her from everything and everyone, including herself."

"What do you mean?"

"Regina, we appreciate your help, but we have a lot to do today, so if you don't mind," Hector says opening the door. "Please, drop by anytime to visit."

Regina pauses as the door locks behind her, smiles, and nods her head. Libitina is in excellent hands, despite their weird behavior. She couldn't have chosen a more perfect family, which she may soon regret, as Jack storms down the sidewalk toward her.

"Regina, I just got a call from Gerald Yarrow. His wife hasn't said a word since they left this house," Jack yells. "Did they threaten her?"

"What? Jack, you're crazy. The Alvarez family plans to adopt Libitina."

"Well, they want her, and I'm going to help them get her," he screams as he sticks his finger in her face. "And if they don't take her, I'll find someone else who will, because that family isn't right for her."

Regina shoves Jack into the side of her vehicle and pokes her pointer finger into his sternum. "First off, don't you ever point your finger and scream at me like that again. Second, the Alvarez's and I know how to fight as well. Libitina is where she should be. As for the Yarrows, Gerald may have wanted Libitina, but judging by Nadine's body language and attitude, she doesn't. So, if you try and fight us, Jack you're going to fucking lose," Regina hisses as she throws her car door aside. "Now get away from me you lazy fuck."

Regina slams her door shut, cranks the sedan in reverse, and barrels out into the street. Her middle finger flies high out of her partially rolled-down window as she rounds a corner and vanishes.

Jack turns, glares at the house, and furrows his brow as Hector smiles through the window. He holds his head up and tries to stroll away with dignity, but the divot between the sidewalk and the lawn catches his foot, and he twists his ankle. A weak seam in his slacks rips open, revealing his brown-stained briefs. He hobbles along with his palm over the gap in his pants like a toddler with an uncomfortable load in their diaper.

Giggling comes from behind him. He peers at the family standing in their front yard with their arms around each other grinning. His face reddens as he crosses the street and wedges himself into the driver's seat of his car.

I ponder over the image Libitina showed Nadine. Is it a premonition of her future, or a form of self-preservation Libitina uses when she feels threatened? There must be a way to find out more.

The Alvarez family attends a weekday evening service once a week. Tonight, Pastor James speaks of protection and the strength of family. It was as though his sermon was meant just for them after their eventful day. The pastor invites members of the congregation to stay after for individual messages. Hector and Lola wait until all the other families have taken their turn before approaching.

Fabiola dances her way to the pastor. "Hello," she smiles broadly.

"Hi, Miss Fabiola. Did you come up for your message?"

"Yes," she shouts.

The pastor sits on the red velvet steps and whispers in Fabiola's ear. She jumps away from him and circles around her father while singing, "I am God's child, I am God's child, and He loves me."

"Fabby, settle down," Hector insists.

Lola and Hector shake their heads as Fabiola sprints around the pews.

The pastor stretches his arms to Libitina. "May I hold her?"

"Oh, I don't know Pastor James. Libitina isn't fond of strangers," Lola says.

"Lola, let him try," Hector insists.

Lola grins at Libitina's long eyelashes and wide-open eyes then blows the air from her lungs through her lips. "Okay, but only for a moment."

Lola allows the pastor to take Libitina, but what everyone, including me, assumed would happen, didn't. A tear slides down Pastor James's face as Libitina grips his finger and smiles.

Huh.

A shadow casts over him, and the pastor's face pales. Hector dives to catch Libitina as Pastor James drops his arms and leaps away from her. The family's hope that Pastor James would bless Libitina with his prayers, support, and God's message for her, now fades as he turns his back on them and leaves them without a word.

"Pastor James!" Lola shouts as she slams through the double doors and chases him.

The lights flicker as I scurry along the ceiling. By the time Lola catches up to him, he's packing his bag and throwing the strap over his shoulder.

"Excuse me," Pastor James says as he moves Lola aside and storms through the emergency exit.

"Wait," Lola yells chasing after him as the door alarm screams overhead. "What did you see?"

"I'm sorry. I can't help you," he murmurs as he shuts himself inside the church van.

Lola pounds the glass with her fist as he turns the car on and shifts it into drive. "Hey, you almost dropped my baby, the least you can do is tell me why."

The pastor hesitates, rolls down the window a quarter of the way, and mumbles, "I'll pray for you, and your family. That's the best I can do."

The clear partition drones back up, and Pastor James guns the gas as Libitina, Hector, and Fabiola approach.

What an odd reaction. I'm dying to learn more.

I float inside his car and penetrate the pastor's holy flesh. Nothing.

It's blank as though he's aware I am here trying to listen to his thoughts. No one can stay there for long, so I'll wait.

He cranks the heat on high, despite it being almost seventy degrees outside. The brakes squeal and the wheel shifts abruptly to the right as he swerves, skids on the loose gravel, and comes to a halt. A deer meanders across the highway and enters a side road, oblivious of the death it just avoided. His eyes fixate on a diamond-shaped, yellow sign with black writing.

"Dead End," he whispers as he reads it aloud.

Here they come. The memories float into his head as he releases his thoughts to me. He's kneeling in the church parking lot chanting the last rites repeatedly. Blood oozes from his knees as tiny stones dig into them. He raises his head as fire envelopes his church and hot embers penetrate his eyes right before he bursts into flames.

"Lord, please save us," the pastor says to his empty car as I vacate his frame.

Save us.

The pastor removes his phone from his pocket and dials a number, one-handed using his thumb. He taps the speaker button as he snaps the turn signal down and pulls back onto the roadway.

"Paster James, how are you," the man on the other end of the line announces with a cheer through the echoing receiver.

"Pastor David, we need to set up a prayer vigil."

"Of course. For whom, where, and when?"

"Tonight, and the Alvarez family."

"Has someone fallen ill?"

"No, it's not like that, David," Pastor James sobs.

"James, what is it? Has something happened to them?"

"It's their new daughter, Libitina, the one they are fostering. She…"

"Libitina? Sister Mary Beth and I discussed this child after her car caught on fire. You have concerns as well?"

"I do."

"Very well. We will meet this evening after dinner. I have some phone calls to make," Pastor David sighs.

"Who are you calling?"

"Everyone."

The dial tone hums and disconnects as Pastor David hangs up.

He's calling everyone. Not a chosen few pastors or nuns. Everyone. At least there is plenty of room for the slew of prayer warriors to congregate outside Libitina's home since the lot beside them is vacant and still up for sale.

As Pastor James enters his abode, a house a few blocks over draws me to it. A woman has pushed her husband down the stairs and blood seeps from his cracked-open skull as she pumps his chest up and down.

Too late now, Deliah. You should have expected him to call you a whore when you cheated on him with his brother. Now the police will lead you away in handcuffs, and your husband is floating away with the angels.

Deliah races up the cellar steps and the next flight to the second floor. She stuffs a duffle bag full of clothes, throws her husband's service revolver on top, and jogs towards her vehicle.

A detective. Really lady? Did you think he wouldn't find out you were cheating, especially with his brother?

Moron.

Too bad the neighbors already called 9-1-1. As she rolls out of the driveway a patrolman blocks her in, but she would rather die than go to prison. She draws her gun, jumps out, and points it at the officer.

Wish granted.

Multiple bullets pierce her body, striking her chest, upper left shoulder, and hip. Deliah drops to the ground, and the officer kicks her weapon away as he calls for an ambulance. He covers the gaping hole in her chest, as she fades into the darkness.

I seize her soul as it floats away from her and drop it on the crimson-covered grass. Deliah gazes up at her former self as I transform into the worst of her. Growling comes from an open portal to her right. She turns and backs away as a shiny black arm penetrates the surface and reaches for her.

And she's running.

I'm not surprised. She did try and run before she died so it makes sense she would do it after as well.

She's sitting behind the wheel of her car trying to figure out why she can't grasp the wheel. Her hand swipes through it several times before she stops and freezes. Beside her, waiting in the passenger seat, a shadowy apparition snatches her spirit and launches it through the window like an Olympic game of shot put. She lands on the edge of hell's doorway and a set of claws grip her around her transparent waist and haul her inside.

Goodbye, Deliah.

Chapter Eighteen
Vigil

Lola rolls the chain of her gold necklace between her fingers. The black sedan with tinted windows across the street has been sitting idle for hours.

Hector returns from showing a house to a couple who work past six. He tosses his keys in the bowl, strolls over to Lola, and pecks her cheek. "What are you looking at?"

"That vehicle has been parked outside a long time."

"Huh," he says glancing at the car a second time. "I'll go find out what they want."

Lola nods as Hector pushes the outer door and heads toward the idling vehicle. He taps on the glass and waits. Nothing. He cups his hands around his face and squints through the windshield. Jack blinks several times as he grips the steering wheel.

"Roll down the window," Hector insists swirling his pointer in a circle.

The divider descends halfway, revealing Jack's sweaty face and releasing a foul odor from inside.

"Why are you sitting out here? And what is that stench?" Hector asks waving his hand in front of the opening.

"I planned on speaking with your wife, but something I ate didn't agree with me."

"Sir, did you poop in your pants?"

"A little. I wish your wife would have come out sooner."

"Well, she didn't. Now you have ten seconds to tell me what you want before I call the police and make a report of stalking," Hector murmurs covering his nose.

"My name is Jack, and I am Libitina's case manager from the hospital. I also work with social services. The Yarrows and I spoke at length. Nadine agreed to adopt, but not Libitina. I don't know what happened in your house, but Mrs. Yarrow would rather care for five non-family members than take responsibility for Libitina."

"Thanks for telling us," Hector says pushing off his window frame. "Now get off my street and don't ever come back."

Jack mumbles under his breath as Hector waltzes away from him and enters the house. As Lola follows his bumper out of the neighborhood, a white church van stops out front.

"I wonder what he's doing here," Lola sighs as she slides her arm around Hector's waist.

"Let me guess, you want me to go see."

"No, we both will."

They step off the stairs as a second van pulls behind the pastors. The brakes of an SUV squeal across the street as a station wagon steers into their driveway.

Pastor James clambers out of the driver's seat, an unknown pastor out of the passenger, and five others hop out of the side door. The other vehicles unload a similar amount of people, including the nun who blessed Libitina without permission.

"Pastor James, what's happening?" Lola inquires.

"Mr. and Mrs. Alvarez, my apologies. I meant what I said at the church. All I, well we, can do is pray for you and your family. You don't have to stay out here or anything. We will just line up and pray."

"I don't understand," Hector huffs. "Is this necessary?"

"Mr. Alvarez, there is power in prayer. The more people the better."

"But why?" Lola questions as a truck clears out.

"Sometimes when something can't be explained, it's better to pray and seek God's protection and ask him to provide us with answers than do nothing and face the consequences later."

"Consequences? Pastor, what are you talking about?" Hector asks as another van approaches.

"The demon," Sister Mary Beth pipes up as Pastor James puts his hand up to quiet her. "Something sinister dwells in the shadows with Libitina, and we are here to bless this house and your daughter and rid them of evil."

A nun with straight, long brown hair, drags the sister away by her robe as the other pastor who rode with Pastor James comes forward. "I'm sorry. My name is Pastor David. Sister Mary Beth isn't well."

"Did she call Libitina evil?" Hector scoffs, balling his fists. "We have a Christian home and attend Pastor James's church more than one day a week faithfully, so for her to come here and say our house and child are evil, is not only rude but unacceptable. I want everyone to leave. Right now."

"Mr. Alvarez, we won't take up any of your time. We will say our silent prayers and go. Please," Pastor James begs with his palms touching.

"Fine," Hector announces as he leads Lola away. "Do what you need to do and go."

The pastor nods and turns to the crowd developing behind him.

When Hector and Lola cross the threshold, they lunge toward Fabiola who is holding Libitina.

"Fabby, what are you doing?" Lola asks as she takes the baby from Fabiola's struggling arms.

"She woke up, so I took her from her swing," she grins as she rocks on her heels.

"Fabby, next time wait for me or Mama. You could have dropped her," Hector moans.

"I won't drop her. I love her," she sobs.

"Oh, we know you do. Don't cry. How would you like to give her a bottle?" Hector offers.

She jumps up and down, vibrating the carpet. "Yes, please."

Lola points to the chair by the window and has Fabiola sit. She rests Libitina in Fabiola's arms, and Hector passes the formula to her.

Libitina sucks her formula as Fabiola crosses her eyes at her. The news starts its nightly broadcast. The weatherman paces before a map of the state pointing out the path for a short storm. Outside, an enormous crowd of onlookers has joined the pastors and nuns. Soon the whispers from the mouths of believers echoes through the walls.

Libitina stirs on Fabiola's lap. She sets the bottle aside and lifts the baby under her armpits. "Mama, can you take her?"

"Sure. Are you done already?"

"No, I have a message," she beams as she throws the door open and skips into the yard.

"Shut up!" Fabiola screams at the top of her lungs, silencing the group.

"Fabiola, why did you do that?" Hector hisses as she wedges past him to get back inside.

"Libitina told me to."

"Fabby, what have we said about lying?"

"I'm not lying."

"Go to your room."

"But Papa, I didn't lie," she cries as she sprints to her bedroom and slams the door.

"Hector."

"Lola, she knows the rules about lying."

"And what if she isn't?" Lola says standing before him. "If Libitina can make people see or feel things when they hold her, what makes you think she can't ask our daughter to tell the people outside to be quiet?"

"You're right. I will go and apologize to her."

She kisses him on the lips and smacks his rear as he walks away. He chuckles and smiles at her. A small punishment for making their daughter cry.

The door creaks open, and Pastor James peeks around the corner. "I'm sorry if the praying became too loud. We didn't intend on disturbing you."

"It didn't bother us," Lola grimaces as she places Libitina on her thighs and pats her back.

"Oh. I thought when Fabiola came out and yelled at us, you sent her."

"We didn't. Libitina did. At least, that's what Fabiola says," Lola explains as she cradles Libitina against her bosom.

The pastor parts his lips to say more, but instead goes back outside. Lola shuts the door behind him and stares out the window. Like a game of telephone, the pastor whispers in Pastor David's ear, then he does the same to Sister Mary

Beth, and she transmits the message to the next person and so on. By the time the original statement makes it to the last person, it has a whole new meaning.

Arguing begins in the center of the group. Pastor James and Pastor David raise their hands and ask the worshipers to lower their voices as the noise level continues to rise.

Libitina whimpers and pouts as Lola bounces her in her arms. After several staggering breaths, Libitina belts out a piercing shriek drawing everyone's attention to the house.

Fire burns through me, and I need it to stop. I jet through the wall and barrel through everyone in the crowd. One person after another goes blank and goosebumps plaster their skin.

Silence. Complete and utter silence. Even the environment around them falls quiet. Drops of liquid force a blink from each person as it strikes their faces, and the sky grows dark. One by one, people begin leaving. First the onlookers, tired of waiting for something more exciting to happen, then the church clergy except for Sister Mary Beth. A cloud burst above her, drenching her clothes, but she did not waver. Her eyes fixate on the bay window where Lola stands with Libitina.

Pastor James snaps an umbrella over her and takes her by the forearm. She shouts towards the house as he ushers her into the van. "I know you are there demon. You will not take this child. We will not allow it."

The door shuts muffling her words. The pastor climbs in as the storm ends abruptly, and the sun burns through the clouds. An enormous rainbow shoots across the sky over the Alvarez home, making cars stop. Lola and Hector carry the girls outside.

Lola laughs as she shakes her head. "Does this look like the work of a demon?"

"Nope," Hector says holding Lola from behind. "We have ourselves a guardian angel."

They are both wrong. Who am I kidding? All of this is wrong. Things used to be simple. I would do my job and move on to the next. But, ever since Libitina's birth, the long list of life's unanswered questions has grown even longer.

Chapter Nineteen
Traffic

Lola throws the bay window curtains aside and gasps. The sun barely lights the front porch, but she doesn't need much light to see.

Flowers cover the whole floor. White and pink roses, cornflowers, blue iris, and massive bundles of jasmine litter its surface. A woman, wearing all white with hair to match, carrying a vase full of lavender, smiles when Lola opens the door.

"Morning," the woman cheers as she rests the floral arrangement in an available opening on the step. "These are lavender. They'll protect your family."

"I know what they are," Lola announces resting her fists on her hips. "And we don't need protection."

"Perhaps not now, but someday you will," the woman says cupping her hands together. "May God be with you."

The woman in white saunters away, dragging the bottom of her dress through a puddle. Lola follows the liquid with her eyes as it races up the cloth absorbing it.

"Pretty!" Fabiola shrieks as she runs out and seizes a pile of flowers. "Are these all for us?"

"Yes, Fabby."

"What is this?" Hector asks as he adjusts his tie. "Did someone die, and we don't know it?"

"The woman who left these says they are for protection," Lola says picking up the vase.

"Really? What about the rest?"

"Excellent question. I'll have to get back to you on that."

Hector glances at his watch, takes a sip of the coffee he left inside the door, and swipes his car keys. "I have to go. Call me if you need anything," he insists kissing her on the forehead and palming Fabiola's head as she plucks the petals of a rose.

Lola moves the gestures aside with her foot and sits on the step. Libitina sleeps in most mornings, giving Lola time to enjoy her coffee.

Something sharp stabs Lola's scalp. "Ouch, Fabby."

"Sorry, Mama. Can I put a flower in your hair?"

"Okay. Be careful."

The long stem of a red carnation digs along the ridge of Lola's ear as Fabiola slides it into her hair. "You're pretty, Mama."

"Thank you, Fabby."

Fabiola jumps around in a circle and runs inside as a brown van with bouquets displayed on the side pulls out front.

A young man, in his late twenties with shaved blonde hair, moves the sliding side door ajar. He flips through pages on a clipboard, nods his head, and raises his eyebrows. "Yep, this is it," he says to himself.

He strolls down the sidewalk and stops before her with a small box in his hand. "This is for you."

She takes the brown container from him, and peers inside. It's full of envelopes. "Excuse me. What are these?"

"They go with all of these," he smiles as he whips the door aside.

The sweet and powerful scent of floral carries to Lola's nostrils in a gentle breeze as the man unloads one vase after another. He hauls the load to the front of the house and lines them up neatly beside the hedges. He returns to his vehicle and untangles a bundle of balloons with different spiritual messages.

His eyes widen and he releases the balloons in the air as something behind Lola catches him off guard. Libitina is upside down in Fabiola's grasp as she struggles not to drop her.

"Fabiola, no," Lola shouts as she lunges to brace Libitina in her arms. "What did Papa and I say about trying to carry her yourself?"

"But Mama. I saw a man in her window, and I didn't want him to take her," she pouts.

"A man? What man?"

"He's behind our house," Fabiola points.

Lola cradles Libitina like a football in one arm and takes Fabiola's hand with the other. "Show me," she steams.

When they round the back corner of the property, no one is there. Lola sloshes through the soggy grass and stops just shy of Libitina's bedroom window. Large footprints sink deep into the mud. Smeared upward fingerprints stain the glass from someone trying to slide it open.

"Fabby, what did the man look like?"

"I don't know. He had a mask on like Papa's."

"You mean like Papa wears when it's cold and he needs to shovel?"

"Uh-huh."

"Okay. Back inside."

Lola ushers Fabiola through the back and grabs her cell phone. Her finger hovers over the nine, as the doorbell chimes, startling her. She peers through the window beside the door. The delivery guy raises his palm and gives her a one-finger wave. "Sorry. I need you to sign for the flowers."

She cracks the door and reaches her free hand through. He places the clipboard under her wrist, and she signs using the string-attached pen.

The door creaks to a close and clicks as she rotates the deadbolt. After taking multiple deep breaths, she calls the local police.

An unmarked cruiser grinds to a stop in her driveway a few minutes later. The man who steps out is not a uniformed officer.

"Morning. I'm Detective William Gerard. I understand you had an intruder?"

"I'm confused. Why did they send a detective to take a statement?"

"I was a few blocks over. My former partner died and I'm handling the investigation."

"I'm sorry to hear that," she frowns as Libitina belches.

"Beautiful baby. What's her name?"

"Libitina."

"Libitina? Libitina Yarrow?"

"How did you know that?"

"Regina and I are close. She raves about how special she is, and the amazing family who has taken her in," he grins as his face brightens. "What's with all the flowers? Someone die?"

"Someone at the church believes a demon stalks Libitina. They came and prayed for us last night and today we woke up to this."

"Nothing threatening?"

"Not as far as I know, but I haven't read any of the letters that go with this bee attractant nightmare."

"Letters?"

Lola lifts the box from behind her rocker and passes it to him.

The detective paws through them and sighs. "Okay. Let me take your statement about the attempted break-in and then if it is alright with you, I'd like to stay and go over these with you."

"That would be amazing."

The detective moseys around Libitina's room taking in the environment. "Which window?"

"This one," Fabiola hollers as she rams into the room with a bottle and points to the one to the detective's left.

He unlocks it and peers over the edge. "Those are some big footprints. I can make a mold of them and if we find a suspect, we can try and match him to the impressions. What did he look like?"

"I don't know. Fabiola saw him, and he wore a mask."

"Fabiola, can I ask you an important question?"

"Okay."

"What color eyes did the man have? Were they like yours?"

"Green."

"Green?" The detective turns to Lola. "Green is good. A lot less common than brown or blue." He turns back to Fabiola. "One more question. Around his eyes was his skin like yours and your mom's, lighter, or darker?"

"It looked like vanilla."

"Mmm. Vanilla is my favorite kind of ice cream. Thank you for your help, young lady."

He smiles as Fabiola skips away then smooths Libitina's cowlick with his thumb. "I'll step out and take that mold then we can read through those cards," he smiles as Libitina smirks.

Will spread the contents of the box on the porch table. The majority are blessings and prayers, a few unsigned, but one catches Lola's attention. The black rose on the white envelope has a wax seal with a pentagram impression. Lola's hand trembles as she slips her finger under the flap and tears. She fumbles over Libitina's bouncer as she drops the envelope and bolts away.

"What?" Detective Gerard asks leaping to his feet.

"Bones."

He kneels, removes a pen from his inside pocket, and tips the envelope to empty it. A folded piece of paper lands on the pile. The detective unfolds a latex glove and stretches it on his hand. Using two fingers, he spreads the note open.

'An offering for the chosen one. May she grow to love the dark creatures of the deep and one day lead us through the fires of hell.'

Lola makes the sign of the cross as the detective shuffles the tiny remains into a small bag. "What is it?"

"Not sure. Kitten maybe?"

"That's disgusting," Lola says as she cringes.

A red coupe with tinted windows stops across the street. A group of teenage girls unload from the car and whisper to each other as they approach the stairs.

"What can we do for you ladies?" the detective inquires.

"We are from the local high school, and we are interested in babysitting for your family," the tall blonde with a pink sweater says through clenched teeth.

"Really? All of you?" Lola asks.

"It's a lesson in teamwork."

"Girls, your request for employment wouldn't involve an Ouija board, would it?" the detective asks, moving his jacket aside, and revealing his homicide shield.

The girl's eyes widen right before they turn, sprint toward their car, and speed away. Will shakes his head and gazes at Lola. Tears glimmer on her cheeks as she embraces Libitina. It's not her fault. It's no one's fault this is happening. It doesn't make things any less stressful for her. Libitina is innocent and she will protect her from everything and everyone.

The detective places one foot on the first step and rests his palms on his bent knee. "Lola, I think you and your family should leave the house for a few days. Just until things calm down."

"I'll talk to Hector when he gets home."

"Here's my card. Call me anytime. If you can't reach me, call Regina. She can track me down."

"Thank you," she sighs as he strolls to his car and drives away.

Fabiola smacks the screen open, and water from the bucket she carries splashes everywhere. She slams the liquid down on the floor beside Libitina and begins plucking the petals from all the roses and dropping them inside the container.

"What are you doing Fabby?"

"Making a bath for my sister."

"She won't fit in the bucket, Fabby."

"I know, but we can put it in her tubby. Please, Mama. I want her to smell beautiful."

"We'll see."

A black panel van slows but doesn't stop as it passes. Chills race up Lola's arms and she scrubs them. Down the street, an elderly couple dressed in matching attire walks towards them carrying a woven basket. Fabiola hops off the porch and meets them on the sidewalk. "What's in there?" she asks.

"Apples for your family. A whole bunch of them. Want one?"

"She does not," Lola shouts. "Fabiola up here with me."

"We don't mean any harm. It's just apples," the wife says while grinning.

"And you are strangers to my daughter and this neighborhood. Leave them if you like, but then be on your way."

"Sure," the husband says as his wife murmurs in his ear. "Can we peek at the baby? My wife loves babies."

"That's not happening. Please just leave us alone," Lola insists as she carries Libitina inside.

She waits by the window until the couple is out of sight, places Libitina down in her bassinet in the living room and goes to retrieve the basket.

The weight of the fruit tugs on her sore shoulder. Playing baseball all through high school did nothing for her besides make her popular and give her an arthritic joint. She lugs the shiny red produce to the sink, removes the top layer, and washes them under the sprayer before placing them in a bowl. The lower she went, the softer the fruit. By the time she reached the bottom, the apples couldn't hold their form. Maggots weave in and out of pitting holes.

Lola shouts and Fabiola comes running. "Mama, what's the matter?"

"Bad fruit," Lola grimaces as she grabs the garbage can and drops the whole basket inside.

Fabiola swipes an apple from the bowl and opens her mouth. Lola slaps it away scaring her.

"Mama these aren't bad."

"They're all bad. I'm sorry."

Lola empties the bowl, breaks a banana off the bundle on the counter, and puts it in Fabiola's hand. "Have this instead."

She grins and runs away as Lola reaches into her dress pocket, removes her cell, and calls Hector.

Chapter Twenty
Haven

After several days in a hotel, the Alvarez family headed home. Despite having to pay over a hundred dollars per evening, Hector and Lola enjoyed not having to worry. But as they round the corner and their house comes into view, their chests tighten, and the worry returns.

Word has gotten out that the child who lives here may or may not have special abilities. Now every lunatic, believer, non-believer, reporter, and anyone else in between has set up in the vacant lot beside their home. The front porch has three times as many flowers, baskets, and gifts as before. Strangers barbeque under a white canopy and someone even rented a portable public toilet.

"We can't stay here," Lola says as she grips Hector's knee.

"I know," he sighs as he hooks his fingers around the door handle. "Stay in the car and lock it when I get out."

Lola nods her head and presses the auto-lock button when he exits. He scales the steps, stomping over anything in his way, and pushes into the house.

Knuckles thump on the glass as the light from a reporter's camera shines in Lola's eyes. "Mrs. Alvarez, would you mind if we asked you some questions?"

Lola ignores her as Libitina starts to cry.

Soon multiple people surround the vehicle, taking selfies and trying to catch a glimpse of the special child.

"Mrs. Alvarez, if you could just step out of the car and answer a few questions, we could make all these people go away," the reporter promises.

Hands slap the roof and fists pound the glass as the mob demands they exit.

Fabiola sobs and covers her ears as Libitina screams.

I dash into the camera's light and shatter it, sending shards of glass in the face of the reporter.

Oops.

Men and women of all ages, dressed in black, push the cameraman and reporter away from the vehicle. They create a human shield around the family, close their eyes, and begin chanting.

'Dark creatures of the underworld, we protect your spawn with our bodies and offer this sacrifice to prove our loyalty to her.'

A man with a black beard and eyes just as dark holds a white rat to the window beside Libitina and slices it open. Entrails pour from its body as the sinister man takes his finger and draws a pentagram on the glass. Fabiola screams, making Libitina shriek even louder. Lola lays on the horn as I dive into the man like an Olympic swimmer and jerk him away from the window. He stands before his followers, lost for words as I force him to the ground, and whisper.

'Leave this place.'

I climb out, and he shakes the dizziness from his head. Another member of his group lifts another rat from a portable cage. The bearded man, who is slow to stand, snatches the member's wrist and hisses in his face, "We have been demanded to leave, so that is what we shall do."

All the members of the dark and dreary group disperse from the vehicle on his order, allowing the others who dare come close access. A new group circles the vehicle on their hands and knees and prays as Libitina continues crying.

Hector bolts out the door, carrying multiple suitcases.

"Move, right now!" he yells at the crowd blocking his path.

Their bodies are too close together, and he can't penetrate the line. I can keep jumping in and out of people, but they will just keep coming. They need outside help. I leave the family and check the house where Deliah killed the detective's partner a few blocks over.

Jackpot.

The detective is taking notes in his car, listening to loud music. I sit beside him and touch his temple. He flinches as a sharp pain stabs through his head, making him turn the music down.

A call for help blares over the radio, and he recognizes the address at once. He slams the car into drive and launches the vehicle in the direction of the Alvarez family's home.

He turns on their street but can't get through the congested traffic and people milling about. His cruiser is still rolling when he leaps out of the car a block away and sprints in their direction.

Bang.

A single gunshot sends everyone scattering like ants on a sidewalk. Hector slowly drops his arms to the side as the detective hustles up the driveway. "Get out of here now.

Call me when you're at a safe distance," the detective insists as he keeps his gun trained on the unruly crowd.

Hector tosses their clothes in the trunk and plops beside Lola, "I called my sister. We are heading to her house."

"That's an hour away. What about work?" Lola asks concerned.

"I'll commute. I don't want you girls anywhere near this house. I will sell it and move us to the cabin in the woods if we need to."

Lola intertwines her fingers with Hector's as he nods through the windshield at the detective. She peers in the backseat. Fabiola has her head leaned against Libitina's, whispering to her. "Fabby, are you girls, okay?"

"I'm scared, Mama," Fabiola weeps as she wipes snot from her nose.

"We are staying with Auntie Marie tonight."

"Yay. Can Libitina sleep with me?"

"We will figure it out when we get there," Hector says to her reflection.

Hector glances at Lola's hand. The fabric of her dress wrinkles in her grasp. He takes her hand, kisses the back of it, and rests it on his leg. She doesn't look at him. Her focus and furrowed brows stare at the trees as they fly by.

"Lola, look at me."

She turns her tear-stained face to him and blows a staggered breath through her lips. "What are we going to do?"

"Let's worry about that later. Right now, let's concentrate on making it to my sisters without the tail that's been following us for the last several miles."

"What?" Lola says cranking her neck.

"Behind us, about three cars back. Watch the silver car," he says as he signals and turns left.

A few seconds after rounding the corner, the silver car pulls onto the street. Hector makes another left turn, and the result is the same. He turns left one more time, bringing them back to the original road, and the car continues to follow.

"Do you still have the detective's card?"

Lola unzips her worn, burgundy leather bag, finds the business card, and dials the number. The detective picks up on the first ring.

"Detective Gerard."

"Detective this is Lola Alvarez."

"I just left your place, and officers are dispersing the crowd. Are you guys safe?"

"Someone is following us," Hector blurts. "Silver car, tinted windows."

"Tell me where you are, and I'll call someone to intercept."

"We just passed the last light in town heading east toward the highway," Hector says glancing behind him.

"On the main road?" The detective asks.

"Yes," Lola answers.

"Okay, once you're on the highway, stay in the right lane. Don't exit, it will make it harder to find you. Even if your exit comes up, pass it. We don't want the person to know where you're heading."

"I understand."

They pass the exit to his sister's house and continue past several more. Hector glances at Lola as red taillights from multiple brake lights slow traffic and bring them to a stop.

Their vehicle inches forward as I float to an accident up ahead. Blood drips from a man's open mouth as he struggles to breathe. His broken body dangles over a guardrail after driving at excessive speeds, and not negotiating a turn.

I wonder what goes through people's minds in that split second as they eject through the windshield and fly through the air. Surely, they feel it coming. A little voice in their head telling them, '*Stop now or slow down before you kill yourself, or someone else.*' They chose to ignore it. Too desperate to get to work on time, evade the police, street race, or whatever reason they are driving so recklessly to start with.

I remove his confused soul and steer him toward the light. He's not a bad man. As it turns out, his wife is in labor, and he doesn't want to miss the birth of his son. Now he'll miss everything. Sure, he can hang around and check in on his family from time to time if he chooses to stay in the in-between, but his predeceased father encourages him to let his old life go. He turns away from his crumpled body as medics rest a white sheet over his corpse.

The Alvarez family creeps by as firemen wave them past the scene. A few vehicles behind them, the silver car switches lanes and gains on them. Traffic speeds up and Hector sits taller in his seat. After a mile, blue and red lights dance in his field of vision as a trooper wedges himself between their vehicle and the trailing car. It tries to slip around the cruiser but another one pulls in beside it, boxing the person in, and forcing them to the side of the highway.

Hector and Lola let out their held breaths in unison as they take the next exit and double back to his sister's city.

Marie lives on a private road up on a hill, so few people have access to it. Hector punches in the security code and the iron gate screeches to the right. They take the winding driveway around a few curves and the white colonial appears. Lola squints and drops her visor as the sun reflects off its clean side. Hector's sister is ten years older than him. She helped him get his first job in real estate and taught him everything about the business.

Marie stands at the entrance with her hands cupped before her smiling face. She hasn't met Libitina yet, and it has been months since they last visited. Marie no longer leaves her home. Ever since two men attacked her while leaving her office in the heart of the city, she can't make it past the front porch without gripping anxiety. It doesn't prevent her from working from home and drawing in clients for her company.

"Auntie Marie," Fabiola cries out as she hugs her.

"Fabby, I missed you so much," she beams.

"I have a sister now," Fabiola says pulling her by the hand toward the car.

Marie pulls back and rubs her palms.

"I'm sorry Fabby," Marie grimaces as Fabiola yanks her again.

Hector rotates Fabiola's head to face him. "Auntie Marie can't leave her porch, remember?"

"Because it's lava?"

"Something like that. Now go help Mama get the bags from the trunk. I'll bring Libitina to Auntie Marie."

Hector pecks the side of his sister's cheek and jogs around the car. He hoists Libitina out of the car seat and kisses her head. Marie lifts the smiling infant and rests her against her chest. A tear slides down her face as Libitina takes her finger and squeezes.

"She's beautiful," Marie announces. "I'm your Auntie Marie."

Marie's face goes blank, and she mindlessly walks off the porch, shocking Hector, and Lola. Fabiola races from inside the house and dances before her. "You did it, Auntie Marie. You walked on lava."

Marie blinks multiple times and tiptoes backward onto the steps as her body tremors without control. "I…I…," she stutters.

"It's okay," Lola says reaching for Libitina.

"No!" Marie shouts.

Lola and Hector glance at each other. Marie backs up further into the house and disappears as they follow.

"Marie? Are you okay?" Hector asks as she gazes at herself holding Libitina in a floor-to-ceiling mirror.

"She makes me feel safe. Something I haven't felt in a long time," she sobs and turns to them. "I didn't understand what you meant before when you said she was 'special,' but I get it now. You can stay as long as you need."

"Thank you, Marie," Lola says as she embraces her and the girls.

"No. Thank you."

Chapter Twenty-One
Fast-Forward

Staying as long as they needed turned into almost a year. Christmas came and went and the time for them to move to their new home has come. Hector took a new job closer to his sister working for her real estate agency.

Fabiola starts pre-k in a few short weeks and unfortunately for me, Libitina can walk. She chases me around the house from room to room. I try and avoid her by dashing through walls, but she staggers along the barricade until she finds an opening and charges after me.

Persistent little shit.

"Are you chasing ghosts again, Libby," Auntie Marie says lifting her from the pristine white carpet.

Things are quieter since they left town and sold their house. Marie wishes for them to stay longer, but they already overstayed their welcome. Besides, the beautiful former farmhouse they bought on twelve acres supplies their girls with plenty of room and privacy. From the time they arrived at Marie's until now, the Alvarez family fought against Jack, who was determined to place Libitina elsewhere. With the help of Regina, the family won and were able to formally adopt Libitina. She now carries their last name, severing any ties to the Yarrow name, and tragic story tied to it.

Lola tucks Libitina's adoption papers in a manilla envelope, along with any files or photographs she acquired for Libitina's future. There is no doubt that one day she will ask about her birth parents and when that day arrives, and Libitina is old enough, Lola intends to tell her the truth as hard as it may be. But for now, she relishes in the girl's happiness as they run around Auntie Marie's foyer one last time.

"Careful, Fabby. Remember your sister isn't steady on her feet."

"Yes, Mama."

Crying echoes through the wall as Libitina smashes her face on a corner after tripping over her own feet. Blood oozes from her mouth as Lola swipes her from the floor, carries her to the kitchen counter, and sets her down. Lola runs cool water on a washcloth under the faucet as Libitina stops crying and sucks the crimson liquid filling her palate. Her front teeth pressed through the skin between her lips and her chin, creating a cross-shaped wound. Lola dabs the injury, and smears triple-antibiotic ointment on it to minimize scarring.

"What happened?" Hector asks, rushing to Libitina's side.

"Libby took a spill," Marie says, taking Lola's stained cloth.

"Will it scar?" Hector inquires as he examines the toddler's face.

"If it does, it will be a worthy one," Lola utters as she makes the shape of a cross with her finger.

"Everything's packed. Are you girls ready to go?" Hector asks as he lifts Libitina from the granite.

"We are."

Marie walks them to the door and kisses them goodbye. Seeing them go may be difficult, but knowing they are close provides a small measure of relief. Libitina and Fabiola blow kisses to her as they drive away from the house, making her smile.

The girls haven't seen their new house yet. So, when they turn into the driveway, Fabiola shrieks with excitement. "Is that a lamb?"

"No, it's a goat, and you can name him whatever you want," Hector beams.

Fabiola whispers to Libitina and giggles. "Asher."

"Asher? Where did you come up with that name?"

"I don't know."

"Asher it is," Lola smiles.

Fabiola bounces up and down, as she waits for Libitina to be free from her restraint. Hector sets her on the grass, and she takes off running with Fabiola in tow. He slips his hands into the pockets of his sweatpants and leans against the hood.

Libitina reaches for the fence gate fork latch, lifts it, and releases Asher from his pen. Hector raises his eyebrows and shakes his head as the girls chase the goat into the tall grass.

"Did you see that?" Hector asks Lola.

"Sure did. She figures things out so fast."

They set their luggage on the porch and take a seat in the oak rockers on either side of the entrance. Their updated farmhouse carries all the amenities of a brand-new home while keeping its charming appearance. The wrap-around porch supplies plenty of room for entertainment, an outdoor dining area, and an attached swing that doubles as a daybed for napping.

The primary yard along the front gives the girls a wide-open field to romp about without losing sight of them. Out back a vast cornfield spreads to the far end of the property behind them. An easement agreement allows them to harvest up to three rows of corn whenever they like without permission.

Crows circle above the swaying meadow, float to the earth and disappear.

"Do you hear that?" Lola asks Hector as she listens to the faint sound of giggling.

"I do. Wonder what is so hysterical," he says as he steadies the rocker, stands, and extends his hand to Lola.

They walk through the mowed yard and enter the high grass. As they wade through the thick blades, the laughter grows louder.

Everything stops. Words escape them, their strength to move forward vanishes, and even their ability to control their eyes as they fixate on the sight before them. Crows create a ring around Fabiola, Libitina, and Asher. The feathered creatures bob their heads and appear as though they are communicating with each other like birds congregating on a telephone line.

Asher steps toward them and the birds walk the goat back, keeping him in the sphere.

"Mama, Papa, look. The blackbirds are playing ring around the rosy with us," Fabiola chuckles.

Libitina staggers to one of the crows and touches it with her pointer finger. The bird takes off into the sky, taking his friends with him. Fabiola claps and Libitina joins her as Asher runs back to the house.

"Well, that was weird," Lola says breaching the silence between them.

"Yes, it was," Hector replies as he plucks Libitina from the tall grass. "Why don't we show you girls your rooms?"

"Yay," Fabiola yells.

Fabiola sprints through the field, leaps onto the porch, and uses her hip to pop the front door open. She pushes the second-floor doors open, searching for her room. Hector rests Libitina on the landing and secures the gate behind himself and Lola. She waddles down the hallway, passes Fabiola's room, and walks straight through her bedroom doorway.

Fabiola jumps out from behind the bathroom door, and into Libitina's room making the toddler burst out in laughter. She surveys Libitina's quarters, pulls the lock of hair from her mouth, and smiles. "My room is bigger."

"Yes, it is. You're a big girl who needs a big girl room," Hector points out as he scoops her into his arms and plops her on Libitina's toddler bed.

"But why does she have a crib and a bed, Papa?"

"Well, that way if she gets tired, she can crawl in bed all by herself and take a nap. Or, if you want to lay in here when she's in her crib you can too. I have an important job for you, Fabby. I need you to make sure you always remember to close the toilet seat. Just like at the old house."

"So, sissy doesn't flush herself down the toilet?"

"Of course, but mainly because she's a baby, and standing water can be dangerous."

Fabiola places her hand on her forehead and stands up straight and tall, "Yes, sir," she says with an emotionless face as she salutes him.

She runs into the bathroom, checks the lid, then skips into her room and dumps her toys.

"I think she watches too many war movies with you," Lola grins.

"You may be right," Hector smiles as he scans the room. "Where's Libitina?"

They search all the rooms and closets upstairs. No Libitina. Hector storms into Fabiola's room, opens her closet, and peers under her bed. "Where's your sister?

"Hector!" Lola screams.

He dashes into the hallway as Lola stomps down the stairs. "The gate is open," she yells.

"What? I closed it myself," he insists.

Lola enters the living room and grabs her chest. Libitina sits on the couch drinking her bottle and watching the news. Bubbles enter the bottle as she cheeses at Lola and Hector standing before her with their fists planted on their hips.

"Well, I guess the baby gates are pointless," Hector says throwing his hands in the air.

"Hector if she can open those and Asher's pen, what if she gets out the front door?"

"I'll put a deadbolt up high where she and Fabiola can't reach."

Hector rotates Lola's necklace, moving the clasp to the back. "I'll make sure to Libitina proof the house," he smiles as he kisses her.

She gazes at his back as he strolls to the kitchen, then sits beside Libitina. Libitina crawls onto her lap, rests her head against her chest, and closes her eyes. Lola places her palm on her spine and pecks her head. Soft snoring begins as Libitina drifts off to sleep, and so does Lola.

Chapter Twenty-Two
First Word

Lola lays in the tall grasses of the field before their farmhouse. The soil beneath her chills her flesh. Vultures circle above her as she fights to move but can't. She's stuck. Halfway between awake, and asleep, the muffled sound of the television alerts viewers of a weekly emergency broadcast test in her living room, but she can't pull herself out of her nightmare.

She's dying, alone and afraid in the overgrown blades. Libitina hovers over her and cups her face with both hands. 'Lola,' she whispers in her dream.

"Lola," Libitina murmurs as she rotates Lola's face back and forth, waking her up.

"Mama, sissy said your name," Fabiola announces dancing around the room.

Lola shakes her head trying to focus on Libitina's lips as the word comes out a second time. "Lola."

A grin spreads across Lola's face. "Hector!" Lola yells.

"What?"

"Libitina said 'Lola,' twice," she replies dabbing her eyes with her sleeve.

"Really? I wonder if I should start calling you Mama, so she learns that instead."

"Hector, don't be silly."

"Lola, Lola, Lola," Libitina chants as she bounces up and down on the couch cushions.

"Lola, Lola, Lola," Fabiola sings joining in.

Libitina climbs off the sofa and follows Fabiola as she marches to the kitchen saying her name. Their arms move in unison like a drill sergeant leading his recruits.

Lola shoots Hector a sideways glance.

"Alright. No more watching war movies with the girls."

"I don't know what Libitina will do without Fabby when school starts on Wednesday."

"She'll be okay. She has you. Lola, Lola, Lola," he sings as he pounds his fist in the air.

"Behave," Lola says furrowing her brow as she slaps his hand down.

They venture into the kitchen together. Lola washes the dishes and watches the girls play near the edge of the cornfield, while Hector chops vegetables for dinner. They take turns cooking. Monday through Friday, Lola makes dinner, and on the weekends, Hector cooks. This evening's dinner consists of stuffed peppers with a side of homemade Spanish rice. Lola's favorite.

"Should I make Libitina something?" Hector asks as he places the peppers in the crockpot.

"Probably a good idea. Ever since she turned one, she thinks she's an adult, and refuses to eat any baby food."

"I'll cut up some peppers real tiny, cook them, and mix them with the Spanish rice."

"Fabby will probably want something else too. You know she doesn't care for stuffed peppers."

"Already covered. I thin-sliced some tomatoes, and plan on grilling her a tomato and provolone sandwich."

"She'll love it."

Lola glances out the window and drops her hand towel. "The girls are gone."

"Probably playing in the corn," Hector says moving the sheer aside and scanning the field. "I'll find them."

He steps outside and calls to them. "Girls? Fabby, Libitina, where are you?"

No reply.

Hector scales the field's edge until he reaches the property marker, then jogs back in the opposite direction. "Fabiola, answer me," he yells as he closes his eyes and turns his ear to the corn.

No response.

Lola taps on the glass of the kitchen window, and he shakes his head. She joins him in the yard just as Fabiola and Asher appear from in between the rows.

"Fabby, where's your sister?"

"We were running, and I turned, and she didn't and now I can't find her," she whimpers.

"It's okay. We will find her together. Take Asher to his pen and sit on the back steps while Mama and I search for her."

"Okay, Papa."

The corn leaves slice into their bare arms as they each take a row and call Libitina's name repeatedly. Birds swirl in the distance and they exchange glances when they spiral toward Earth.

"Are you thinking what I'm thinking?" Lola asks.

"Follow the birds?"

"Yep."

They push through the razor-sharp crops and stop at the farmer's scarecrow. Standing next to it, a motionless man with brown hair, and dirt smudges on his sharp jaw, dressed in jean overalls with a white tank top underneath, holds Libitina. He does not acknowledge their existence or speak when they approach. He's gazing down at Libitina, holding her hand.

"Hello?" Hector says waving his palm in the man's stoic face.

Nothing.

I manifest beside them, confused.

The man lifts his head to face Lola, right before his eyes roll back into his head and he topples over. Libitina lands on the farmer's chest and rolls onto the ground. Hector scoops her up and steps away as Lola places her ear against his sternum.

"He's not breathing, and I don't hear his heart," she announces as she begins compressions. "Call an ambulance."

Hector removes his phone and dials while I hover by, waiting for his soul to decide if he's coming or going.

In and out he goes, like a game of whack-a-mole.

Above them, birds circle much like the nightmare Lola dreamt of earlier, making her fight for him even harder. Lola hesitates, then continues as one of the man's ribs cracks under her palms. Hector sets Libitina down and places his hand on Lola's shoulder. "I think it's too late."

"I'm not stopping until they get here."

"Lola, let him go."

She cranks her neck, stopping for a brief second. "If it were you, I would never stop."

When she turns back, Libitina stands beside the man's chest and topples forward onto his diaphragm.

The farmer bends upright and inhales a deep, noisy breath. "Save us," he whispers to Libitina as she cups his thin cheekbones and rests her forehead against his.

Everyone falls silent. The sirens of an ambulance grow closer as the man embraces Libitina and repeats, "Save us."

"Sir, are you okay?" Lola asks.

The farmer glances at her, and Hector. "Who are you?"

"I'm Hector Alvarez, and this is my wife, Lola. We moved into the remodeled farmhouse."

Lola seizes Libitina around the waist and lifts her onto her hip.

"Wait. Who is she?"

"This is our daughter, Libitina," Hector replies as a paramedic breaches the corn stalks.

"Sir, do you have a history of heart trouble?" the paramedic inquires.

"It doesn't matter."

"Sir, it does matter. I think we should take you to the hospital and check out your heart."

"It's a test. She's testing me," the farmer says pointing at Libitina. "I let Jesus in my heart a long time ago little one. So, test me all you want."

The paramedic squints his eyes and gazes at Lola. "What is he talking about?"

"I have no idea. Our daughter is waiting for us, so we are heading back. Also, I think I broke a rib."

The paramedic nods and turns his attention back to the old man as Lola and Hector vanish between two rows.

Libitina smears the bloody cut on Lola's arm as they track through the crops back to the house. Fabiola plucks the petals of a daisy on the porch when they appear from the corn.

"Why does sissy have a hand on her face?"

Lola spins Libitina around to face her. A perfect red handprint stains her forehead. Hector leaves her side, goes to the kitchen, and returns with a washcloth. He cleans Libitina's face, and Lola's arm as a vehicle steers into their driveway. After a brief pause, Detective Gerard and Regina climb out of the car.

Will and Regina vowed to stop at least once a week to catch up and see the girls once the family moved into their new home. When they were staying with Marie, Regina, and Will didn't come around as often because they didn't want to intrude or make Marie uncomfortable. Although Will is a homicide detective, it still brings back painful memories from Marie's interview with the detective on her mugging case. Sometimes, the Alvarez family would meet Regina and Will for dinner at a family restaurant, but it wasn't the same.

"Hi, girls," Regina says, waving at them.

"Regina," Fabiola screams as she runs up and hugs her legs. "Did you bring presents?"

"Fabby, that's rude," Hector scolds.

"Well, she isn't wrong," Will announces popping the trunk.

He lifts out two giant stuffed animals, a vanilla-colored horse, and a shiny-haired, black-and-white goat.

"It's Asher," Fabiola says with wide-open eyes as she crushes it in her grasp.

"Who's Asher?" Regina asks as she shakes the horse in front of Libitina who pounces on it.

"Asher is their goat," Lola smiles as Libitina rolls in the grass with her new stuffed animal.

"You got them a goat for a pet?" Will inquires raising his eyebrows.

"It's a pygmy. We planned to buy a second one, once this one is comfortable."

"You let it run free with the girls?" Regina asks as she pets Asher's head.

"Well, we keep putting him back in his pen, but Libitina keeps letting him go. So, we let him wander."

"Libitina?" Regina says to Lola as she accepts a lemonade from Hector.

"Yep. Baby gates don't work for her either," Lola says shaking her head.

"Come up and have a seat," Hector offers pointing to the outdoor seating.

They scale the porch steps and sink into the conversation set at the far end of the porch.

"So, what brings you two here?" Lola asks.

"Well, for one we wanted to check out your new house."

"And two?" Hector asks as he sets his empty glass on the aluminum table.

Regina nods, and the detective removes a letter from his inside jacket pocket.

"I'm not sure if you want this or not, but I think you should at least read it."

"Who is it from?"

"Mr. Thaddeus Yarrow."

Tightness grips Lola's chest at the mere mention of his name. Hector steadies her bouncing leg and slides the letter from the detective's grasp.

"What does it say?" Hector says without opening it.

"It's an apology to Libitina. He wants her forgiveness for what he has done."

"How can he expect her to forgive him at her age?" Lola says confused.

"Listen. It's up to you if you want to read it, but he's insisting it is done right away."

"What do you mean by insistent?" Hector asks.

"That's not the first piece of mail. It's the seventy-fifth letter he has sent me. The last one said he won't quit sending them until you read it to her."

Lola stands from her seat. "Why is he doing this?"

"All I know is, from what I read, he is still a little cuckoo," the detective states making a circle with his pointer finger beside his temple.

Regina follows Lola as she storms into the house. "Lola, I know you're upset but if we don't deliver his message, he won't stop."

"So, tell him you did," she huffs raising her voice.

"We can't. Mr. Yarrow wants proof."

"Proof? What kind?"

"A letter back."

"Have you lost your mind, Regina?"

"If you just write, 'I received and read your note to Libitina' and sign your name, I'm sure it'll be enough to pacify him. Will can mail it from the station."

"And what if it isn't? What if the letters keep coming?"

"Then we can request his postal privileges be revoked."

Lola eyes the girls as they play with their stuffed animals. Asher chews on the ear of the goat one as Fabiola fights to release it from his clenched teeth. Libitina sits on her horse like a future jockey.

"I'll talk to Hector. If we do this, it's the first and last time. Understand?"

"I couldn't agree more. One and done."

Lola ignores Regina when she says goodbye and heads out to the front porch. I slip inside and listen to her thoughts.

'Be compassionate like the Lord says, Lola. Who am I kidding? Mr. Yarrow doesn't deserve our time or energy. God give me the strength to do what I must.'

I float out of her.

She rubs the goosebumps from her arms, rolling her bandage off in the process. The wound resembles a sickle and Lola traces it with her finger. Hands slide around her waist as Hector holds her from behind. "Are you okay?"

"I don't know."

"We don't have to read it," he insists spinning her body to face him.

"I know, but we should. If not for her, for us."

Hector slips the note from his pocket and places it on the table. They take a seat across from each other and stare at the folded piece of paper.

Chapter Twenty-Three
The Letter

Unlike Lola and Hector, I want to know what Mr. Thaddeus Yarrow has to say. I stick my head inside Hector's and whisper.

'Open it.'

Hector slaps the college rule paper and snaps it open. Lola holds her breath, then releases it slowly. "Wait," she says stopping him from reading. "Let's set Libitina in the room. That way we won't need to read it again."

She gets up and hustles to the living room. Libitina is in a deep sleep in her toddler recliner, so Lola is careful not to disturb her. The seat jars to a stop when it hits the floor, startling Libitina awake.

"Lola," Libitina smiles as she stretches her arms. Lola chuckles and shakes her head.

"Come here, silly girl."

"Are you sure you want her to hear this?"

"Hector, she's too young to remember. Let's get this over with."

He smooths the paper flat on the wood surface and begins reading.

Libitina,

I'm sorry for everything. Now I know the pain I have caused. You come to me in a recurring nightmare. Only, you are no longer a child. You are a hurt and broken person who releases her wrath on the world.

Not everyone is like me, Libitina. There are still good people in this world. Don't give up on us. Please forgive me. I don't want to die, but if that's the fate you chose for me, then take me. Take me and leave everyone else. I will be your sacrificial lamb. I am the one who set you on this path of destruction with my selfishness, so I deserve your punishment. Killing people is wrong and a sin. Remember that before you do anything you might regret.

Love,

Dad

The paper crumples and launches across the room. The chair under Hector topples over when he stands abruptly. "Who does he think he is? Dad? Libitina a murderer?"

Lola scoops the balled-up letter and drops it in the trash. "Hector, you're her father, and you always will be. We did our part. We read it. Now we need to respond."

"To hell with that!" Hector shouts making Libitina pout.

"Hector, language."

"I'm sorry," he says removing Libitina from Lola's arms and hugging her. "I didn't mean to shout. Papa is just upset."

Lola wraps her arms around them both. Fabiola enters the kitchen and joins in the family group hug. "Why are we hugging?" Fabiola asks as she gazes up at Hector's red face.

"Because you are my girls, and I will do anything to keep you safe," Hector smiles down at her while stroking her cheek.

"Okay, Papa. Can Libby and I play with Asher?"

"Sure," he says setting the toddler down.

Libitina saunters to the trash can, removes the ball of former wood pulp, and straightens it back out. She examines the page for a few seconds then tosses it in the air. It floats to the floor like a molted feather as she takes Fabiola's hand and leaves the room.

"I think she doesn't care what he says," Lola points out.

"That's what I got out of it too. Grab a paper and pen."

Lola pulls open the kitchen drawer, and removes a pen, paper, and envelope. She puts the address on the front of the envelope but leaves the sender part blank as Hector begins writing.

Mr. Yarrow,

We have received and read your message and so has Libitina. God may forgive you, and someday perhaps so will we. As for Libitina, that is not for anyone but her to decide. To say she will one day kill people is preposterous. As long as we are around, she will never be like you. Perhaps the dream you are having isn't Libitina punishing you at all. It's just you, putting someone else in your place so you don't have to face what you have done when your time comes. I don't know what you're looking for, Mr. Yarrow, but you won't find it here.

Hector and Lola Alvarez

The pen rolls off the table when Hector sets it down. He pushes the letter to Lola and waits for her to scan it.

"Do you think it's enough?" Lola asks, resting her palm on his fist.

"I don't know," he sighs as he rests his other hand on top of hers. "Call Detective Gerard and let him know it's done."

Lola nods as Hector slips his hands in his pockets and peers out the window. The girls are playing with their stuffed toys in the front meadow. Fabiola plucks a wild daisy and bonks Libitina on the top of her head. The toddler giggles and runs circles around her sister. He laughs through his nose as Lola stands by his side.

"Will and Regina are coming by later. I invited them to dinner."

"What are we having?" Hector asks twisting his waist to look at her.

"Macaroni and cheese."

"That's everyone's favorite."

"I know. I thought it would be a good meal considering the day we are having."

"You're right as always," Hector smiles as he gives her a smooch.

Detective Gerard pushes his glasses up his nose and passes the letter to Regina. She raises her eyebrows, folds it, and stuffs it inside the envelope. "Perfect. Will can mail this first thing tomorrow."

"Is it possible to request he no longer sends anything?" Lola inquires.

"We can make a request on your behalf," Regina offers.

"Thank you," Hector nods.

Libitina jams a twisted macaroni noodle into her mouth with her knuckles, then pulls it back out. It sticks to her fingers, and she shakes it hard to release it. The pasta flies up and lands on her head. Fabiola bursts into laughter as the detective passes beer through his nose. The entire table erupts in a well-deserved bout of hysterics. Libitina seizes a handful of food and launches it across the table at Regina. Regina's eyes widen, and she takes a noodle and throws it back at her. Food flies everywhere, in all directions, as they wage an all-out food fight in the dining room. Lola's famous comfort food paints the walls, ceiling, floors, and everything in between.

Rain pounds on the black metal roof, making everyone look up and smile. Lola unbuckles Libitina from her belt, and they all run outside to rinse off in the free shower nature provides.

Through the darkness, Detective William Gerard bends his knee before Regina and opens a black velvet box. She cups her hands around her mouth and nods. No one can hear his words through the thunderous storm, but the question he asks is obvious and so is her answer. Hector shakes Will's hand and Lola hugs Regina as the girls stomp through puddles oblivious of the transaction that just happened.

Regina whispers in Will's ear, and he smiles. "All we can do is ask."

"Lola, Hector, do you think we could have the wedding here?"

"Of course, you can. We can even cook if you like," Lola offers.

"Can my sister and me be in the wedding?" Fabiola asks as she tightens her grip around Regina's thighs.

"Are you kidding? Do you think I would leave you out? You two are my flower girls."

"Yay," Fabiola sings as she raises her open mouth to the sky to catch the falling water.

Lola goes inside and returns with a pile of white towels. They stand on the porch and dry off as the rain slows to a trickle. Hector inhales the scent of bleach as he pats his face with the terry cloth then scrubs Fabiola's sopping locks.

Libitina strokes her silky hair and then does the same to Lola. "Mama."

Everyone freezes and glances at Libitina, as tears of joy join the rain on Lola's face and race to her chin.

"That's Mama," Hector smiles. "And I'm Papa. Can you say, Papa?"

"Mama," Libitina repeats.

"Don't worry, Hector. She'll get to you in time," the detective says reassuring him with a hearty slap on the back.

They all stare into the dining room. Macaroni moves at a turtle's pace down the wallpaper and plops on the floor. Even the dangling light over the table has bits of cheese hanging from it. Lola carries in a bucket of soapy water and washcloths. Regina takes one, dunks it in the soap, and starts scrubbing. "Sorry about this."

"Don't be sorry. It was worth it," Lola grins.

Libitina takes a cloth and copies Fabiola. A pool surrounds them as they dip and wash without wringing the cloth first.

Such a night will live in their memories for the rest of their lives. It is one night, one moment where they thought of nothing else, but each other's happiness. Not work, bills, health, or even Mr. Yarrow could ruin this for them. Time is a precious commodity so why waste it on things you can't control or change?

Chapter Twenty-Four
Wedding Day

Time passes in the blink of an eye. One day we are sending Fabiola off to her first day of pre-k and the next we are decorating for Regina and Will's wedding. Libitina displays astonishing growth. Over the last year, she has gone from eating with her hands, needing help getting on the couch, and someone changing her diaper, to using a fork and spoon, pushing a plastic folding step stool around to get to places she's too short to reach, and using the toilet on her own. I've even caught her humming the chorus from Madam Butterfly. She warms my silhouette as she runs by and ignores me.

Odd.

I don't sense temperature from any other human.

She disregards my existence on purpose. Before it was due to a busy toddler mind.

Everyone is happy. Nothing could ruin this day, not even rain. The forecast calls for a gorgeous fall day, so no one is worried.

Lola smooths Regina's satin gown and adjusts a few pearls. The backless ballgown flows beautifully over Regina's hourglass frame. Fabiola carries a tiara with an attached veil and rests it in her mother's palm. The girls wear tea-length rust-colored satin dresses with hair ribbons to match. Libitina's short, wavy brown locks curl around the shiny material, while Fabiola's rings bounce behind hers.

Outside, Hector straightens Asher the goat's bowtie as Pastor James adjusts Will's collar. The intimate wedding only has a select number of attendees. A few officers and detectives from the force, Regina's parents, and her brother. The farmer dropped by with a card and left. He hasn't said much of anything, and they rarely see him since the incident in the crops, but they drop in on him on occasion and bring him dinner. Hector gazes at the empty seat reserved for his sister. If only she could leave the house to see this.

It wasn't for lack of trying. Hector brought Libitina to Marie's house. After she displayed comfort with Libitina at their first meeting, he thought it was worth a try. She made it to the car, but the approaching unfamiliar mailman sabotaged their efforts, and Marie retreated inside her sanctuary.

Hector plans to videotape, and send it to her, but it's not the same.

"I want the dark one," Fabiola says as she picks up the bundle of red mums mixed with crimson roses. "Here Libby, take this one," she offers handing Libitina the bouquet with orange mums and lilies.

"Thank you, sissy," Libitina smiles squeezing the white stick.

I float around the yard, listening to the few people in attendance. I don't have to be here. But things are quiet now, and I have nothing else to do. Libitina stops before the barn entrance I'm waiting beside. "Dark One," she says reaching for me.

I'm sure she's just mimicking what her sister said to her, but how fitting she chose those words to copy.

I partially immersed myself beneath the earth's threshold so I could gaze into her eyes on her level. She tips her chin down, glares under my shadowy hood, and whispers, "You don't belong here."

I plaster myself against the barn wall and gaze at her pointing finger as she gives me a direct order. "Leave."

The nerve.

Does she really think I need to listen to her? I moved towards her but pause as a man approaches.

"Who are you talking to?" Regina's brother asks as he crouches beside Libitina who's staring at a vacant wall.

Her finger touches me as she points sending fire through me. She does it again as the man hoists her into his arms and walks away. Smoke billows from my apparition as the steam of my false flesh burns.

The demons of the underworld are the only other ones who cause me such pain. Is she one of them who walks among us? Could she be a spawn of Lucifer? She smiles at me over the man's shoulder. Before today the most she's ever said to me was, 'Hi.' Now I have a new name.

Dark One.

I am dark, but I'm not evil. I can't say the same about her. I still haven't figured her out yet. To make matters worse, now she's communicating with me like an adult, ordering me to leave, like a boss, and causing me pain like shingles.

How?

Until she's older, I may never know.

Pastor David plays the 'Bridal Chorus' on a small white piano he brought in the church van. Regina steps off the porch, with Lola by her side as the girls walk across colorful petals decorating a silky red walkway. Everyone stands as she passes and joins Will under the arbor. Decorative leaf chains wrap around the archway, and battery-operated acorns cast an orange hue on Regina's face.

Crows caw in the fields picking off the remnants of the earlier crop in the background. The music stops when the final note plays, and Pastor James reads from the bible. Libitina giggles as Fabiola makes faces at her across the aisle. Lola rests her palm on Fabiola's knee and whispers to stop the antics. Hector places Libitina on his left, removing her from Fabiola's line of sight.

Pastor David stands in the center aisle, holding a wooden crate, as Will kisses his new bride. The pastor lifts the latch and releases multiple white doves into the air. Libitina hops from her seat and dances in a circle. The crows join the doves and descend toward the crowd. Everyone moves. Everyone except Libitina.

She stretches her arms to her sides, and the birds land on her. "Birdies," she smiles as everyone stares at her with their mouths open.

The birds associated with good and evil launch from her limbs and disappear into the sky. A talon scratches her skin. She smears it with her finger and points at me. "Dark One."

Dying fields and a few sparse clouds floating by the sun are the only things they notice when they follow the direction she points in.

She can't represent both sides, like the heads and tails of a coin. Could she? The crows make sense. Up until today, I assumed she was steering toward evil, but the doves rebuke that. Perhaps we have reached a crossroads. Libitina grows and changes every day. Who am I to assume what, or who she shall become?

Hector takes his handkerchief from his breast pocket and wipes the blood from Libitina's arm. "Come here my little ringmaster," he says tossing her in the air.

Ringmaster?

This isn't the circus. She's not training the animals to come to her, they are gravitating towards her on their own.

"How did you get those birds to do that?" Detective Gerard asks as he glances up at the last remaining dove that's visible.

"You're the detective, Will. You tell me," Hector insists.

Pastor James shakes Will and Hector's hands, followed by Pastor David. "Aren't you two staying," Lola asks.

"Tonight, Pastor David and I have a dual sermon with multiple messages. So, we cannot stay."

"Thank you for performing the ceremony," Regina says hugging them both.

Neither Pastor uttered a word about the incident, but their eyes and facial expressions spoke volumes. I imagine the sermon they originally planned to make changed once they saw the birds coming to Libitina like a flock of sheep to a shepherd.

The family takes their places at the autumn-decorated table and prepares to eat once the clergy vanishes from sight.

Libitina refuses to sit. She runs around the table multiple times while Hector fights to grab her. Regina turns her seat to face her and opens her arms. Libitina slows down and stops. She takes Regina's belly in both hands and whispers. "Hi, baby."

"Baby?" Will laughs. "No baby yet."

Regina's face pales, and she turns to him. "Would that be so bad?"

"Oh, my goodness," Lola cheers. "You are?"

"Wait, what?" Will says, turning her face back to his. "Am I going to be a father?"

Regina bites her lip and nods her head. "I planned to tell you tonight. Who knew Libitina, of all people, would ruin the surprise? Are you mad?"

"Mad? Come here love," he says as he scoops her up in his arms and spins her around. "This is the best wedding gift I could ever receive. Better than me surprising you with a trip to the Bahamas."

"Are you serious?"

"I wanted to tell you tonight, but…"

She gazes into his eyes. "I love you, Mr. Gerard."

"I love you, too, Mrs. Gerard."

They give each other a passionate kiss, and Fabiola frowns. "Gross."

"Gross," Libitina repeats.

Will shuffles Libitina's hair with his palm, and she takes off with Fabiola and Asher.

A blue pick-up truck steers into the driveway hauling a small animal trailer. Will waves at the driver, and exchanges smiles with Regina.

"We got you guys something," Regina murmurs as she holds Will around the waist.

"Us? It's your wedding?" Lola insists.

"Yes, but you let us have it here, decorated, and cooked everything. We wanted to repay your kindness."

The girls both squeal when the driver rounds the back of the trailer with a goat.

"Another Asher," Fabiola screams.

"Not just another Asher. This one only has one horn like a unicorn," Regina whispers. "It's a rescue. Our vet was treating it when we brought in my cat for some shots. I told her I knew the perfect family to adopt him. Didn't you used to have a cat?"

"We did. Luna never came back after the tornado. I stay in contact with my old neighbor. He promised to let me know if she shows up. Thank you, both," Hector says shaking Will's hand. "I've been meaning to get another but haven't had the time."

Libitina and Fabiola pet their new friend while Asher inspects his competition. "Karma, come!" Fabiola shouts a command as she slaps her leg.

"Karma and Asher. I don't know where these girls come up with these names," Lola says gritting her teeth. "Boy, I hope they are careful. That horn looks sharp."

"Here. I almost forgot," the driver says handing her a tennis ball from his back pocket. "Stick it on the horn."

"It's better than a beer can," Will grins.

"True. Green ball on his head it is. Girls, bring Karma here," Hector yells.

Fabiola takes the goat's leash, and Libitina holds it behind her. They stop in front of Hector, and he pops the round toy on its pointed horn.

"Papa, he looks silly," Fabiola insists as she tries to remove it.

"No. Fabby, you must leave it on. That horn is sharp. It's for you and Libby's protection."

"Karma silly," Libitina says as she slaps her hands against her sides and rubs her belly.

"Hungry?" Lola bends her knees and hovers at eye level with Libitina as she rotates her fists in her eyes.

Libitina wraps her arms around Lola's neck. "Sleepy."

"It's been a long day, hasn't it," Lola grunts as she lifts the toddler onto her hip.

"I'll take her in," Hector offers removing her from Lola's clutches. "Come here, big girl."

Her eyes droop, and close as he scales the front steps and enters the house. He places her in her toddler bed and covers her with a plush pink blanket. "I love you."

"Papa," she mutters in her sleep.

Hector turns into me as he heads for the door. He pauses and stares at the rising hair on his arms. "Whatever you are, if you ever try and hurt her, or my family, I will go to the ends of this earth to find someone who can rid her of your presence."

I shudder when he continues through me and leaves the room. I have no doubt he would do anything to protect his family, but who will protect us from her?

"No one," Libitina whispers.

I came closer, thinking she was talking in her sleep.

I'm wrong.

She's sitting up in bed and staring straight at me with an ever-so-slight smile tugging at the corner of her mouth.

"What did you say?"

"You heard me." Her voice echoes in my head, but her lips don't move.

"How can you know my thoughts?"

"I know everything."

"If you know everything, then why not tell us God's plan?"

"Why would I do that? So, you can warn them?"

"Warn who?"

"You know who."

"Why do you speak in riddles? Why not answer my questions?"

"Because you already know the answers to the questions," she sighs as she turns her back to me and covers herself. "You're just afraid to accept them."

"I'm not afraid of anyone, or anything."

"We shall see."

Chapter Twenty-Five
Time for Baby

It seems like yesterday Libitina blew the whistle on Regina's pregnancy. Now Lola, Hector, and the girls are hustling down the crisp white floor tiles of the hospital hallway hoping they make it on time for the birth of Will and Regina's baby girl.

I'm already here, so I didn't have to float far.

Regina's brother sits in the waiting room, with his elbows vibrating on his bouncing knees when the family whips around the corner.

"Bob, what's happening? Regina's not due for another four weeks," Lola murmurs sinking into the faux leather couch beside him.

"The baby has other plans."

"They'll both be fine," Hector insists patting him on the back.

"Let's hope so," Bob nods.

"Hope," Libitina murmurs.

"Come on Libby," Fabiola insists steering her toward the book rack.

Bob stands and paces the room, creating a wear pattern in the commercial teal green carpet. Lola and Hector exchange quiet words as Fabiola reads to Libitina.

Duty calls so I leave them to their worries and float to the nursery a few doors down. A baby boy, born three months too soon, fights to survive. His parents console each other as the doctor informs them, he won't make it.

"Adam's heart is too weak, and his underdeveloped lungs are failing fast. I'm sorry."

"Can I hold him one last time," Adam's mother asks.

"Of course. The nurse will take him out when you're ready."

These ones are hard. I can't imagine what it's like for a mother to carry her child inside, only to lose it to fate.

The nurse enters, lifts the covered bassinet open, and asks the mother, "Ready?"

"Yes."

"Disconnecting now," the nurse says with a deadpan face.

How people in this field can turn off their emotions at a time like this, I may never understand. Perhaps they venture home and cry about it later, but this staff member is as solid as they come right now. She rests baby Adam on his mother's bare chest and wraps a receiving blanket around the doll-sized infant. The nurse disappears through the doorway, giving them their privacy.

Adam's mother cups his tiny head in her palm, closes her eyes, and prays. Her husband leans in and prays with her.

It's not working. An angel appears through the ceiling and hovers beside me.

It's time.

I reach for Adam's soul but stop as the doors drone open, and Libitina saunters inside. She touches Adam's father's leg, startling him.

"Joy, someone's kid is here."

"What?"

Libitina rotates to me, and scowls. "No."

I ignore her. Who is she to tell me how to do my job? I remove the infant's soul from his frame and pass it to the angel.

Libitina seizes the baby's soul, rips it from the angel's grasp, and pushes him back inside his body. "Nooooooo!" Libitina screams.

The angel shrieks at Libitina for interfering with fate, then turns to me to try again. Adam's parents gawk in horror as smoke billows from Libitina's empty palms as she snatches the angel's wing and my arm and forces us to touch. The heavenly apparition and I launch through the fluorescent fixture, rupturing its bulb as baby Adam stirs under his mother's palm, then latches onto her breast.

Adam just needed more time, and Libitina gave it to him. Joy and her husband burst into tears as their son defies the odds. The nurse and doctor rush in, drawn to the sudden darkness in the family's room. Using his cellphone flashlight to guide him, the pediatrician flicks on the light behind the mother's elevated bed. Whisps of smoke remain, but Libitina is gone.

"Impossible," the nurse murmurs gawking at the nursing infant.

"No, it's a miracle," the doctor says as he rests his stethoscope on the baby's wrinkled spine.

"Where's the little girl," Joy asks scanning the room.

"What little girl?" the nurse inquires.

The husband and wife glance at each other and then back to their surviving son. Who are they to question the will of God? Joy gazes at the space above her and thanks the Lord for giving her son a second chance.

Libitina is more powerful than I ever imagined. I'm not the only one she can hurt. Having the ability to see and touch the employees of the afterlife is an amazing gift. The power to snatch a soul from us, and send it back to its physical form, saving the person's life, is another.

What is she? Is the boss downsizing? Did He create a creature who will replace all reapers, demons, and angels? One person to the job of many. How many of them exist? Are we the last of our kind, as she is the first of hers?

Nursery chimes jingle overhead. Another baby joins this forsaken world. I levitate down to the waiting room.

"Baby Hope," Libitina announces coming into the room from the hallway.

"Where have you been, young lady?" Lola asks.

"Dark One," she smiles and glares at me.

"Playing with your invisible friend again?" Hector grins lifting her from the floor. "Time to go, Dark One," Hector orders to the empty corner Libitina points in. "You're not putting a damper on this day."

Well, no kidding. Libitina already did.

Will bursts through the double doors with a giant smile on his face, and his eyes wet with tears. "I'm a father."

Lola hugs Will, and Hector and Bob take turns shaking his hand.

"Baby Hope," Libitina repeats pulling Will's pant leg.

Will swoops Libitina up in the air and catches her right before she hits the floor. The toddler laughs hysterically as he does it a second time, and grins. "Hope. I like it. Let's go sell it to Regina."

The family crowds into the room, eager to lay eyes on the new baby.

"Where's her hair?" Fabiola asks, rubbing the top of the baby's head with one finger.

"Some babies are born without it, and it comes in later," Regina sighs.

"Hope," Libitina smirks as she pecks the infant's forehead.

Libitina places her hands on either side of Regina's face and repeats. "Hope."

A single tear flickers from Regina's lid as she nods in agreement. "Hope it is."

Fabiola plops down on the foot of the bed. "Can I hold her?"

"Go sit in the rocker," Regina requests.

The chair punctures a hole in the wall as Fabiola throws herself into it.

Hector rolls his eyes and shakes his head. "Settle down."

He rests Hope in her arms. Libitina holds Hope's hand as Fabiola rocks her. The infant opens her eyes and smirks at Libitina.

"Beautiful baby," Libitina blurts.

"That's a big word for a little girl," a nurse chimes entering the room and checking Regina's water pitcher.

"She likes the expression on our faces when she repeats harder words. Wait until we teach her Spanish," Hector says raising his eyebrows.

The nurse folds at the waist and whispers to Libitina. "Can you say gorgeous?"

"Gorgeous," Libitina mimics.

"Huh. Well, I suppose I need to stop procrastinating," she proclaims over her shoulder.

"Procrastinating," Libitina smiles.

The nurse pauses at the door and then continues through it.

She tested Libitina, and she passed without a problem.

The nurse returns a few minutes later clutching a board book.

"This is from the neonatal ICU waiting area. I disinfected it. It's full of difficult words," the nurse smiles handing it to Libitina.

Libitina takes the book, sits on a pillow, and begins reading.

"Can she read?" the nurse asks.

"I guess we shall see," Regina exhales.

"Tired?" Will asks Regina.

She nods her head and shuts her eyes. Hector directs Lola to the door with his head. "We should go."

Will walks them out of the room.

"Farewell, Regina," Libitina utters as she speeds out the door dropping the book.

Will exchanges glances with Lola as Hector chases the girls down the corridor.

Lola swipes the colorful board from the tile, and thumbs through the alphabet, stopping on the letter 'F.'

"F is for farewell. A fancy way to say goodbye."

"Do you think Fabby read that to her and she mimicked it?"

"I don't know, but I think I need to buy her more books to find out," Lola smiles.

They meet the girls and Hector in the hallway and stop at the viewing window. A couple gazes into an incubator at their tiny baby boy. A blue index card, decorated with construction vehicle stickers, highlights the preemie's name. Adam. Libitina yanks on Hector's pants. "Up Papa."

He hoists her up, and she presses her forehead against the glass. The couple standing with their premature infant drops their jaws at Libitina. They rush from the nursery to speak with Lola and Hector.

"Is this your daughter?" the husband inquires.

"Yes, why?" Hector asks.

"Our son almost died, but she came in and we think…," the husband's voice trails off. "Well, my wife and I believe, she may have saved him."

Lola rolls her charm between her fingers but doesn't respond. Will slides his hands in his pockets and stares at the floor. Hector prays to himself as he hugs Libitina tighter.

She's special. But is she capable of saving an innocent child from certain death?

Interfering with the natural order of things sends a powerful message. If she can stop us as a child, what will her capabilities be as an adult? What if someone hurts her? Will she hurt them back? Libitina can save lives, but can she take them as well?

No.

It's not possible. Angels, demons, and reapers can't cause death. Whether by natural causes, accident, the hand of another, or disease, they don't have a hand in it. It must occur on its own. Our job comes after, always has.

I've never been afraid of anything, or anyone, but God. Now I fear He may have created something even more fearful than Him.

The question is, why?

Chapter Twenty-Six
Pre-K

After the nurse gave the book to Libitina at the hospital, Hector and Lola took Libitina for an evaluation. As it turns out, she is capable of starting kindergarten despite her age. Since many preschool programs permit children to attend at the age of three, and Libitina is only a few months shy, the district made an exception, making her the youngest student in her class. If it were up to them, they would send her to kindergarten, but the law doesn't allow it.

The camera snaps as Lola takes a picture of Libitina and Fabiola's first day of school. Libitina wears a plush purple unicorn backpack, and Fabiola carries an iridescent one.

"Mama we are going to miss our bus," Fabiola groans rolling her eyes.

"One more," Lola beams taking another photo.

The bus screeches to a halt at the end of the driveway and the girls take off running. The door cranks to the side, and they disappear inside. As the yellow transport rolls away, Lola wipes her face of tears.

They didn't even say goodbye. The screen door creaks open, and Lola saunters to the kitchen. The quiet house depresses her, zapping her energy. She gazes into the living room and debates watching television.

A shadow moves across the dark screen, and Lola leaps from her chair. "Hello?"

"Lola?" Regina says peering around the corner.

"Regina, you scared me," Lola gasps clutching her chest.

"Sorry. Hope and I thought you could use some company."

"I certainly would," Lola insists taking the baby from her. "Boy, she's growing fast."

"She sure is. My parental leave is almost up. That's why I'm here," Regina grins. "I have a question for you. It's okay if the answer is no. I understand."

"I'd love to babysit Hope when you go back to work," Lola says as her face lights up.

"Oh, thank God. I didn't plan on interviewing anyone else."

"I wouldn't allow it," Lola says raising her voice. "She's my goddaughter, and I'd be honored."

How sweet.

I levitate to the school, and into Libitina's class. She's sitting at her desk with her hands folded on its oak surface. A little boy behind her flicks her ear, making her cry out.

"Ouch."

She turns to glare at him and notices me hovering in the corner by their cubbies.

"Go away," she says frowning.

"Who are you talking to?" the bully asks, looking behind him.

Libitina doesn't respond. Instead, she removes a piece of construction paper and some crayons from her desk and starts drawing. Squares and shapes soon turn into an image of a shadow with eyes filling the space in the back of the classroom.

The teacher stops at Libitina's desk and slides the page from under her wrist. "Who's this?"

"Dark One," Libitina murmurs.

The entire class erupts in laughter.

Libitina's face reddens, and Ms. Thomas raises her hand. "Quiet."

She reaches behind Libitina and takes the bully's coloring page. She goes on to collect everyone's and tapes them up on the wall. "Come here. I want you to take a minute and examine each other's artwork."

The children move from their seats and glance at every picture posted.

"Everyone, line up," the teacher orders pointing to the yellow tape on the floor.

The children fall in like soldiers given a direct order by their superiors.

Ms. Thomas walks the line, turns on her heels, and stops. "Do you know what I see when I look at this wall? I see one picture that's worthy of display in the hallway for all eyes to see. It doesn't belong to you, or you, or even you," she insists pointing at the bully and two others. "It belongs to Libitina. Remember that next time you laugh at someone for their talent."

The teacher removes Libitina's art from the wall of shame, and steps into the hall with a roll of Scotch tape. She tapes it to the left of her class door and smiles. "Perfect. Now, back to your seats."

"Thank you, Ms. Thomas," Libitina says hugging her.

"You're welcome. Now go take your seat."

Ms. Thomas may be old, but with age comes wisdom, and intolerance. She straightens her pleated skirt, adjusts her white-pressed blouse, and sits in her rolling chair. The bully tugs Libitina's hair.

"Stop," she whines.

Ms. Thomas smacks her ruler onto her desktop. "Thomas James you may have gotten away with bullying in Mrs. Barney's class, but I will not tolerate it in mine. Now get in the corner."

The boy puts his head down and mopes his way to the corner chair I am hovering beside. Libitina turns and smiles at me. She doesn't need to say anything for me to know what she's thinking. I flicker the light above Thomas, and he stares at it, then glares at Libitina. She smirks and points to the corner as the sun comes through the window, revealing my silhouette to him. He fumbles from his seat and lands hard on the unforgiving tile.

The children turn and gasp. Thomas's pants are wet between his legs. I thought Libitina might consider this funny, but I was wrong.

She stands from her seat, removes her sweater from its hook, and hides his shame. "I'm sorry," she says holding her hand out to him.

Thomas swats her hand away and runs from the room.

Ms. Thomas leans to Libitina. "That was a nice gesture, but you don't have to apologize for something that wasn't your fault."

Libitina puts her head down and returns to her desk. The other children giggle.

Ms. Thomas issues a stern warning. "Enough. I will not allow this in my classroom. If it continues, no one will attend recess."

The room quiets as Ms. Thomas draws on the board with chalk. A bell chimes overhead, making the class jump. It's lunchtime. She sends the children into the hall in alphabetical order. Libitina leads the group down to the cafeteria.

Fabiola waves at Libitina from a far table, and she runs to greet her. "Hey, Fabby."

"I know she's not sitting with us," a haughty blonde, dressed in a red plaid skirt, with a white shirt and blue sweater insists. "She's a baby."

"She's my sister, and she can sit wherever she wants. If you don't like it, you can go somewhere else," Fabiola says pressing her palms on the table and leaning in the girl's face.

"You should sit somewhere else," the snob challenges.

Fabiola snatches the girl by her hair and yanks her backward onto the floor. The blonde scrambles to her feet and storms toward Fabiola. Libitina steps in between. "No fighting."

"How cute. Your baby sister is protecting you." The girl snarls, seizes Libitina by the arm, and slings her out of the way.

Libitina slams hard into the next row of tables and screams. A crack of thunder rattles the entire building, and the lights go out. In the dark, the blonde straddles Fabiola, and punches her in the face.

Libitina dives on the girl, takes her by the shoulders, and shrieks a blood-curdling screech in her face. Libitina's face distorts, changing into a creature I have never seen in life or in death, and then switches back again. The blonde's face pales, and she scrambles away from the sisters. The generator kicks on and illuminates the room.

Fabiola holds her bleeding nose, while Libitina sits beside her eating a chicken patty with no mayonnaise. The entire cafeteria stares at the blonde girl when she finally stops screaming.

She bolts from the room, as the principal helps Fabiola to her feet. "Let's take you to the nurse and have your nose checked. I will deal with Tonya later."

Fabiola glances at Libitina. "Are you okay, Libby?"

"I'm fine, sissy."

Libitina sucks down her chocolate milk and unwraps her oatmeal cookie as Fabiola walks away, and Thomas James inserts his legs under the bench beside her. "I'm sorry, Libitina," he mutters.

"I forgive you," she shrugs handing him part of her dessert.

Thomas splits the half she gave him and shares it with the girl across from him. "Here Daisy."

"Thanks," Daisy smiles taking a bite as he gets up and switches to a different table. "Thomas is my brother, and he can be a jerk sometimes."

"He has time," Libitina says without looking up.

"Time for what?" Daisy asks wiping her mouth with a crumpled napkin.

Libitina stands up and leaves without another word. She heads to the playground and sits on an empty swing. Rain soaks her clothing and hair. Ms. Thomas splashes through a puddle, springs open an umbrella, and hovers it over Libitina's dripping locks. "Libitina, come inside sweetheart. You're going to get sick."

Libitina slides her buttocks off the swing and takes Ms. Thomas's hand. She glances at me and turns to Ms. Thomas. "Can you see it?"

"See what?"

"The Dark One," Libitina points to the brick wall beside the entrance to the cafeteria. "It's right there."

"Honey, I don't see anything."

Libitina drops her hand and pulls away from Ms. Thomas. "Why can't you see what I see?"

"I don't know, Libitina. Perhaps your eyes are playing tricks on you."

Libitina bows her head and allows Ms. Thomas to guide her back to class. She stays quiet for the rest of the day and refuses to join the afternoon reading circle. Instead, she stays at her desk drawing. When the bell rings, Libitina removes her unicorn backpack from her cubby and leaves without saying goodbye.

Ms. Thomas bites her fingernails as she reviews the schedule for the following day. She closes her scheduler and stuffs it in her rope-handled canvas tote. As she turns to leave, a paper sitting on Libitina's desktop catches her attention. The flipped-over page doesn't reveal its image. She takes a deep breath and turns it right side up.

A white-haired stick-figured woman lies beside her desk with a shadowy creature towering over her and an angel on the ceiling. A stick figure little girl stands crying by a door. Ms. Thomas exhales her held breath, grabs her bag, and speed walks out of her classroom. She bursts through the main exit and searches for Libitina. The lined-up buses and mass amounts of children filtering onto them make finding her difficult. Her eyes pan left to right and stop when she spots Libitina standing with her sister preparing to board her bus.

She jogs over to her and wiggles the paper before her eyes. "Libitina, who is this?"

Fabiola removes the paper from the teacher's hand and stares at it. "Looks like you to me. You should probably call a doctor," she smirks passing the drawing back to her. "Come on Libby, let's go home."

Ms. Thomas blinks several times then shakes it off as the bus pulls away from the curb.

Banging comes from the bus window and Ms. Thomas glances up. Libitina waves goodbye with a smile through the glass, but the teacher doesn't wave back. She wads the drawing in her palm into a ball and drops it into the trashcan by the sidewalk.

Chapter Twenty-Seven
Tough Day

Fabiola and Libitina exit the bus and walk slowly towards their house. The first day of school didn't go how either of them hoped.

"Libby, what did you show Tonya to make her run from the cafeteria?"

"Herself."

Fabiola sighs and stops walking. "Libs you didn't have to help me today."

"You're my sister, Fabby. I will always protect you."

"When did you get so grown up?"

"When I was sleeping."

The girls giggle as they scale the porch steps. Lola slams the front door open, startling them both. "Let me see your face, Fabby."

"Mama, it's not that bad."

"Not that bad? She gave you a bloody nose."

"Time heals everything, Mama," Libitina murmurs.

Lola gazes down at Libitina. "Well in the meantime, I'm going to continue to be upset until the bruising vanishes. Suspending that girl for three days isn't enough punishment."

"Libby punished her enough," Fabiola chuckles as she passes through the doorway.

Libitina lowers her head and walks around Lola. She puts her arm across the door frame, preventing Libitina from entering. "What did you do?"

"I grabbed that mean girl and screamed. My face felt funny, like it was moving, and the lights went out and she ran away," Libitina confesses hanging her head. "I showed her herself only I think her face was inside out."

Lola rubs the fabric of her dress between her fingers. A tear splatters on the porch surface as Libitina cries softly.

Lola tucks her palm under Libitina's chin and lifts her head. "Thank you for telling me. Tomorrow, I want you to apologize to Tonya."

"But Mama."

"Libby, I know you were protecting your sister, but scaring the life out of her, and showing her the wrong side of herself, may affect her in the future. Everything that happens in life, whether to us or to others molds them into who they become as an adult. It's like throwing a tiny pebble into a pond. Sure, it doesn't raise the water by much, but what it does do is create a ripple. Understand?"

"No."

"It's okay. Someday you will. Now go inside and eat your snack. I'll start dinner soon."

Hector steers into the driveway, and races towards the house. He hops out of the car and hustles up the steps.

"Hector, what's wrong?"

"They're here."

"Who?"

"Those lunatics who killed the rat in front of the girls at our old house. I saw them at the general store. Lola, we need to take the girls and go before they find us."

"No," Libitina says opening the screen door. "Let them come."

"Libby this isn't up for discussion. These people kill animals and worship the devil."

Fabiola comes outside and stands with Libitina. "We aren't moving again," she says crossing her arms.

"Fabby, what happened to your face?"

"A girl at school hit her and Libitina stepped in," Lola says standing beside the girls.

"What's this? Three on one. Lola let's talk about this in private," Hector insists.

"Hector, we can't keep running."

Hector swipes his face with his palm. "Lola, these people are dangerous."

"I'll protect us, Papa," Libitina says cocking her head.

He blows a staggering breath through his lips and places his hand on her head.

"That's my job, Libby."

"No, Papa. It's our job," Fabiola insists taking his and Libitina's hand.

Lola takes Hector's hand and Libitina's creating a circle. They rest their heads together in the center. "Together then," Hector announces.

I thought the night would be more entertaining, but so far none of the cult members have shown up. Libitina stares at me in the corner as she lays on her side in bed. Sometimes she talks to me, but tonight she's quiet. Perhaps not being normal weighs heavy on her mind. I thought about starting a conversation, but what's the point? When she's like this, solemn, sad, and depressed, she won't engage. Besides, the last time Lola caught her talking to an empty wall, she advised Libitina that if she needed to talk to anyone, it should be her, not her invisible friend.

We aren't friends.

I'm here for the sole purpose of collecting information for myself and the others. They too, have questions. It's not like we have meetings or anything, but occasionally when other reapers and I cross they ask what I've learned thus far. My answer has been the same, every damn time.

Nothing.

I mean I have some suspicions, but nothing concrete or based on fact. If only God would just tell us all what is happening like a yearly board meeting that would be great, but as of right now, we are all in the dark. Angels, demons, reapers, and even Libitina aren't aware of His plan. Perhaps as she grows in age, she can share what God's plan is to us when he finally lets her in on His big secret. Until then, we sit and wait.

Headlights shine into the family home. Hector pops his head up from the back side of the couch and peeks through the blinds. Multiple cars park by the road and unload a massive number of individuals. Hector rolls off the couch, not wanting the trespassers to see his silhouette. He shakes Lola who's sleeping in the recliner awake. "They're here," he whispers.

Lola springs from the recliner, and they move quickly to the girls' room. They wake Fabiola first and then enter Libitina's room together.

"Libby, the people have arrived."

Libitina sits up in bed and grimaces. "Stay here."

"No, Libby. We agreed we would do this together as a family," Hector announces.

"Okay," Libitina sighs.

Asher and Karma bleat at the people invading their space. The family walks through the back door with their heads held high and hustle to the barn. Inside, the leader of the group holds a knife to Karma's neck.

'The sacrifice of this mystical creature will show our dedication to the Dark Lord's spawn.'

Libitina screams at him. "Don't you touch my unicorn!"

"Sweet child, don't you know this is what our master wants?" the dark-bearded man insists.

"Come here if you are so loyal," Libitina requests.

"You are but a child. I take my orders from the master below."

"And what would your boss say if he finds out you defy her orders?" Fabiola presses. "You're scared of Libitina aren't you?"

"I'm scared of no one. I am Damen, leader of this flock."

"Come closer," Libitina orders.

The man refuses to budge from his position. He holds the knife against Karma's throat. Libitina releases her father's hand and moves within a foot of him. "Take my hand, and I will show you your truth," she proclaims.

The man reaches for her but hesitates. Libitina snatches his arm and yanks him close to her. She wraps her arms around his waist, refusing to let go. He thrashes about as she floods his mind with images of his grisly death.

Fire melts his flesh, and he dives into salty water to avoid the flames. A creature of the sea clamps down on his limbs and drags his mortally wounded frame into the dark depths of the raging water.

Libitina drops away from his trembling body and rejoins her family. "Leave us alone," she demands.

The man says nothing to his people. He picks up the knife he dropped from the hay-covered ground, carries it back to his SUV, and drives away.

His people bend their knees and rest their foreheads on the Earth before them. Libitina walks the row they create with their bodies and touches each one of their crowns. "Take this message to everyone you meet. You still have time to change. If you do not, the end will be swift and unforgiving."

Lola, Hector, and Fabiola exchange wide-eyed glances. Where are these words of wisdom coming from? Libitina speaks beyond her years and issues a stern warning that seems to come straight from God himself.

Does she speak for Him? Or is she issuing a cautionary tale based on the power she possesses?

It doesn't matter. What matters is her message works. The members nod their heads, turn, and leave as Libitina returns to the house, leaving her family in the barn. She climbs into her twin-sized bed, pulls her plush rose covers up to her neck, and closes her eyes.

My hand sizzles as I place it on her head. I hoped that by doing so, she would show me what her purpose was, but all it did was cause me more pain without supplying the answers I seek.

The bedroom door creaks open, and Lola peers through the opening. "She's asleep," she says quietly to Hector.

"Then let her. If she wants to talk about it tomorrow, we will listen."

"She has school tomorrow," Lola murmurs.

"We can wait until she gets home. I'm not asking her over breakfast," Hector insists.

The door closes without any sound, and Hector and Lola retreat into the living room.

Fabiola slips inside Libitina's room and crawls in bed beside her. She places her arm around her waist and pulls her close. "Are you okay?"

"I wish I was normal, like you," Libitina whispers.

"I'm glad you're not." Fabiola squeezes her tighter. "Don't be afraid to be yourself. You saved Karma's life tonight, and that wouldn't have happened if you didn't use your voice. I love you, Libby, but stop hiding who you are to make us more comfortable. We are your family, and nothing you could do or say will ever change that, understand?"

"I do, and I love you too, Fabby." Libitina flips herself over to face Fabiola. "Starting tomorrow, I'll just be myself."

"Good," Fabiola says as she kisses Libitina on the forehead. "Now get some sleep."

Chapter Twenty-Eight
LIBITINA SPEAKS

No one talks during breakfast. You'd think now that I found my voice, and as of last night began using it, there would be more to say.

Fabby never has been big on questioning what I can do. Sure, she presents me with an inquiry from time to time, but when I am vague, she doesn't press the issue. I'm not evasive on purpose. It's just, how can I explain to my family that despite being in Pre-K, I feel like an adult trapped inside a small child? I try to play the role of a youngster, but last night I refused to allow that lunatic to kill my beloved pet.

Perhaps it wasn't me who did the talking. It may have been my shadowy friend that hangs around so much speaking through me.

Who am I kidding? Last night I spilled a secret I've been withholding for almost a year. From the minute my first word passed through my lips, I knew I could spew an all-out speech if I wanted to, but God came to me in my dreams that night. He spoke of patience, time, and trust, but he also told me that He chose me for an important task. One that, in time, He will reveal to me.

I thought I already figured out what it was.

Last night, I protected my family from those who trespassed against us, and before when a storm nearly killed us, I cast a shield to ensure our safety. When I spoke to God about this, He rested His illuminated palm on my scalp and said, 'You are not the protector, that is my job.'

I glance at the ticking wall clock, wipe my lips, and go to my room. My purple backpack rests on my unmade bed. I feed my arms into it and sling it onto my back. The Dark One blocks my doorway. Now that it's aware I'm capable of communicating with more than a few words, I expect it will drill me with more questions that I can't answer.

"Not now," I sigh.

"What is your purpose?"

"I said, not now."

It floats away from me, allowing me to leave.

"Who are you talking to, Libby," Fabiola asks meeting me in the hallway.

"The Dark One."

She stops walking and pulls me back by my backpack. "Libby don't talk to it. You don't know what it is."

"But I do."

"Care to share?"

"Girls, you're going to miss the bus," Papa yells.

Fabiola let the question go for now. We run outside, as the bus drives away from our house.

"Well, I guess I'm dropping you girls off on my way to the office," Papa says, resting his hands on our upper backs as he stands between us.

"Sorry, Papa," my sister and I say in unison.

"It's fine. Get in the car, I'll be right there."

Fabby and I sit silently beside each other when Papa climbs in. He gazes through the back window as he backs down the driveway. Every few minutes of the quiet drive, he peers in the rearview mirror.

I sense his words hanging in the air like dust floating through a sunny window. Fabby rests her hand on top of mine and squeezes it as we park at the curb in front of the school. "Talk later?"

I nod and kiss Papa on his cheek before climbing out. Fabiola veers to the right and I go left. The school only goes up to seven grades then students attend high school once they graduate from fifth. Parents expressed their concerns when the district placed sixth graders in with mature high schoolers, but the board was all about balance. Now there are seven grades divided equally between two buildings. The people in charge decided to divide each building in half, creating sides to pacify the angry parents.

A lot of sense that made. Now three grades are on the left and four grades are on the right, defeating the purpose. Though Fabby and I are in the same building, I miss her. The only time our paths cross is lunchtime.

I stuff my bag inside my cubby and drag my feet back to my desk. A note with four words written in red ink waits for me.

See me after class.

I flub my lips and flip it over so no one else reads it. Ms. Thomas draws the word of the day on the chalkboard.

Reverie.

"Can anyone tell me what this word means?"

I remain quiet despite knowing the answer. Thomas James blurts from behind me. "Sports person."

"That's a referee, but good guess Thomas," Ms. Thomas smiles.

I murmur the definition under my breath as Ms. Thomas passes my desk. "What did you say, Libitina?"

"Daydream," I whisper.

"That's correct. Good work, Libitina. This is something everyone in this room does. Daydream. Nice work," Ms. Thomas nods at me before returning to the front of her classroom.

A shadow pushes through the door. It's here to take Ms. Thomas. I leap from my seat and cry out. "No!"

Ms. Thomas turns away from writing and gawks at me. "Libitina, what's wrong?"

Through the ceiling, an illuminated circle serves as a portal for the angel coming to retrieve my teacher's soul.

"Help!" I yell, trying to gain the attention of a passing teacher through the outside window with my waving arms.

Everyone laughs. Everyone, but me. Ms. Thomas takes one step towards me and falls forward onto her face. She stays motionless as the classroom becomes void of noise. The Dark One pulls out her soul. I run up front and seize its limb. It squeals and releases Ms. Thomas's apparition, but the angel snatches her fast and disappears. I charge at the Dark One, but it vanishes through the closed door. When I throw it open, a teacher from across the hall stands in my path.

"What's going on in here?"

"Ms. Thomas is dead," I announce.

"What?" He moves me aside and kneels beside Ms. Thomas.

I return to my seat, rest my head on my forearm, and weep. Why didn't I try harder to stop it? Perhaps I sensed she didn't have the will inside her to fight anymore. Baby Adam, although small, fought with every ounce of his tiny being. She didn't. Has life treated her so poorly that she didn't care if it ended?

"Hey," a man's voice says while shaking me. "Come on."

Everyone has left the room, except for me. The teacher offers me his hand. I accept it, and he escorts me to the back of the room, and out an emergency exit.

An ambulance and police car turn into the lot with their lights on, but no sirens. They climb from their vehicle with no sense of urgency. I sit under the only tree that provides shade with my crying classmates, waiting for our parents to pick us up.

"Libby!" Fabiola shouts from across the lawn as she jogs towards me.

She wraps me in her arms and combs my hair with her fingers. "Are you okay?"

"I saw them take her."

"Who?"

"The Dark One took her spirit, and an angel carried her to heaven," I whimper.

"I'm sorry, Libs," Fabby says tightening her hold on me.

Children leap into the arms of their parents as they arrive. Some are inconsolable while others stay soundless as their mothers and fathers press them for information. My tears are dry by the time Mama comes for us. She clutches her purse strap as she barrels across the pavement and pulls my sister and me into her warm embrace. Behind her, Papa sprints towards us. Mama must have called him.

We hold each other as a family, and no one wants to let go. Papa lifts me and carries me to his car, and Fabby rides with Mama.

He signals left and falls in line behind a row of people waiting at a fast-food restaurant. It's my favorite place, but not today. Papa passes me the box containing waffles fries and chicken tenders with barbeque sauce. I remove a fry, but the pit in my stomach prevents me from putting it in my mouth, so I close it back inside its container.

When we arrive home, Fabiola waits on the porch with food from the same place. She too, didn't eat. Asher and Karma gallop to me. I feed them my waffle fries and pet their heads. Fabby joins me, and we feed them our entire meal together.

"Do you want to talk about it?" Fabby asks me.

"Not really," I reply without looking at her.

"Mama and Papa want to know what happened. I can talk to them for you if that would be easier," she offers.

"Okay."

Fabby kisses my head and strolls away from me. Having her tell them calms my shaking hands, but only a little.

"Why are you here?" I say to the Dark One as it appears beside me.

"Why are you?"

"God wants me to do something, but not until I'm older."

"What?"

"I don't know," I grimace and walk away from it.

Answering a question with a question annoys me. I sense it following and turn to face it. "Don't follow me."

It stops floating and dissipates into the air. I enter the barn and sit on a bale of fresh hay. Karma nudges me with his tennis ball.

Asher stands in the doorway, waiting for Karma.

"Go on. Play with Asher."

The goat nudges me one last time before leaving.

Knuckles thump the frame around the barn door.

"I don't want to talk, Papa."

"You don't need to. Just listen. I don't know why God gave you this gift, but He always has a plan. If you need to talk to us about how you're feeling please don't be afraid. You are not alone, Libby, and you never will be."

I turn to him, and he catches a tear running down my face with his finger. "Thank you, Papa."

He draws me against him, keeping his hand on my shoulder as Asher enters the room and drops a messy pile of feces in front of us.

Papa chuckles. "Is that a chicken nugget?"

"He may be a goat, but he eats like a pig," I laugh covering my nose to shelter it from the stench. "Let's go."

Chapter Twenty-Nine
Mandatory Counseling

I don't need to be here, but I couldn't return to class until after I attended at least one session. After speaking with the school counselor, he referred my parents to a child psychologist. Telling him I drew my teacher dying the day before, and I tried to stop it didn't help.

I couldn't lie. That's not who I am.

I sit with my hands folded neatly in my lap, in a stained blue fabric-covered chair, and wait for the doctor to come and retrieve me. I glance over Papa's head at the time. It's five minutes past my scheduled appointment time. The substitute sent work home for me with Fabby, and I am eager to complete it.

A woman, with jet-black hair trimmed above her shoulders, opens the door. "Libitina Alvarez?"

"You're late," I say rolling my eyes and entering her office.

"Libby, don't be rude," Papa says raising his voice.

Papa shakes his head at the psychologist, and she closes the door. I sit on a brown leather couch against the wall of her peach-painted office. I run my finger on the walnut trim behind the window casing.

"Libitina, my name is Dr. Inez. Please take a seat in front of my desk."

"Sure."

My feet dangle above the hardwood floors, so I swing them back and forth while flicking my fingernails.

"Libitina, you don't have to be nervous."

"I don't want to be here."

"And you don't have to be, but if you don't speak with me the school board won't allow you back in school."

"I don't need to go back."

"Libitina, all kids need school."

"I'm not like other kids."

"Yes. I read your records. Even if you're too smart to be around children your own age, it's still necessary for your social growth to interact with people of all ages."

I make raspberry noises with my lips and drum the arms of the chair. A book on one of her shelves catches my attention.

I slide it from the shelf and open it. "Do you believe demons cause mental health issues?"

"Well, Libitina, that book's just one person's opinion."

"That's not what I asked you."

"Do you think you have a demon?"

"Avoiding the question. Super. Can I go now?"

"We haven't talked about what happened in the classroom."

"If you know, will you let me out of here?"

"I will march you right through that door myself."

I push the book back into its rightful alphabetical location and lean against the front of her desk. She pulls her hands away from mine when I reach for them. I snatch them hard and slam them on the wooden top.

Images flood through her like drugs through an IV chilling her flesh. Everything I remember from my birth until now slams through her brain in a matter of seconds. Her body shakes violently, and the whites of her eyes reveal themselves to me, so I release her.

Sweat soaks Dr. Inez's blue button-up shirt. She yanks a tissue from its box and blots her brow with it.

"Now you know everything," I hiss.

"Libitina, you've known this whole time you were adopted?"

"That's what you're going to ask me after what I showed you?"

"Who are you?"

"Someday, God will tell me, but I can't answer that question right now."

I push myself off her desk and meet Papa in the waiting room.

"Did you tell her everything?"

"No. I showed her."

"Oh, Libby. You probably shouldn't have done that."

"Sorry, Papa."

"It's okay. We will deal with whatever comes of it."

Dr. Inez stares at us through her office window as we back out of our parking space. I wave at her, but she doesn't return the farewell.

Mama waits for us on the porch when we pull up. I try and pass her, but she stops me. "Everything, okay?"

"Ask Papa. I need to do my homework."

The phone rings in the kitchen as I enter my room. I hold the work Fabby brought home to me. Goody, more coloring pages.

For once when I gaze into the corner it's empty. The Dark One must be too busy to bother me with its annoying questions. I breeze through my schoolwork and sit on the edge of my bed.

Something's coming. My hands shake and bile elevates from my vacant stomach to the top of my esophagus where it waits like an airplane on a runway. Footsteps stop outside my room. They're hesitating, I sense it. The doorknob shifts and Papa enters. He sits next to me without a word, gathering his thoughts.

"Libby…"

"They're not letting me back, are they?"

"No," he sighs.

Here it comes.

I take off from the room and crash through the bathroom door. Vomit launches from my throat, and nose, burning them like acid.

A hand presses my back as I wipe my lips.

"I'm sorry, Libby," Mama whispers.

"I wanted her to understand. I needed her to see."

"Everything will be okay. Dr. Inez and I spoke at length about homeschooling. She sent me the information for testing. That way we can tailor your studies to your specific needs."

"What kind of tests?"

"Intelligence, and Achievement."

"When?"

"Whenever you're ready," Hector chimes in as he swings the door open wider. "Libby, there is no rush."

Papa passes a warm washcloth to me. "Wipe your face, brush your teeth, and come to the table when you're done. Mama made dinner."

"I'll be right out."

After they leave, I sit on the closed toilet lid. Kicking a child out of school at my age within the first week must be some kind of record. I never got to apologize to Tonya. Perhaps Fabby can pass her a note for me.

It's in here. I sense it close by. The shower rings clank together as I whip the curtain aside. "If I turn the water on, will you melt?" I ask.

"No."

"Go away."

"I have questions," Dark One says floating before me.

"And I don't have the answers," I scold as I exit the bathroom and storm to my bedroom.

It's bad enough the school expelled me, now I must deal with the Dark One hovering all day when he's not busy taking souls. I kick off my sneakers, change into pajamas, and slide my feet into my fuzzy pink unicorn slippers. One of these days, I need Mama to take me to the mall so I can buy clothes for my true self instead of a toddler.

Steam floats above the goulash sitting on the cartoon placemat in front of my booster seat. I roll my eyes, unbuckle the seat, and remove it from the chair. Mama stands from the table, grabs a fabric placement, and replaces the cartoon one.

They all smile when I sit. My eyes barely breach the surface of the table. I'm not afraid to admit when I'm wrong. "I might need the seat for a little longer."

Fabby peers into the living room. "I have an idea."

She tosses a towel over the coffee table, throws one thick pillow on the floor, and puts out four placemats. "Come on. Let's eat out here," she announces.

Papa carries her plate over, and Mama and I carry our own. The pillow elevates me closer to their level.

"I know we can't do this every night, but at least for today, Libby can feel more like one of us," Fabby proclaims.

I lean over and kiss the side of her head. "I love you."

"Love you too."

We each interlace our fingers, and close our eyes, as Papa thanks God for our meal and our family. I peek through my squinting eyes and grin at Fabby's smiling face. She feels good inside, and it shows in her expression. I turn my eyes to Mama and Papa. Their fingers wrap around each other as Papa prays.

It is a blessing to have such an amazing family, but not telling them that I know my entire history from start to finish bothers me. I'm sure they plan to tell me one day, but I don't want there to be any secrets between us. I have to tell them.

I need to tell them.

Chapter Thirty
Confessions

The sun warms my face, waking me from a deep slumber. A shadow crosses the end of my bed and stops in the corner.

"I'm not talking to you today," I say to the Dark One.

"Why do you hurt us?"

I ignore it and wrap my comforter around myself as I head for the door. The Dark One blocks my path.

"Move," I sigh rolling my eyes.

"Answer me."

"I don't know why. Now get out of the way," I order.

It doesn't budge. I'm not sure what it thought hovering in my personal space would accomplish.

I ask one more time, but this time with a warning. "Move, or else."

"You know something," it says pointing at me with its smokey finger.

It's gone too far. I'm hungry, and tired of it holding me against my will. I clench my lids shut and charge into it.

The screeching from it hurts my ears, like music blaring from the speaker at a concert, but I hold my position.

The Dark One needs to learn.

Heat makes me sweat as I scorch it from the inside out. That's enough for today.

I push through to the other side and turn my bedroom doorknob. "Don't ever try and stop me again," I say over my shoulder without looking back.

Mama and Papa are sitting at the table eating when I enter the kitchen. Fabby left for school already, and Papa is still in his pajamas.

"Papa, why aren't you dressed for work?"

"I'm staying home." He cups his hands around his coffee mug. "Mama and I wanted to talk to you about something."

"I have something to say as well."

"Let me get you some food first," Mama insists getting up from her seat.

Papa avoids eye contact. He's nervous. Perhaps they want to tell me the same thing I plan to tell them. I need to go first.

Mama carries over the booster seat. She straps it down and places a shiny, floral placemat on the wooden surface before resting the steaming plate down. I raise my arms, so she can put me in my chair.

"Thank you, Mama," I say as I stab my scrambled eggs and fork them into my palate.

"Libby, we have to tell you something." Papa pauses to wipe his mouth.

"Papa, I know what you're going to say."

"You do?"

"I know everything."

"And by everything you mean?" Mama inquires.

"I'm adopted. My mother passed away giving birth to me. My father killed two people, and you are not my biological family."

"Libby, how do you know?" Papa asks.

"I have a photographic memory. My mind and language skills are beyond my physical years. From the time I came out of my mother's belly until now, I remember every moment. It's all up here," I say pointing at my temple with my finger.

"I'm so sorry, Libby," Papa sighs.

"There is nothing to be sorry about. You fought to keep me. I love you. You are my family."

Mama and Papa raise their eyebrows, and each takes one of my hands. "We love you too," Mama smiles.

"And if you have any questions, don't be afraid to ask us," Papa insists as he grips my palm.

Bacon crunches in my mouth, as I debate asking them about my father. Mama lets my hand go, bites the tip off a piece of sausage, and leaves the table. I swirl maple syrup into a spiral on my pancake and cut it into small pieces. Mama returns holding a manilla envelope.

"What's that?"

"It's everything we collected about your case; from the time we met you until now. I don't know if you still want to read it."

"I will."

I parted my lips to ask about having one of them take me to visit my father, but the doorbell stops me.

Regina turns the corner, cradling Hope. I slid from my seat to the floor and run to meet them. She's chubbier than before. Her tiny fingers resemble the sausages on Mama's plate. I place my pointer in Hope's palm, and she pushes it into her mouth.

"Ouch." I yank my finger away. "Does she have a tooth?"

"No, but she's teething so she's chewing everything," Regina says shaking her head.

Hope fusses when Regina passes her to Mama. Regina sighs and strokes her daughter's hair. "I miss you already, beautiful."

Today is Regina's first day back at work. I imagine leaving her is difficult. Mama follows Regina to the door. Hope wails at the top of her lungs and flails in Mama's arms.

Regina dabs her eyes with a tissue and then hustles to her car. Fog limits visibility, but I can still make out Regina crying as she backs out of the driveway and disappears.

I sit in the living room recliner and rest a crochet blanket on my thighs. "Bring her here, Mama."

Mama grins and kisses the screaming baby girl before placing her in my arms. I cup my palm over her forehead and enter her mind. Hope fears her mother is leaving her, never to return. I send images through her mind of Regina coming back for her. Her distress dissipates and turns into a mild whimper as Mama pops her formula into her mouth.

"Thank you," I say as I take the bottle holding over.

"Nice work, Libby. You'll make an amazing mother someday."

"No, I won't."

"Of course, you will."

"It's not possible," I say elevating my voice.

"Why?" Mama inquires as she kneels beside me.

"Because I can't have children."

"Libby, that's ridiculous. I mean physically your body isn't old enough to carry a child, but someday it will be."

"No, Mama. God told me I will never have children."

"Perhaps He's mistaken. When you're older in years, we can take you to a specialist," she insists as she pushes off the floor and stands. "Even if it proves to be true, there's always invitro, surrogacy, or adoption."

She lifts sleeping Hope from my arms and takes her to my old crib. Mama doesn't understand. If God says I can't have children, then I can't have children. She's in denial.

"What's got you so deep in thought, Libby?" Papa asks entering the room.

"I don't want to talk about it," I murmur. "Papa, when can you take me to see my father?"

Papa's hashbrown hovers before his open mouth. The question catches him off guard. He returns the fried potatoes to his plate and rests it on the side table. Mama comes in and sinks into the cushion beside him. "What?" she asks, staring at his paling face.

"Libby wants to visit her father."

She stays silent. Her fingers rotate the material of her cotton floral dress. Mama does this when she's nervous or upset; right now, she's both.

"You don't have to worry. You are my parents and nothing he says or does will ever take me away from you. I only want to speak with him one time. It doesn't have to be right away."

"Libby, I think seeing your biological parent will provide you with the closure you seek, but I think it would be best to wait until you've at least started high school. Your father lives in a mental institution now. I believe if his daughter comes in appearing to be a child and has a full-on adult conversation it may not be so great for his mental health," Papa points out.

"I didn't think about it that way," I say to myself. "You're right."

"I know I am," Papa says stuffing the hashbrown into his mouth with a smile.

I chuck the couch pillow at him, and he throws it back. Mama seizes the toss pillow beside her and slaps Papa in the chest with it.

Hope cries from the other room. Our shenanigans woke her up. Papa and I grimace as Mama goes to attend to her.

"Libby, why do you need to see him?"

"So, I can tell him I forgive him, but it won't save him."

"What do you mean?"

I scurry away, avoiding the question. God only supplied bits and pieces of my purpose, but no more than I can handle. He will divulge everything once my numeric age and body catch up with my mind. But for now, I will share as little information as possible. Keeping quiet takes a toll on me, but it's for the best. I swing the door to my room closed, revealing the Dark One floating behind it.

"I'm sorry I hurt you," I say to it.

"Why did He give you this power?"

"I only know what I think."

"What do you think?"

I sit up in bed, place my hands on my knees, and sigh. "I think it's to keep you from stopping me from doing what needs to be done."

"And what is that?"

"I don't know yet."

It moves to my side. "You can put souls back, but can you take them as well?"

"I'm not sure."

"If so, what about us?"

"You're worried He's consolidating angels, reapers, and demons into one like some kind of corporate merger?"

"Wouldn't you be?"

"I may not know what I'm fully capable of, but I don't think God's plan for me is to slap you and your kind with a pink slip and send you on your way."

It vanishes through the door.

Everything will come in time, and I'm not in a rush to grow older.

The reaper pushes through the wall. "We want you to come with us."

"We?"

Above my head, an angel breaches the ceiling and floats beside the reaper. A hole grows in my floor and a black claw digs into my carpet as the demon hoists itself to the surface.

It's an ambush.

"Where do you want me to go?"

The angel's voice resembles the strumming of a harp. It comes out soothing with a comfort and reassurance I can't deny. "To the hospital."

"You want to test me?"

"Are you afraid?" The demon bellows like a poorly played violin.

"No."

"Good," the reaper murmurs reaching for me.

They each place part of themselves on me, and we vanish from my room. Flames surround us as they catch fire, with me in the center. They release my sweating body onto the lawn of the medical center.

A portal opens and the smoking demon crawls inside and disappears. Above the angel, a ray of sunshine envelopes its apparition and carries it to heaven. The Dark One changes from glowing embers back to its normal self as it cools. Bringing me here took courage and strength. They must be desperate to endure the pain my touch causes.

"I'm not sure if I can do what you think, but whether I can or can't, none of you will ever do this again."

"We understand," the reaper says with a forty-year smoker voice.

The hospital doors slide open, and I walk straight into Regina.

"Libby? Honey, what are you doing here, and where are your parents?"

"I'm being tested."

"Do your parents know?"

"No."

"Well, I don't know what's going on, but you are coming with me," she insists as she scoops me off the tile and walks through the reaper.

She stops and peers behind her as the hair on her scalp rises and chills flood her skin. "I don't know what this is about, but Libby is too young for your kind of tests," Regina says in the blank space where the reaper levitates.

I smirk at the reaper as it hangs its head. No answers today, or any other day as long as Regina is around.

Chapter Thirty-One
Fast-Forward

In the back of my mind, I always knew I was smart. I just didn't know how smart until now.

Mama and Papa were curious, so we did an online intelligence test Dr. Inez recommended. My results put me right up there with Cleopatra and Albert Einstein.

We talked it over and decided that I would return to a regular school once I turned sixteen, and officially began high school. That way, Fabby will be a senior, and if I need her to get me through the first year she's there for support. Even though my mind will be ahead of the other students, Mama and Papa think it's important for me to make friends, so that's what I'm going to do.

The Dark One slowly stopped asking me so many questions over the last ten years. Instead, it follows me around wherever I go. I can't even use the bathroom in peace.

I asked it one day, why it stalks me now more than ever. All it said was, 'Someday you will understand.'

A useless answer.

Today, Mama, Fabby, and I went shopping for school clothes. Fabby's excited to start ninth grade and needs a whole new wardrobe. She spins before a floor-to-ceiling mirror and gazes at her backside. "Do these make my butt look big?"

I roll my eyes at her. "Fabby, you don't even have a butt."

"Libby, when you turn sixteen, please don't give me a hard time like your sister," Mama sighs.

"Oh, I won't."

"I'm not giving you a hard time I just want to look nice for my first day," Fabby says, raising her voice to Mama. "Libby, do you like this shirt?"

The peach-colored material crisscrosses the front of her chest with faux buttons running from her cleavage around to her hip. Fabby has filled in over the years, and any weight she gained landed on her chest. The rest of her is petite. My breasts are mounds compared to her mountains.

"It looks good on you, but don't you worry it gives too much away?"

"Too much of what?" Fabby inquires.

"Your boobs for heaven's sake," Mama blurts. "Anyone taller than you can stare down your shirt."

"I'll wear a sweater then," Fabby insists.

I slap my forehead with the palm of my hand. "Fabby, unless the sweater buttons to your throat, it won't make a difference."

"So, don't get the shirt?"

"No," Mama and I say in unison.

"Fine," she scoffs. "I'll try something else."

The white curtain rings clank as Fabby tosses it aside and disappears behind it. I shake my head at Mama and stroll to the front of the store. The sales associate sets up a new display of dress pants. I check out the display as a woman and her son bike past the window.

Screeching tires followed by deafening screams draw a crowd from across the street. Multiple people run by the store, as Mama and I step out onto the sidewalk. A cargo van ran the red light, striking the small child head-on. His mother wails for someone to help her, as shocked onlookers gawk at them. I push the rubber neckers aside and kneel beside the child. Blood oozes from his mouth as he struggles to breathe. His rib pokes through the side of his chest. A ring of light encapsulates his body as an angel descends from heaven to retrieve him.

The Dark One levitates beside the boy but doesn't reach for his soul. It's waiting for me, and so is the angel.

I can't save him, and they know it. They're here to see if I can do their job.

I can.

But up until this point, I kept that a secret. Now I have no choice. If I don't do it, he'll be stuck haunting his family for the rest of his life, and that's not fair to him. I place my hand on his chest and gaze into his mother's eyes. "I'm sorry."

The boy's soul levitates from his body, and I toss it toward heaven like a graduation cap with a quick flick of my wrist. His mother struggles in the arms of a stranger as a paramedic shakes his head, and locks eyes with me. "Thank you for trying."

Mama grips my bicep. "Come on Libby. Give them some space."

The crowd parts as I move out of the street and onto the sidewalk. The store tag hangs from Fabiola's shirt as she opens her arms and pulls me into her. The store clerk stands behind Fabby, her arms crossed, staring at us. Mama removes more than enough money from her wallet, passes it to the woman, and clears her throat. "Keep the change."

The woman snatches it from Mama's grasp and charges back inside.

Is there no understanding left in this world? Here a woman just lost her child to tragedy, and all the store associate cares about is that Fabiola left without paying.

Fighting erupts on the street as the boy's father arrives on the scene. The police struggle to contain the situation, but it gets out of control fast. The father stomps the driver of the vehicle that struck his son with his steel-toed boots. Over and over again, he raises and lowers his foot in a rage. Blinded by his broken heart, he doesn't realize what he's done until it's too late.

Once again, they're waiting for me. The Dark One and the demon from the black portal wait beside the driver for me to do their job.

I am not a circus act, nor will I allow them to treat me as such. I slide my arm around Fabby and turn my back on them.

As I scoot into the back seat, and peer out the back window, the clawed creature seizes the driver and stuffs him into the cavernous deep. The police handcuff the boy's father and push his head down as they load him into the back seat of a cruiser. The mother is on her hands and knees screaming at the sky. She has lost them both, and there is nothing anyone can do about it.

Cell phones drop back into pockets, and the crowd disperses as people go back to business as usual.

The show's over.

A vehicle with a crumpled front end, a mangled bike, emergency responders, and the boy's mother are all that remain. She sits on the curb, clutches her son's helmet, and sobs.

Mama glances at my reflection as she turns the corner. "Do you want to talk about it?"

"No, Mama."

Fabby puts her hand on mine, and we ride in silence all the way home. I'm not sure I would have reacted the same as the father did. I imagine as a society it would depend on the situation as well. Some people with children may defend his actions and would have done exactly what he did. I'm not sure I would have, but then again, I've never been in a situation to test that theory, and I hope I never will.

Papa jogs to the car when we come to a stop. Mama called him from the car on our way home. He opens the door, and peers inside. I ignore him, keeping my eyes forward. I didn't do anything wrong but feel guilty, nonetheless. I did take that boy's soul and send it to heaven when it wasn't my place to do so. I could have left it to the reaper and the angel, but I knew they wouldn't stop testing me until they had their answer.

Papa's knees crack as he squats beside me. "Libby?"

I turn to him. He wipes the tear from my cheek, pulls me out of my seat, and onto his legs. Gravity tips us backward onto the grass, but he doesn't let me go. Mama and Fabby join us on the ground and wrap their arms around Papa and me. This is where we stay for a long, long time; crying, praying, and comforting each other. No one wanting to let go, and all of us with the same thing on our minds.

What if that happened to us?

Life can go awry at any moment and thoughts of our own mortality humble us.

Karma breaks the circle with a jab of his tennis ball. We sit back from each other and smile as Asher bumps him with his head. They play in the middle, like siblings vying for their parents' attention.

I break away to be alone in my room, but it's not empty when I arrive. They're here. All of them.

They bombard me with multiple questions at once. As they try and speak over each other, I cover my ears. It's too loud.

It's too much.

"Shut up!" I scream, shattering a lamp against the wall they bicker in front of.

They fall quiet, but only for a few seconds, and begin again.

I'm tired, upset, and not in the mood for their bickering. "Go away," I scream as I run through them. They shriek, and light on fire. My eyes heat up as they burst into flames and turn to ash. A black outline stains my wall where they used to stand. I run my finger over the lines and swirl the soot between my fingers. Something about this outburst felt different.

Multiple feet stomp down the hallway. Papa, Mama, and Fabby burst into my room each carrying a weapon. Mama spins her favorite cast iron skillet in her palm, as Papa trains his bat on an unseen foe. Fabby stands between me and the wall, her fists high, ready to strike. I hang my head, and sigh. "They're gone."

Mama tosses the pan on my bed and hugs me. "If you want us to hire an exorcist, just say the word."

"Thanks, Mama. All I wanted was to be by myself, but now that you're all here, I'd like for you to stay."

Fabby leaves, returns dragging her sleeping bag behind her, and shakes it straight parallel to my bed. Mama whispers in Papa's ear and they both leave. Me and Fabby furrow our eyebrows and exchange glances as the sound of scraping fabric on wood directs our attention to the doorway.

Mama bends her and Papa's mattress around the corner, and Papa pushes it inside. Air shifts a lock of my hair as the mattress flops onto the floor by the wall. They leave again and return carrying the television from their room as well. Fabby plugs it in and passes me the remote. "Your room, your choice."

"How about we decide on something together?" I offer as I begin scrolling through the channels.

"Sounds good to me," Papa says, leaning against the wall and sliding to the floor. "We will stay with you as long as you need us to."

Fabby places her hand on his and Mama rests hers on Fabby's creating a stack. I slap mine on the pile, and say, "I wouldn't have it any other way."

Chapter Thirty-Two
Unexpected Visitor

Today was Fabby's first day of high school. Even though we've been apart before, this is different. Teenagers can be cruel, and I hate that I'm not present to watch over her the way she does me.

Hope doesn't start school until tomorrow, and since Mama is sick today, I volunteered to keep an eye on her so she can rest. Hope can pretty much do everything herself, except cook. After she burned a perfect circle on the countertop when she set a hot saucepan on it, we decided she needed a bit more guidance.

"Good grief, Hope. You smell like the goat's barn," I say to her as we stand outside waiting for Fabby.

"It's the eggs. They give me gas."

"Well, maybe you should avoid them, like forever," I grimace waving the rancid air in front of my face.

A hint of yellow peeks through the thick trees. The bus slows to a stop by our mailbox, and Fabby steps off. Her cheeks inflate as she blows out a massive breath and bubbles her lips.

Hope jogs beside me as I rush to her. "How was your day?"

Fabby's eyes light up as she smiles. "It was amazing. I met so many new people," she says wrinkling her nose. "Eww. Libby was that you?"

"No. It's Miss Nasty Pants over here." I point with my thumb.

Hope rolls her eyes and whistles. "Could have been the goats."

"Liar," Fabby says pushing her away. "How's Mama?"

"She's been sleeping on and off all day. I made her some soup, but she barely ate it. Her fever is down, so that's a plus."

The girls enter the house, and Mama meets them in the living room wearing a mask.

"Mama, get back in bed. You need to rest," I insist resting my hand on her elbow and steering her back to her room.

"I wanted to see how Fabby's day went," she murmurs as she turns herself around and heads back to the living room.

"Mama, she's in the bathroom. I'll have her come in and see you after."

I cover her up, and swing her door around, but don't close it. As I pass my room, I catch a glimpse of the Dark One sitting on my bed.

I roll my eyes and sit beside it. "I'm sorry I drove you away. I know you have questions, but I can't answer them."

"Although your apology seems sincere…"

Something's wrong.

This is not the Dark One. The deep voice belongs to a different reaper. I leap from my bed and take a few steps back as it continues.

"…what you did, erased the others from existence."

"What do you mean erased?"

It towers over me as it stands within inches of my mortal frame. "I mean they are gone, dead, kaput, vanished, no longer here, you will never see them again. Not in this life or the next," it announces with a raised voice. "I know you don't know everything about your powers yet, but now that you do know this aspect, I hope you will be more careful in the future."

"I just wanted them to leave me alone. Are you Dark One's replacement?"

"The truth is, Libitina, it shouldn't have been here to begin with. It dragged the others into it as well, and they too suffered the consequences. I'm not sure why God allowed it to continue, but He has asked me to be here today to tell you that going forward, if you need to ask a question of me, an angel, or a demon for that matter, ask. Otherwise, you won't see us any longer unless you are nearby when death occurs."

It disappears through the window, and out of view.

I can kill them. Why would God give me this ability?

Hope yells at the television in the other room. Regina bought her a new video game, and she gets upset when her virtual person dies. I guess we have that in common now.

The corner where Dark One used to stand mocks me with its emptiness. I should be glad, but I'm not. It just wanted answers, like the others, and I destroyed them for it. They are not the monsters. As it turns out, I am.

I push past Fabby with my head down on my way to the bathroom and close the door. Vomit launches from my mouth and splashes onto the side of the sink and wall. The toilet seat slams open as more bile races into my esophagus.

I'm a murderer.

Knuckles thump the door. "Libby, are you sick?" Fabby's voice muffles through the partition.

Am I sick? A loaded question that I don't have the answer to.

"I don't know, but don't come in. I made a mess."

I unfurl a wad of toilet paper and smear the vomit from my lips. Mama keeps old rags under the sink, so I reach under, pull them out, and start cleaning. I flick the fan switch. It spins noisily as I spray and scrub my bodily fluids. My stomach tightens and rolls as my bowels rush up, over, and down my intestines and land violently at the bottom. I rotate fast and drop my rear on the seat just as everything I ate for the last twenty-four hours exits violently. My face prickles and goosebumps blanket my skin. Perhaps this is punishment.

I deserve it. I'm a terrible person. Am I even a person?

Heavy footsteps stop outside the door. "Libby, can I get you anything?" Papa yells.

"No."

"Okay. Regina came to pick up Hope and wanted to see you."

"I can't right now. I'm sick to my stomach," I holler back. "Can you tell her I said I'm sorry, and I love her?"

"I will."

I break down as soon as his steps fade. If an empty bucket sat beneath my face, it would fill fast with my guilty tears. They splat on the floor, creating a small transparent puddle. My elbows dig into the space just above my knees as I drop my forehead into my palms. Odor stifles the air in the small space, so I flush the toilet. Water splashes my butt cheeks, grossing me out. I lean over to the tub and turn on the shower. Steam fogs the mirrored cabinet above the sink.

I wipe, wash my hands, shed my attire, and climb into the falling water.

Squeaking comes from the direction of the mirror above the sink. I shift the curtain aside as words slowly appear on the fogged medicine cabinet.

'Not a monster.'

"Who are you?" I ask.

One word appears, and I scream, "No!"

I trip out of the tub, falling to the floor as I scramble to grab a towel to surround myself. I barrel past Fabby and Papa as they run towards me. I slam Mama's bedroom door aside and leap onto her bed. I seize her arms and shake her. "Mama!"

Her eyes pop open as Fabby and Papa come into the room. "Libby, what's the matter?" Mama says furrowing her brow.

"I thought that. I mean the only way you could have written on the mirror is…"

"Libby, what are you talking about?" Fabby asks taking me by the forearms.

I release myself from her hold and return to the bathroom.

It's gone.

"Not Mama," I whisper to myself as Papa enters. "Mom."

"Libby, tell me what's wrong."

"The mirror. It had writing on it, and when I asked who it was, it spelled out…" I sit on the tub edge and adjust my towel.

"Spelled out what?" Papa inquires sitting on the closed toilet lid.

"Mom."

"I see. And when you saw that, you thought Mama was doing it which only could mean one thing."

"That she was dead," I cry.

He places his hand on the back of my head and presses his forehead against mine. "Libby, if she is here, it is because she thinks you need her."

"I know."

"What did she write?"

"That I am not a monster."

"Of course, you're not. Why would you think that?"

"Because I got angry and vaporized the spirits. They're gone forever, Papa."

"Libby, just because they disappeared doesn't mean they are gone for good."

"Papa, a different reaper came to me today before I got sick. He told me what I did made them go away forever."

"Like an exorcism?"

"I guess so."

Mama rubs her nose as she leans against the doorway. "Is everything okay?"

"Libby's birth mother paid her a visit," Papa says as he stands.

"Do you think it is because of what Regina told us?" Mama inquires.

"About what?" I ask standing up.

"Libs, they are transporting your biological father to a new facility closer to here. He contacted Will and asked him to ask you if when the move is complete, you would come and see him."

"Yes." It came out without hesitation, and I didn't expect it. I divert my eyes from them. I don't know why, but a sense of urgency comes over me.

"You don't have to decide today. Why don't you take a few days to…" Papa pauses as I interrupt.

"No. I want to go. I don't need time to think about it."

"I'll let Will and Regina know to set it up," Mama says as she takes Papa's hand. "We support your decision."

Papa kisses the back of her hand and guides her out of the bathroom. They may support my decision, but I sense they don't agree. I don't even know what I am going to say to him when we meet.

Fabby waits for me when I enter my room. "Are you okay?"

"Yes," I sigh as I let my towel fall to the floor when she passes me my pajamas. "Just tired." I yank the cotton pinstripe top over my head, then stick my feet in my underwear holes, and pull them up. She passes me the matching bottoms, but I throw them on my dresser and crawl under the covers.

"Can I come with you?" Fabby asks as she turns off the light, lifts the sheets, and climbs in beside me.

"If Mama and Papa say it's okay, then yes," I whisper to her silhouette in the dark.

Fabby interlaces her fingers with mine. "I'll be by your side every step of the way."

Her breathing shallows as she drifts off to sleep. I roll onto my back and stare at the ceiling. A tiny spider creeps across it, heading to the corner where the reaper used to hover. As much as Dark One drove me nuts with all its questions, I miss it being here. I never meant to vanquish it for good.

Perhaps it was right about me being their replacement. Why else would God grant me the power to get rid of them, and do their jobs?

The door creaks open, and Papa peeks inside. "Night, girls."

"Night, Papa," I whisper.

The door closes, and I shut my eyes. A chill frosts the back of my neck. I roll over to check my window. My eyes widen as the rocking chair in the corner shifts, and my birth mother sits down. She gazes at the crescent moon shining through my window and hums softly to herself.

Chapter Thirty-Three
Mother

"Why are you here?" I whisper.

The rocking stops, and the humming ceases. Even in death, my mother is striking. Her long brown hair cascades over her shoulders as she grips the chair arms and stands. I glance at the photo I framed of her on my dresser. She wears the same dress in that image as she does at this very moment. I've seen it before, many times, in a photo album Mama put together for me. It must be her favorite.

I freeze when she touches the side of my head. Not because I'm afraid, but because I didn't want to hurt her.

Her cool touch warms my heart. She's safe with me.

"Don't be afraid," her voice echoes in my head.

"I'm not," I murmur as tears drip on my pillow. "I'm sorry I killed you."

"You didn't. You are where you should be, and I am too."

"Libby, are you talking in your sleep?" Fabby asks sitting up on her elbows.

"No. I'm talking to my mother."

"Hi, Mrs. Yarrow," Fabby says waving to the empty space beside the bed. "Are you taking the Dark One's place?"

My mother kisses my cheek and vanishes, but not before responding.

I roll over and face my sister. "She's happy you are here with me. Then she said something odd."

"What?"

"She told me that when the time comes, not to be afraid."

"Afraid of what?"

"I don't know."

"Do you think she knows you're going to see your biological father?"

"Maybe."

"Huh. Well, I guess it's a good thing I'm going with you," she says turning her back to me. "Because if he tries anything, I'll kick his butt."

"Thanks, Fabby."

"No problem. Now get some sleep."

Fabby's gone when I wake up. I glance at the empty rocker in the corner and sigh. My comforter slides to the floor as I roll out of bed, and saunter to the window. Asher and Karma are by the barn devouring shredded carrots out of Papa's hand. Regina's car sits in the driveway, and muffled voices filter through the wall.

I pull on my pajama bottoms and slide my feet into slippers. The cool morning air chills my skin, so I grab a long cardigan and wrap it around me. Mama and Regina are in the kitchen making breakfast.

"Morning," Mama says as she passes Regina a cup of coffee.

"Morning." I take a seat at the table and stare out the window beside me. "Regina, when is the transfer?"

"Well, Libby, that's why I'm here. The facility transferred Mr. Yarrow last night."

"So, he's here," I say keeping my eyes on the car idling at the end of our driveway.

"Yes," Regina says sitting across from me. "I made an appointment for you to see him tomorrow. But if that's too soon, I can reschedule."

"No!" I shout startling Mama.

"Libs, what's the matter?" Mama asks, dragging the chair out next to me and sinking into it.

"My mother came to see me last night. She told me not to be afraid when the time comes."

Regina drums her fingers on the table. "Libby, you don't have to worry about a thing. Will and I are taking you."

My eyes dart to Mama. "But what about Fabby?"

"Papa and I think it's best if she stays home."

"But I need her," I whimper.

"Libby, I'm sorry. If it were up to us, you wouldn't be going either."

"I know Mama."

Stones pop under tires as the vehicle idling at the end of our driveway steers toward our house.

"Someone's coming," I announce.

Papa walks out of the barn and strolls to the four-door steel gray sedan. Regina moves the curtain aside. A massive tattooed bald man, with a tight black t-shirt and black jeans, climbs from the vehicle. My eyes widen when the man swings at Papa but misses.

Regina snatches her purse from the counter and jogs out the front door. I leap from my chair, and Mama blocks my path. "Stay here, Libby."

"Mama, I can help," I insist trying to break free from her grasp.

"Not this time. Let Papa and Regina handle it," she says, forcing me to my room and closing the door.

I ran to my window. Papa struggles with the man on the ground while Regina riffles through her bag. The man outsizes Papa, but he's not fast, and Papa quickly puts him in a chokehold. A single gunshot echoes as Regina fires into the air and trains her weapon on the assailant. I yank my door open and race outside. Papa takes zip-ties from Mama and secures the man's wrists. Regina puts her weapon away and grabs her cell phone to call for help.

Papa flips the man over and sits him upright. "Who sent you?"

The man's chest heaves in and out as he tries to catch his breath. He opens his mouth to speak but stops when he notices me. "It's you," he whispers as he twists his legs behind him. "Forgive me," he pleads. "I should never have taken this job."

"What job?" I inquire as Papa and Mama stand on either side of me.

He mumbles under his breath and lets his body fall to the side.

"What job?" Papa yells while clenching the man's shirt and shaking him.

"To kill her."

Papa releases him and backs away. "What did you say?"

"Someone paid me fifty thousand to kill her."

Regina walks behind the man and lifts his shirt. She unclips a sheath from his belt and slides a large, curved hunting knife from inside.

"Give it to me," I demand.

"Libby, I don't think…" Mama starts.

"I'm not asking," I stress.

Regina leans over the man and puts the blade in my hand. I turn it and grip the pearl handle.

"Please don't kill me," the man weeps.

I drive the blade deep into the soil beside him making him flinch. "I'm not going to kill you. Sit up."

The man flops around until he's upright and facing me. My knees touch his as I kneel before him. "Who sent you, and why?"

"I don't know. Some guy in an all-white fancy suit, with blonde hair and blue eyes approached me on the street. Someone gave him my information. I'm the muscle for a busy casino and have a large amount of gambling debt. He offered to pay them off and then some if I...."

"Killed me?"

"Yes."

"Did he say why?"

"The guy is crazy. He didn't make any sense, but I needed the money, so I accepted," he says avoiding eye contact.

"What did he tell you?" I ask, putting my face an inch from his, forcing him to look at me.

"He said you're a demon sent to this world to wipe out anyone worthy of God."

"Libby don't listen to him. He's clearly lying," Papa advises.

"Only one way to find out," I announce.

I take both my palms and grab his head. The man bucks backward, and I land on his abdomen. Regina lunges for us and I shoot her a nasty stare. She retreats with her hands up. I close my eyes, and dive into his memories. He's telling the truth, but that doesn't excuse what he did.

I release him and unmount his body. Flashing lights flicker through the trees by the road. The police are coming. I don't have much time.

The man turns onto his side. "I'm sorry."

"So am I." I seize his head once more and shriek in his face. The earth sinks, lowering us an inch as I give him an order. "When that man contacts you, give him a message for me."

We sink another inch as an unmarked patrol car steers in our direction.

"Tell him if he wants a job done, come do it himself," I demand forcing us down another inch. "Then he can be the one I put into the ground."

I can't let him go.

I'm so angry. This man came here to kill me and swung at Papa. There must be consequences. Everything inside me quakes, and my blood rages through my veins. The pounding in my head grows louder and louder. Steam billows from my hands as rage forces out of me, burning the man's flesh while he screams for mercy.

"Libby!" Mama cries out. "Let him go."

Her voice sounds so far away. I screech to the sky at the top of my lungs and clouds blacken out the sun. Lightning strikes the barn light busting its bulb as torrential rain stings our skin.

Why can't I let go?

The screen door to the house rips off and launches across the lawn. A light illuminates the entranceway as my birth mother floats through it and approaches me.

They can see her too. Mama, Papa, and Regina move from her path as she crawls on her hands and knees toward me. "Libby Rose, let him go," she whispers wiping my mortal tears.

I remove my hands from the man's face, and Papa lifts me away from him. Two blistering handprints scar his cheeks. "I'm sorry. I didn't mean it," I cry releasing a staggering breath. "I couldn't let go."

My birth mother vanishes as the sun peeks through the clouds, and the storm dissipates. They're all staring at me when I turn around. "I'm sorry. I…"

"Libby, we aren't mad. It's not your fault," assures Mama.

A marked police vehicle parks at the end of the driveway and two uniformed officers exit. "Are they coming for me?" I inquire backing away from everyone.

"No, of course not," Regina says walking toward me.

I run into the house, down to my room, slam the door, and lock it. My legs fail and I collapse on the rug. What have I done? What that man did was wrong, but what I did was worse. He'll never be the same. Heat warms my left arm as reaper number two penetrates the door, and crouches beside me. "Your mother can stop you. How?"

"Please, go away."

My door vibrates with an insistent knock. "Libby, it's Will. Open the door."

They're coming to take me away. I made a mistake and now I'm paying for it. The reaper waves his shadowy appendage in front of my eyes. "Answer the question."

"Get away from me," I yell as the knocking turns into pounding.

"Answer," it insists.

"I don't know. Now, go away!" I scream.

It disappears as Will bursts through the door with his gun drawn. He sweeps the room before holstering it and pulling me into his embrace. "No one's going to hurt you, Libby."

"But I hurt that man. Am I going to jail?"

"Of course not. Do you think I would allow it?"

"I couldn't stop. I don't know what's wrong with me."

He strokes my hair and speaks softly in my ear. "There is nothing wrong with you. You protected your family. What you did is no different than if I had to hurt the guy subduing him when I got here."

Will holds me at arm's length. "Regina and I love you just as much as we love Hope. We will always protect you."

I wrap my arms around his waist and hold him tighter than I ever have. Regina comes in and holds me from behind, sandwiching me between them. "We love you, Libby," Regina whispers.

"Love you too," I sob.

Papa leans on the door jamb. "Will, one of the guys wants to talk to you."

"I'm coming," he says letting me go.

Will shuffles by Papa, and Regina follows leaving Papa and I alone. I put my head down, and he tilts it up with his knuckles. "Next time, stay in your room like Mama says," he chuckles.

"Not funny Papa." I move away from him and sit on my bed. "I hurt him."

"If you stayed put like your mother asked it wouldn't have happened," he says grabbing the broken door and wiggling it. "Guess I'll have to put a new one on this weekend."

The knob pulls from its hole and the door falls, crashing into my mirror. Papa gazes down at the glass shards littering my carpet, and smiles while nodding his head. "And now you need a new mirror."

"Yep."

He rubs my back, steers me out of the room, and into the kitchen. "Hungry?"

"Starving."

Papa removes a frying pan from underneath the cupboard and cracks some eggs. I peek through the kitchen window as a paramedic moves the bald man's face from side to side and examines his burns. He unwraps sterile gauze, covers the injury loosely, and glances in my direction. I avert my eyes but sense him staring.

The radio on the counter statics, then turns on, as my birth mother levitates by Papa, and sits beside me.

She warms the back of my hand as she holds it, hums to the song playing on the radio, and sips her transparent coffee.

Chapter Thirty-Four
Guilt

I don't know how everyone can be so understanding. They don't judge me or punish me for what I've done, but they should.

Today, Regina and Will are taking me to visit my biological father. What if I hurt him? Now that I know I can, what's to stop me?

Asher gallops towards me, with Karma trailing behind him. I shake open the bag of leftover fresh spinach, seize a handful, and offer it to them.

Brakes screech at the end of the driveway, and Pastor James rolls towards me. Papa must have called him. I dump the rest of the greens on the ground and stuff the bag in my pocket. The pastor exits his vehicle wearing a stained t-shirt, old, ripped jeans, and a paint-splattered hat.

"Is it laundry day?"

"No. I'm helping your dad put a coat of paint on the barn today."

"Oh. I thought you were here for me."

"I'm always here for you, Libby."

"I hurt someone yesterday."

"I know."

"Pastor James, why has God made me this way?"

He stares at the grass and smiles. "God never does anything without a good reason. You have a purpose, Libby. And in time, He will reveal it to you."

"I'm afraid."

He walks over to me, rests his palm on my shoulder, and smiles. "Libby, I'd be concerned if you weren't." The pastor steers around me, and waves at Papa.

Another vehicle approaches, and my stomach churns. Regina and Will are here. I hold my arms to steady their shaking. Karma and Asher stand on either side of me and nudge my hip, but I can't move. It's like my brain forgot how to communicate with my legs, and now I'm stuck. The valves of my heart slam open and close as they stop in front of me. "Libby, are you okay? You're pale," Regina asks.

Prickling plasters my skin as a sharp pain pierces through my head, and black spots dance before my eyes. Will speaks to me, but I can't understand what he's saying. The scent of burning rubber filters through my nostrils, and that's when I knew. For the first time since I was a baby, a seizure forces me to the earth.

Fabby appears beside me as Regina turns me on my left side. Muffled words come from her lips as she strokes my hair. She's saying the same thing repeatedly, but I can't understand it.

The quaking stops, and my head bobbles a little when I sit up.

"You're okay," Fabby says hugging me.

"I think we should cancel the visit," Mama insists.

"No. I'm fine. You're overreacting," I say to her.

I brush off my pants, and storm to Will and Regina's car. "I'm going," I say as I whip the door open, and plop myself inside. I cross my arms as they stare at me through the window. The six of them talk amongst themselves in a circle. I wipe a tear from my cheek as Papa strolls to the car and taps on the window with his finger. I press the button, and the window glides down halfway. "What?" I scoff.

"Libs, Fabby is coming with you," he insists as the door on the other side of me opens, and Fabby slides in. I nod and turn to him. "Thanks, Papa."

"Thank Pastor James when you get back. He convinced us."

"I will."

He slaps the roof of the car and walks away. Will climbs in and glances at Fabby and me in the back seat. "Ready?"

"Yes," we say in unison as Regina moves her seat forward, giving me more legroom.

Houses give way to trees as we drive out of town. I rub the palms of my hands on my thighs removing their sweat. Fabby releases her seatbelt, scoots beside me, and rests her head on my shoulder. "You scared me today."

"I know."

Regina passes a water bottle to us. "You should hydrate, Libby."

"Thank you," I say taking it from her. "How long until we get there?"

"Another twenty minutes or so," Will says to our reflection.

Water dribbles down my top and Fabby giggles. "Got a hole in your lip?"

I wipe the liquid with my fingers and flick it at her.

"Hey," she laughs using her shirt to clean her face. "Snot."

I smirk and return to staring outside. My thoughts drift somewhere unknown. I'm sitting on a beach with my toes in the water. It's so clear I can see the bottom. In the distance to my left, multiple children run into the ocean laughing hysterically. I smile at them as I rest my head on my knees and close my eyes.

"Libby," Fabby says shaking me awake. "We're here."

I rub the crumbs from my lids and glance at the brick building. In its center are double doors with a camera mounted above them. The door beside me staggers open. Regina blocks my view of the place with her body, and takes a deep breath, "Libby, there is something Will and I didn't tell you, but now that we are here, we think we should." She gazes over the roof of the car at Will and grimaces. "He's sick."

"Of course, he is. He wouldn't be in this place if he wasn't," I say furrowing my brow.

"No, Libby. Not that kind of sickness. He has cancer."

"What? Why would you keep that from me?"

"Will and I wanted to make sure that you came for the right reason, not because it was a dying man's wish."

"He's dying?"

"Yes, Libby."

Fabby takes my hand and squeezes it. The front entrance scrapes open, and a man wearing all blue pushes a female patient wearing all red in a wheelchair down the ramp. The woman talks to herself as they pass us and stop before a white van. Another employee jumps out, and they lift the wheelchair inside and close the door.

"If you've changed your mind, I understand," Will says as I flick my fingernails against each other.

"I haven't. Let's go."

Fabby and I hold hands as the security door buzzes and slides inward. Patients in green mill about in the first-floor hallway as we approach the elevators. Regina punches the button to the third floor, and we jolt upward.

A staff member, wearing black dress pants, a gray button-up shirt, and shiny black loafers leans against the wall when the doors open. His slick black hair and pale skin remind me of a vampire as he extends his bony hand to Will. "Detective Gerard, nice to finally meet you in person."

They shake hands, and he waves us into his office. I lean against the wall as the man removes a folder from his top drawer. "I need all of you to sign this waiver of liability. Even though Mr. Yarrow is ill, he's still a red-level threat. We can't be responsible for his actions if you choose to see him."

"That's what the colors are for, Mr.?" I ask stepping forward to sign my copy.

"Apologies. It's Dr. Edwin Eckert. My patients call me Dr. E. And yes, the colors are according to the threat level. Green patients are of little to no threat and stay on the first floor. Yellow and red are on the upper levels with added security and staff to care for them."

I set my pen down, and it rolls in slow motion across the desk and onto the floor. Dr. E. didn't even try to catch it. Regina picks it up and places it on the desk where it once again rolls to the floor.

"Don't bother. When maintenance brought my desk in here, they snapped off two of the leg levelers. The whole desk tilts to the side now. I must pick up my pen a hundred times a day," the doctor laughs as he stands up and walks around us. "Mr. Yarrow's room is this way. I must warn you; he's not doing well."

We round the corner and stop at the first door. Dr. E. swipes a keycard, and the door clicks open. "If you need me, I'll be in the lounge across the hall," he says pointing behind us.

"Thank you," Regina says.

Fabby grabs my shaking hands with hers and pulls them to her chest. "You got this. I'm right here with you."

I nod and force myself through the door.

Birds chirp on a high small windowsill beside his bed. His disheveled hair sticks up in every direction, and his eyes twitch in his sleep. I sit in a plastic chair by his headboard and whisper. "Hello."

His eyes flicker open, and tears flood his face at once. "You came," he whispers. "You look like your mother."

I didn't know what to say to him. What do I say to the man who killed two people and tried to kill me? I know his mind wasn't right and still isn't, but I'm at a loss for words. His eyes dart from Fabby to Regina and then to Will. "Is this your family now?"

"Just me," Fabby announces crossing her arms. "I'm her sister, Fabiola."

"Thank you for…." He coughs multiple times, covering his mouth with a tissue. Blood stains the white paper as he drops it in the garbage by my feet. "Sorry. Thank you for coming."

"Why did you want to see me?"

He glances at the others and then back to me. "Can we speak alone?"

"Whatever you need to say to her, you say to us all," Will insists.

"We have no secrets in our family," I inform him as my mother floats through the wall and hovers beside me.

"Can you see her?" his voice strains as he struggles to breathe. "She's standing right beside you."

"I know."

"She's here to watch you take me."

"What?"

"I'm dying, Libitina. I'm going to hell for what I did, and I want you to send me there."

"I can't do that," I say backing away from him.

"Of course, you can. I saw it in a dream."

"Libby, I think it's time to go," Regina says taking me by the elbow.

"I agree," Fabiola says turning towards the door.

My mother floats through Regina, raising the hair on her neck and making her let me go. She whispers to me, "Don't be afraid, Libitina Rose."

"Can you hear her?" he asks as he coughs more blood from his lungs.

"Yes," I reply. "I'd like to be alone with him."

Fabby's eyes widen as she objects. "Absolutely not. You can't let her be alone with him," she yells at Will and Regina.

"It's her decision Fabby," Regina replies. "Besides, we all know she's capable of protecting herself."

"But I want to stay," Fabby pleads with me.

"I'm sorry, Fabby. Not this time."

She frowns and stomps out the door. Will bends down and speaks in my father's ear. "If you do anything to hurt her, I'll send you to hell myself."

He nods at me and leaves the room, closing the door behind him. Air wheezes through my father's bluing lips as his breaths shallow, and his chest heaves. "Come closer."

I sit down and place my hands on my lap. "I still don't understand why you want me to do this."

"I…"

He gasps for air, as he reaches for me. I take his hand and move closer.

"I want…"

His eyes close, and he forces them back open, fighting to stay awake.

"Forgiveness," he mumbles as his hand goes limp beneath mine.

He can't keep his eyes open any longer as he whispers one last time. "Forgive me."

I shouldn't feel compassion for this dying man, but I do. He has one last wish before leaving this world and that is for my forgiveness. I look at my mother, and she nods.

I take a deep breath and hold his head in my hands. His eyes open slightly, and I whisper, "I forgive you."

A slight smile tugs at the corner of his mouth, and his head falls to the side. A reaper appears beside me, and a demon crawls out of a swirling black circle in the middle of the room.

"You're not needed," I say to them as I snatch my former father's soul by its arm and launch it into the hole.

A light appears above my mother and an angel floats to her. She's leaving.

I take her face in my hands, warming them with my touch, and kiss her goodbye. "I love you."

"I'll always be watching," she smiles as the angel lifts her, and they vanish through the ceiling tiles.

I wipe the tears from my face, open the door, and hug Fabby. "It's over. He's gone." I turn to Regina and Will. "Can we go home? I need my Papa."

"Of course, Libby," Regina says wrapping her arms around me and kissing my forehead. "Of course."

Chapter Thirty-Five
Vacation

Papa's chest rises and falls beneath me. When I came home from the facility, I went into my parent's room, crawled in beside him, and fell asleep.

When he asked me what happened, I didn't reply. I don't want to talk about it. I don't even want to be here anymore. How can I explain what I did to my family? I gaze through the window as the sun breaches the sill and warms my face. Papa's heartbeat thumps in rhythm against my ear as I listen to his breathing. I slide out of bed, careful not to wake him, and tiptoe to the empty kitchen. The chair by the window scrapes when I sit down and think about the day before. Forgiving him wasn't my intention, but how could I not? If it wasn't for him, I wouldn't have met my family.

A bag drops on the kitchen floor, and slides in my direction.

"What's that?" I ask Papa as he sits across from me.

"Pack some clothes. We are staying at the cabin this weekend."

"But I thought you had houses to show."

"I did, but we haven't taken a vacation in some time, and after the last couple of days, I think we've all earned it. Don't you?"

"Yes, Papa."

He knocks on the tabletop with his knuckles and stands. "I'm sorry about your father. I know you didn't know him, but I imagine seeing him after all this time, and in the state he was in, was difficult."

"It was, but I'll be okay."

"Libby, you're not alone in this. If you ever need anyone to talk to besides us, just say the word."

"Thanks, Papa."

"Why are we up so early?" Fabby asks entering the room.

"We are going to the cabin for the weekend," Papa says as he passes her.

Fabby swipes her eyes with the back of her hand, and yawns. "We haven't been to the cabin since we were little."

"He wants to spend some time together as a family."

"Do you remember the last time we went? We both ventured far into the woods and wandered into poison ivy."

I laugh through my nose and pick up the bag Papa left for me. "I remember telling you we should stop before we get lost, and you told me no."

"I guess I should have listened to you," she grins, pouring two glasses of orange juice, and passing me one. "Drink up, buttercup."

I chug the drink fast and head to my room to pack. I'd stay behind and hide out in my room if I could. I suck in my abdomen and jump up and down while yanking up my zipper. My clothes are getting tight, but I haven't told Mama. She's been so busy teaching Hope how to cook and helping Fabby with after-school activities, that I don't want to burden her with one more task. I pull my slouchy socks over my bare ankles to hide how short they are and lace up my favorite sneakers.

Fabby tosses her backpack into the trunk as I step off the porch. "We are stopping at Auntie Marie's on our way to try and get her to come with us. Papa said they used to go all the time as kids. He thought between you, and her memories of the place it would be worth a shot," she announces taking my bag from me.

"I don't know why we keep pushing her. She needs to be ready to leave on her own without outside influence."

"I have to try, Libby," Papa says coming up behind us.

"But why? She's clearly petrified. Yet, we are constantly trying to make her leave the house when we visit."

"Let it go, Libby," Mama insists as she wedges a cooler in the back seat.

"But I just want to understand."

"Because it's my fault she was attacked!" Papa shouts startling everyone. "I was supposed to meet her after work, and I took an appointment to show a house instead."

"Papa, you couldn't have known that was going to happen. It isn't your fault," Fabby says.

"It is my fault, girls. I chose business over family, and I will never do it again."

"Is that what this trip is about?" I ask.

"Yes, Libby. We need each other right now, and I am not letting my job get in the way of being there for you when you need me."

"I'm sorry I upset you." I lean into the front seat and peck his cheek. "I love you, Papa."

"I love you, too."

Several vehicles line Auntie Marie's driveway when we arrive.

"Is she having a party?" Fabby asks.

"I doubt it," Papa says shifting the car into park. "Stay here."

Papa disappears inside the house. A woman wearing an apron, carrying a caddy full of cleaning products rounds the front of the house. "Mama, look."

"Marie cleans her own house, always has," Mama replies removing her seatbelt. "I'll be right back."

Mama walks over to speak to the woman as another cleaning lady strolls out the front door. I remove my seatbelt and climb out. "Mama, what is going on?"

"Your aunt fell down the stairs while carrying laundry and broke her leg."

"What?" Fabby yells and runs inside.

Auntie Marie is talking to Papa on the couch when I enter the living room. Crutches rest against the cushion arm, and emergency room paperwork litters the coffee table. I step over her pink cast and sit beside her. "Are you okay?"

"Oh, Libby, I'll be fine. The broken banister, on the other hand, didn't fare so well."

"Why didn't you call us?"

"Well, you all have a lot on your plate, and I didn't want to add to the pile."

"I get that," I nod as I think about unbuttoning my tight jeans so I can breathe.

"We are staying here to help you," I insist.

"No, no. That isn't necessary. You have plans, and I'm not ruining them."

"Auntie Marie, do you really want all these strangers working in your house?" Fabby asks.

She stares past us into the foyer as another maid leaves with a garbage bag. "Not really, but what other choice did I have?"

"You could have called us," Mama says entering the room and pressing her hands on her hips firmly. "You're being stubborn, Marie. We are staying, and that's that."

Papa smiles at his family's display of unity for his sister. I'm not happy she broke her leg, but I am happy that we aren't going to the aging cabin. Staying here to help ensures everyone stays busy instead of asking me what happened behind closed doors at the institute.

Mama leaves to dismiss the cleaning staff, while Papa and Fabby go outside to unload the car. I flick on the television and lean against Auntie Marie. "I'm glad you're okay."

"Are you okay?"

"What do you mean?"

"Libby don't be coy with me. Your sister called me from the facility when you were alone with your biological father. She was concerned about you."

"I'm fine."

"Short and sweet answer. That won't do. Libby, we know you're capable of great things, and there is no reason for you to keep secret what happened in that room."

"I sent him to hell," I blurt. "His last wish before dying was for me to remove his soul and send him there myself."

"Having his daughter send him to hell normally would have been punishment. Libby, he made it his last dying wish to give you a piece of revenge for not loving you as he should, even if you didn't want it."

"I didn't want revenge for what he did. If it weren't for him, I wouldn't have met any of you."

"I know, sweetheart."

Papa, Mama, and Fabby all come in and sit down. No one says anything, but their unspoken words float between Auntie Marie and me, stifling the air. They're waiting for one of them to build up the courage to ask me what happened. Luckily for me, Auntie Marie did it for me.

"Libby took her estranged father's soul and stuffed it in Satan's basement. Any further questions you don't care to ask?"

"Nope. I'm good," Mama says slapping her palms together. "I'm going to make us some lunch."

Papa stares at her all the way to the kitchen and sighs. "Girls, can you give your aunt and me a moment alone?"

"Yes, Papa," we say in unison.

Fabby and I take a walk around the grounds. Strawberry Hydrangeas dot the perimeter of the house. The gardener prunes them into trees and shapes the flowers into a teardrop resembling cotton candy. We make a pit stop in the garden. Snap peas twist around three-foot stakes, and tangle into each other.

"You're quiet today," Fabby says folding her shirt into a basin, and filling it with fresh peas.

"Can I be honest?"

"Always."

"If it weren't for you, Mama, and Papa, I would have run away by now," I frown rubbing the prickled surface of a mini cucumber.

"Listen to me, Libby. We will always be here for you. Don't ever think that we don't want you with us."

I reach into her pile of peas and take one. "I sent him to hell," I say as I de-string the outer shell with my fingernail, and pop it in my mouth.

"Is that what he wanted?"

"Yes."

"Then that's all that matters," she shrugs and drops her harvest in a mini plastic bucket. She lifts the pail, starts walking, then stops abruptly. "So, you can hurt people while they are still alive, and send them to hell when they die. Does that mean you can send them to heaven too?"

"I think so."

She starts walking and stops again. "And you can kill angels, reapers, and demons?"

"Yes. Why?"

"Maybe God created you to take his place," she says as she bends over, takes a huge bite of the cucumber I'm holding, and keeps moving.

"What? That's ridiculous."

"Is it?" Mama waves at us in the distance, and we wave back. "Because from what I've seen and heard, you can do most everything He can, and you're still young."

"Fabby there is only one God, and no one can take His place."

"There is a first time for everything, Libs."

I pause on the porch and stare at the back of her head as she pushes the front door open. I suppose she could be right. I mean, I exist, and I don't think there is anyone else like me.

When we enter the dining room, Regina, Will, and Hope fill the normally empty chairs at the eight-person table. Hope smiles broadly when I sit beside her. I kiss her cheek, and she wipes it off.

"Are you here for lunch, or something else?" Fabby asks.

"Both," Regina pipes up as she removes a manilla envelope from the canvas tote by her legs, and hands it across the table to me.

"What's this?"

Regina exchanges glances with Papa. He stops eating, rests his elbows on the tablecloth, and interlaces his fingers. "Libby, it's paperwork. Your father had a life insurance policy through his work before he went to the institute. It sat in an account and accrued interest. Now that he's deceased, and in the ground, the remaining proceeds go to you as his beneficiary."

I didn't know what to say. Why would he list me as a beneficiary, even after he knew he didn't want me? Perhaps he knew one day he'd realize his mistake and thought this would buy me back.

I slide the paper from its sleeve. Attached with a paper clip is a check for fifty-seven thousand dollars. I flip it over. Tears well in my eyes. I don't want this. I'd rather give it away. I gaze at Fabby and smile. "Want a new car?" I ask as my watery eyes spill over. "Get me a pen."

Fabby seizes the corner of the check and flips it over. "Holy cow. You're giving this to me?"

"I'm giving it to my family," I announce choking up.

"Libby, you don't have to do that. You can use the money for college or a new car for yourself," Mama points out.

"Mama, that's not who I am."

"I know, Libby. But if you're going to do this, I need you to promise me one thing."

"Anything."

"Before we go off and buy your sister a car, I'm taking you to the mall and buying you a whole new wardrobe," she says wiggling her finger at me.

"Is it that obvious?"

"Libby if your pants get any tighter you might have a blowout in the back. I don't know how you can even breathe in those things," she chuckles.

"I can't."

"Take them off. I have some sweats you can wear," Auntie Marie says as she grabs her crutches and hobbles away.

Fabby jogs into the room and passes me a gold fountain pen with black trim. I turn the check back over, endorse it, and skid it over to Papa. "Buy Fabby whatever she wants, Papa. Then the rest is up to you."

He takes me by the side of the head and pulls me to him. "Thank you, Libby."

He wipes tears from his face and rubs my shoulder. "Thank you."

Chapter Thirty-Six
Empty Inside

After buying a new car for Fabby, Papa spent over a year teaching her how to drive. Despite a lot of bumps in the road, and concerns over her parallel parking, Fabby passed with flying colors.

She can't drive without a parent in the overnight hours, but let's face it, who wants to go out after dark on a school night anyway? We travel to the mall every weekend. Mama gives Fabby and me an allowance for doing all the chores she has little time for. Then we take that money, put gas in the car, and buy anything we want. For me, it's usually clothes.

I've shot up almost two inches since I turned fourteen. Mama says I should have my period by now and scheduled an appointment for today. I told her before that I couldn't have children because God told me so while I slept, but she thinks my dreams are just dreams sometimes, so here we are.

The packed waiting area leaves no room for us to sit when we arrive. I lean against the wall beside Mama. She shifts her weight from one foot to the other repeatedly. Her feet trouble her a lot these days. The doctors aren't sure what is wrong with them.

A little boy leaps from his seat and runs to Mama. "You can have my seat," he smiles with his finger in his mouth.

"How sweet of you," Mama says as she hobbles over to the empty chair.

"My husband will be here any minute," the boy's mother states as she covers the chair cushion with her palm.

Mama grimaces and moves back against the wall beside me. I bend sideways and whisper in her ear. "Do you want to wait for me in the car?"

"Of course not. I'll be fine."

The boy runs back to me and tugs my sweater. "You're pretty."

"Thank you."

"Are you an angel?"

I crouch down to his level and gaze into his baby blues. "Yes," I murmur.

His eyes light up, and he skips back to his mother. Her face reddens as he relays the message of my partial job title to her. She drops her purse on the floor beside her chair and storms over to me. "You shouldn't lie to children."

"I don't lie."

"He said you told him you were an angel."

"I am."

"Well, you and I both know that's a lie."

"If you say so," I grin turning away from her and staring at Mama.

"You want to know what I think?"

"Not really," I frown turning back to her.

"You're no angel," she huffs. "You're nothing but a devil. A spoiled, entitled, teenage devil."

"Now you listen here," Mama says pushing off the wall and approaching the woman.

I rest my arm across her frame. "Mama, I got this."

The woman crosses her arms and turns her nose up in the air. "What are you going to do now send me to hell?"

I seize the woman's forearm, and images flash through her head. It wasn't what I expected. Her husband isn't coming. He is too busy with having his way with her sister at a hotel down the street. I let her go.

The woman blinks several times, then glances at Mama who passes her purse to her son. "I think you and your mother are leaving now," she says to the little boy.

A tear slides down the side of her cheek as she turns to face me. "It's not true," she sniffles.

"If you leave now, you can see for yourself," I whisper.

Her legs move swiftly as she gathers her belongings, takes her son's hand, and pushes through the door.

A nurse, wearing stork-themed scrubs, comes into the room from the hall and calls a name several times. She crosses the name off her list and sweeps the room. "Alvarez? Libitina Alavarez?"

"That's us," I say waving from across the room.

I offer Mama my elbow. We walk down a long, purple hallway with ultrasound images hanging on white cotton twine and attached with clothespins. Mama stops before one of the images and smiles. "Look, it's Hope," she says pointing.

The nurse clears her throat and directs us into an exam room with only one seat. I offer it to Mama. The exam table crinkles when I sit down, and the paper rips under my palms when I apply pressure. Mama and I giggle as the nurse rolls her eyes and shifts her stool closer to the computer. "So, you're here because you haven't had your period yet."

"I can't have a period," I say as I fixate on a crack in the floor tile.

"And why would you think that?" she asks, typing with two fingers on her keyboard.

"Because God told me so."

Her pointers pause an inch above the keys, and she turns to me. "God said so, huh?"

"Yep."

The nurse turns to Mama who offers her no further explanation. Her stool creaks as she turns her attention back to the screen and types a long answer in my chart. "You do know that periods can come as late as sixteen in some teens," the nurse says over her shoulder.

"My daughter isn't some teen," Mama frowns as the woman turns to her and furrows her brow.

"Okay." The nurse stands and strolls out the door leaving it open.

"She's rude," Mama huffs as she stretches her legs, and crosses them at the ankles.

"Most people are."

A few minutes later, a doctor swoops into the room and swings the door around. "Libitina, I'm Dr. Farr. I understand you have concerns about your ability to have children."

"I don't. Mama does. I already know I can't."

"Well, Libitina your body changes all the time at this age and can make you have strong feelings that may be out of the realm of what's perceived as normal."

"It's not hormones. It's God's will."

The doctor raises his eyebrows and circles a few things on the chart he's holding. "I need you to sign these consents, then I'll have you change into a gown," he says pulling a paper robe from beneath me and resting it behind my back. "Everything off from the waist down and cover yourself with this." He slaps a square folded paper blanket on the counter beside Mama.

"No," I say to his back as he pauses with his hand on the doorknob.

"No? I need to look inside to see if everything is as it should be."

"Then do an ultrasound because your hands aren't violating my body."

"Miss Alvarez having exams is a normal part of life. You will have many in your lifetime," the doctor explains.

"No, I won't. Now, if you're not going to do the ultrasound, then we are leaving," I say as I hop off the table and reach for Mama.

"Fine. I will have the technician take you for an ultrasound. But if we find nothing wrong, then I'd like you to come back when you are more comfortable and have a full exam."

"I won't be back, Dr. Farr. I already know what's wrong," I say inches from his face.

He backs away and shifts his glasses up. "Mrs. Alvarez, may I speak with you in the hallway?"

"No. Whatever you have to say, you can say in front of Libby. We have no secrets in our family."

"Okay. I'd like to do some bloodwork to check your hormone levels as well."

"That won't be necessary," I grimace. "You're not sticking anything in me today, or ever."

Dr. Farr glances at Mama who shrugs. "It's her body and her choice."

"Very well," he says as he leans down, and types in the order for ultrasound.

He leaves the room and the door open. Mama stands from her seat. "I'm sorry if bringing you here made you uncomfortable."

"I'm not uncomfortable, but they are."

Mama laughs through her nose as the ultrasound tech speeds into the room. "Miss Alvarez, right this way," she says in a cheery voice.

We move to a room across from us, but there is no chair for Mama. I hustle back to my earlier room and carry one in for her.

"Thank you, Libby," Mama smiles sitting down.

I kiss the top of her head. "You're welcome."

The technician pats the paper, and I lie back on the cushioned bed. She lifts my shirt. "Can you unzip and pull your jeans down a little?"

I do as she asks.

She tucks paper between my skin and zipper, then squirts warm gel on my lower abdomen. The transducer glides through the goop and explores my reproductive system. Mama stares at the screen as the technician takes several images.

"I know I can't have children."

"Now, Libby. Let the woman do her job I'm sure there is a reasonable explanation."

"She's right," the technician says as she wipes the sludge from my stomach with a clean white towel. "There's nothing there."

"What do you mean, nothing there?" Mama says standing from her seat.

"I'll have the doctor come in and speak with you," the technician says getting up and curving around Mama.

Mama grabs the woman's arm. "No. You tell me."

"Your daughter doesn't have a uterus," the technician says yanking her arm away from Mama. "I'll get the doctor so he can tell you more."

"That won't be necessary," I say to her as I button my pants. "Come on, Mama. Let's go home."

Mama stays quiet in the car. She was hoping I was wrong, and she couldn't hide her disappointment. "Libby, I'm sorry God chose this path for you, but I want you to know that there are so many other ways to have children if you choose to have them in the future," she explains wiping her nose with a crumpled tissue.

"Don't cry, Mama. I'm not upset."

"I know you're not sweetheart. I just don't understand why?"

"God has bigger plans for me."

"What are they? Because I'd like to know why He took away your future," Mama sobs.

"God didn't take my future away. He's paving my path. I just need to stay on it until it reaches the crossroads and go from there."

Mama steers into the driveway and rolls to a stop before Papa and Fabby who are waiting for us. I climb from the car, and say to Papa, "Mama needs you."

Fabby jogs to catch up to me. "What did they say?"

"You know what they said."

"So, your dreams, they're real?"

"Of course, they are."

"Can you see our future?"

"God only lets me see what He wants me to see."

"Libby, did He ever tell you what you are?"

I stop outside my room and gaze at her. "Fabby, what I am is your sister, and you're my family. No matter who, or what I turn out to be, that will never change."

Chapter Thirty-Seven
Back to School

It seems strange that today is my first day of school after so many years without it. Summer flew by, and August came upon us before we knew it.

Fabby holds the passenger side door of her car open with a smile. She's a senior this year, and she's been looking forward to driving me to school for months.

Mama slams the screen door aside. "Wait! I need my annual first-day picture."

Fabby and I exchange smiles and lean against the hood of her car.

Mama takes several photos on her cell phone. Karma and Asher trot in our direction. I put my arm around Karma and Fabby does the same with Asher. Mama takes one last photo as Regina rolls towards us. She always comes to our house after she drops Hope off at school, has a quick coffee, and then goes to work. We wave to her as we climb in the car and buckle up. Fabby adjusts her mirror and shifts into reverse.

A massive number of students mill about when we pull into the front lot. Parking goes by seniority, and now that she's in her final year, Fabby can park in the closest lot.

As we make our approach, a group of girls runs toward us. "Fabby, is this your sister?" A curly-haired blonde girl with ripped jeans, and an oversized red tunic sweater asks.

"Yes. This is Libby. Libby this is Janette, Kensie, Anna, and Kayla."

"Hi," I say softly.

"Did you see the new boy who transferred in? He's not even thirteen and starting the ninth grade. Some kind of whiz kid I guess," Anna says peering through the crowd of students by the entrance. "Look, right there. Do you see him?" she says to me as she points to a short teenage boy dressed in khaki pants and a polo, carrying a plaid backpack. "Isn't he cute? His name is Adam."

I stop walking, and the girls do too.

"What is it? Do you know him?" Kensie asks as she swipes her brown bangs away from her eyes.

Could it be the same Adam whose life I saved years ago? What are the chances our paths would cross again? Fabby grabs me by the elbow and moves me forward. "Let's get you to your first class, Libby," she says changing the subject.

"You do know him," Kensie says with a sinister smile and raised eyebrows. "Did you guys ever kiss or anything?"

"Let it go," Fabby snaps as she pulls the front door open.

She walks with me down the freshman hallway to find my locker. I open it on the first try and hang my sweater inside. I stare at my shaking hand as I swing the metallic partition closed.

Fabby curls her fingers around mine and eases my nerves. "I'm here if you need me. Down there are all the senior classrooms. Here's my schedule. Come get me between classes if you're having a hard time, okay?"

"I will."

My first class is directly across the hall from my locker. I clutch my notebook tight to my chest, take a deep breath, and move towards the doorway. Adam appears before me, stopping me from going in.

"Hi. I umm sorry about this, but I umm saw you outside and thought you looked familiar. Have we met?"

Have we? The only way to find out is to touch him and visualize his past, but if I do that, he'll see it too. He extends his hand for me to shake. "I'm Adam."

"I'm not interested," I say as I swerve around him and find a seat in the classroom.

He strolls in with his hands in his pockets.

Crap. He's here too.

Please don't sit behind me. I think to myself.

And he sits behind me.

I stand up and take another seat in the middle. Other students occupy the seats around me. Adam places his elbow on his desktop and picks his teeth with his fingernail. I sense him staring at me, but I keep my eyes focused on the instructor standing at the front. Fabby warned me about this guy. He likes to throw out a history test before he even starts teaching the class.

His fingers drum a stack of stapled papers. "Some of you may have heard of me, and some not. If you have then you know what these are," he says slapping the pile. "I am Mr. Maitland, and this is your first lesson. Knowledge is power. The more you know about history, the more you will discover what it can teach us," he announces as he drops one on every desk. "You have thirty minutes. Bring the test up and set it here in this basket when it's complete."

There are fifty multiple-choice questions, and I breeze through them effortlessly. I stand after only five minutes and drop the packet in the basket. Mr. Maitland furrows his brow and scoops it up as I sit down. He holds his red pen in his hand, then sets it back down and takes off his glasses. Adam gets up, glances at me, then hands his answers to the teacher. Once again, he picks up his red pen and sets it back down. We both have a perfect score in record time.

Mr. Maitland stands and leans against the front of his desk. He taps his teeth with the arm of his bifocals as other students glance at us. "You two, in the hallway. Right now," the teacher orders.

I sigh and carry my notebook with me.

"Explain yourselves," he says crossing his arms and shifting his eyes from me to Adam and back again.

"What do you mean?" Adam asks.

"You cheated," he accuses. "No one has ever got a one hundred on my test. Let alone finish it so fast. The only way the two of you could have is if you both cheated."

"I didn't cheat," I say rolling my eyes.

"I didn't either." Adam scoffs and turns to me. "Your sister goes here. Perhaps she told you the answers."

"Fabby doesn't have to tell me anything. I'm not an idiot," I argue.

"I'm not an idiot either."

"Enough," Mr. Maitland says. "Go to the office. Both of you."

Wow. I'm only on my first day, and first class, and I already have detention. Fabby said the first day can be tough, but I didn't think it would be like this.

Adam and I sit opposite each other in chairs lining the glass windows of the waiting area. The principal enters carrying two folders and waves them at us. "Come with me."

He has us sit at a round table across from each other while he stands in between. "Mr. Maitland thinks you two are cheaters. Does either one of you care to tell me the truth?"

"I didn't cheat," Adam and I say together.

"Well at least you have your stories straight," he sighs.

"Test us," Adam sneers. "If you and Mr. Maitland are so sure that we cheated, then test us. Make one up right now and give it to us both. Then we will see who the real cheater is."

"Fine. I will. Ten questions. I will make them up myself according to what I know and have learned about history through the years. I'll make it easy. It will be all dates," he smiles stuffing his hand in his breast pocket and removing a pen as he leaves the room.

"Why can't you just tell him the truth," Adam asks slapping the table with his hand. "If I get detention because you cheated my dad will kill me."

"First of all, your dad won't kill you, and second I didn't cheat."

"Okay, whatever."

The clock in the room stops at nine. I stare at it and wait for it to start again, but it doesn't. The principal carries two pages and one cardboard divider into the room. He sets the partition between us and then drops the tests in front of us. "Three, two, one, and go," he says as he clicks the timer on his phone.

Once again, I finish first. I set my pen down, flip the paper over, and toss the partition aside. "Done."

Adam is only seconds behind me and does the same. We cross our arms, lean back in our chairs, and glare at the principal. He takes the papers, places his glasses on the bridge of his nose, and reviews them. "Huh. Back to class kids. Nice work."

I snatch my spiral notebook from the table and throw the door open. Adam hustles to catch up to me. "Wait. I'm sorry."

"You should be. That's what's wrong with people these days. No one has faith in anyone anymore."

Adam grabs me by the shirt and pulls me back. "Please stop for a second."

"Don't touch me," I order.

"Can you at least tell me your name?" he sighs, putting his head down.

"Libby."

He extends his hand to me. "I'm sorry, I accused you of being a cheater, Libby. Can we start over?"

"We can, but I'm not shaking your hand," I insist as we round the corner and near our classroom.

"What are you a germaphobe? Shake my hand," he insists grabbing my arm and shoving his hand into mine.

It's him. The Adam I saved has found his way back into my life. He's had a good life thus far. He's an only child. His intelligence score fell one number shy of mine, and his parents planned his future all the way through medical school, but he didn't want to be a doctor. He wants to be a pastor. I've let him see enough. I place my hand on his as the bell rings overhead, and peel his fingers off me. "Like I said before, don't touch."

His mouth hangs open as I turn away from him and search for my next classroom. He runs ahead of me and stops me. "You're Libitina," he whispers.

"I am."

"My parents told me a story growing up about a little angel who saved my life. They said her name was Libitina, and she was one of God's special children."

"We are all God's children, Adam. Now if you'll excuse me, I don't want to be late to my next class."

"I won't tell anyone," Adam says to my back.

"Good to know," I say as I turn into my English class.

Fabby and I meet in the cafeteria for lunch. Mama and Papa worked with the school to ensure our lunches were at the same time. I stick my legs under the table and sip my juice. Kayla and Kensie sit across from me sharing French fries with ranch dressing. "Oh, my gosh. He's staring at you," Kensie says nodding behind me and to the left.

Fabby and I both glance at where she is signaling. Adam is two tables over and facing us. He nods at me when we make eye contact, and I do the same.

"You do know each other," Kayla says exchanging smiles with Kensie. "Do tell."

"There is nothing to tell," I say biting into an apple.

"Leave her be," Fabby says as she takes a sip of her milk.

"We just want to know how they know each other, that's all," Kensie insists.

"If I tell you, will you stop bugging me about it?"

"Libby, don't," Fabby says shaking her head.

"We won't say another word," Kayla says making a zipping motion across her mouth.

"Fine. When I was little, I wandered away from my parents in the hospital. Adam was born prematurely and died in his mother's arms. When the Grim Reaper came to take him and send him to heaven with an angel, I snatched his soul from them and stuffed it back inside his body, saving his life. Any more questions?" I ask, wiping my lips and standing up.

Both girls burst into laughter as Adam walks up beside me. "Hey, Libitina want to get some dessert?"

"Libitina?" Kensie giggles. "Your real name is Libitina?"

Kayla types something into her phone and then shows the screen to Kensie. "Libitina means death or goddess of funerals. That's weird. Why would your parents do that to you?" Kensie asks.

"Don't answer that, Libby," Fabby says getting up.

"Ignore them," Adam says grabbing my books from the table for me. "They're clearly too dumb to see how special you are."

"Oh, she's special alright," Kensie says as she flops her hands in front of her face and sticks out her tongue.

Fabby seizes her by the back of the head and slams her face into her salad. Everyone stops talking. Not just the few people surrounding the table.

Everyone.

"Apologize," Fabby demands as she grips her hair tighter.

"I'm sorry, Libby," Kensie says as Fabby lets her go and walks away.

Three years of friendship disappear as Fabby chooses me over her friends like she always has. She rests her hand on the small of my back, and we take a seat at another table with Adam.

Friends come and go, but family is for life. It's too bad the principal didn't understand that. He stops in front of our table and crosses his arms. "Ladies, my office. Right now."

Chapter Thirty-Eight
Grounded

Mama waits for us on the porch. Fabby and I exchange glances. "We're grounded," we say in unison as we smile and climb out of the car.

"What in the world were you two thinking?" Mama says resting her knuckles on her hips.

"Sorry, Mama," we say to her with our heads down.

Hope leaps off the steps and runs to us. "Tell me everything," she insists.

"The adults are going out to eat," Mama announces turning away from us. "And you two have extra chores to do."

"Hey, we are adults," Fabby points out.

"Not today you weren't. You two can't be drawing so much attention to yourselves. Do you want Libby to have to leave school again?" Mama asks.

"No," we answer.

"Good. I'm going to clean up. Papa will be home soon, and I'm sure he'll have more to say to you."

She scales the steps and vanishes into the house. Hope pulls Fabby and me toward the barn. "Let's go feed the goats, and you can tell me what happened."

Asher and Karma aren't in their pen when we open it. I walk out the other door and, in the distance, Karma stares at us over the hill. "What is he doing out there?" I say glancing at Fabby as she sets their bucket of vegetables down.

"I don't know. Come on."

When we reach the top, Karma trots down the other side and over to Asher who's lying on the ground crying. "Asher," I scream, running towards him.

A spring-loaded trap bites down on his lower back leg. I seize it with both hands and squeeze my eyes shut. A hunter set it there this morning, just on the edge of the property, in hopes of catching an elusive grey fox.

"Can you open it?" Fabby asks me.

I open my eyes and stare at her. "You and Hope go see if Papa is home. He will have to carry Asher home and call the vet."

"What about you?"

"I need to see a hunter about a fox," I say as I force the teeth apart and remove Asher's leg.

Fabby steers Hope back to the hill, and they hustle back to the house as I enter the woods. I pick up a heavy stick and carry it with me. Several feet in, I discover another trap and slap it with my branch. I keep going, following the direction of footprints in the mud. One after another, I spring the traps.

I slowly approach a small fire, and tent in the center of the forest. I peer inside, but it's empty. A backpack sits beside a tree trunk. I sit down and open it.

"Emmit Jeffrey Travers," I say aloud.

"Yeah, that's me," a voice says startling me from behind. "I'd appreciate it if you wouldn't go through my stuff," he says as he sets down a bundle of fish.

"And I'd appreciate you not setting traps near my family's property," I insist tossing his bag on the ground.

"Well, near and on are two different animals, young lady."

"One of your traps injured my goat."

"Then your goat should stay out of the woods," he snickers as he picks up his pack and tosses it in the tent. "Now if you don't mind, I need to make dinner."

"You're hunting out of season, and I want you to quit."

"Or what? You'll call the cops on me. Please, they have better things to do with their time."

I storm towards him, and he backs away. "I said stop."

"No," he says leaning over me.

I grab his arm but let go after only a few seconds.

He lives here. That's why he won't stop. It's how he pays for his food and survives. After his wife passed, the insurance company found a loophole so they wouldn't have to pay him benefits. He lost his house and had nowhere to go. No employer wants to hire him due to his age. This isn't how someone who spent years protecting our country should be living.

"Come with me," I say reaching for him.

"How did you do that?" he asks, rubbing his arm where I held him.

"It doesn't matter. You're not staying here for another minute," I insist as I remove his backpack from the tent and start walking.

"Wait," he says running to catch up to me. "Where are we going?"

"Home."

"Home? I don't have a home."

"You do now," I smile and hike his bag farther onto my shoulder. "What do you go by, Emmit, or Jeffrey?"

"Emmit."

"Nice to meet you, Emmit. I'm Libby."

"Well, Libby that's a nice gesture, but I don't think your parents would appreciate you bringing a stranger home and offering their house to live in."

"They'll understand," I say without looking back as we breach the tree line and Papa walks towards us with his shotgun.

Emmit freezes and puts his arms in the air.

"Papa, this is Emmit. Put your gun down. He needs a job and a place to stay," I advise him as I walk by and head up the hill.

"Libby, I need a bit more information than that," Papa says with his gun still trained on the hunter.

I turn around and stagger down to him. "Papa, he lives in the woods. No one will hire him, and he lost his home after serving his country for over forty years. He's staying with us, and we are helping him." I take the rifle from him and continue up the hill. "How's Asher?"

"Put your hands down," Papa says to Emmit ignoring my question. "I'm Hector."

"Pleasure to meet you, but you don't have to help me. I can take care of myself."

"I'm sure you can, but we aren't going to let you," Papa says guiding Emmit forward.

"So, your daughter tells you she's bringing a stranger into your home and you're okay with it," Emmit says raising his gray eyebrows.

"If she trusts you, then so do I."

"God bless you, son," he says wiping tears from his bloodshot eyes with his blue plaid sleeve.

When Papa, Emmit and I near the house, the traveling vet exits the barn. "How's Asher?" I ask.

He glances at Papa and shakes his head. "I'm sorry, but between his age and injury, I had to put him down."

"What?" I cry.

"Young lady, the truth is I don't know how he lived this long. The same goes for his unicorn friend. You took good care of him, and he had a good life.

"I'm sorry," Emmit says to me, and Papa.

"It's okay," Papa says patting Emmit on his back. "He's in goat heaven now."

Karma mopes out of the barn and trots towards the house. I shake my head as he walks up the stairs and goes into the house when Will opens the door. He's already missing him.

"Everything okay?" he asks, moving his blazer aside and revealing his badge.

I put my head down, hiding my tears.

"We're okay. This is Emmit," Papa says as he climbs the steps. "And we are eating in tonight."

"Huh," Will says shaking Emmit's hand and staring at me. "Your idea?"

"Yes," I sniffle and wipe my running nose. "Asher is dead."

He sighs and hugs me. "I'm sorry, Libby."

Mama wrinkles her nose when Emmit shakes her hand. "Emmit, before you sit down at my table, you need a shower. Come with me, and I'll show you around."

Regina drops an extra placemat at the table, and whispers to Will.

"I already know," I say to them as my glass thumps on the table. "You're having another baby. That's what you wanted to tell Mama and Papa over dinner, isn't it?"

"Boy, we can't get anything past you, can we?" Will asks me.

"Want to know what you're having?"

"We'd like that," Regina says holding Will's hand.

"Come here," I say waving her to my side of the room.

Regina stands before me, and I rest my palm on her lower abdomen.

"Well, that's unexpected," I say removing my hand and taking another drink of water.

"Libby, don't play games and leave us in suspense. Are we having a boy or a girl?"

"Guess," I smile at them.

"Boy," Will announces.

"No, it's a girl I just know it," Regina insists.

"Both," Hope shouts from across the room.

"Ha, ha, very funny young lady," Regina giggles looking from Hope to me as I raise my eyebrows.

"No," Regina says covering her mouth. "Are you serious?"

"Serious about what," Mama says entering the room.

"They're having twins. A boy and a girl," I say to Mama over Regina's shoulder.

"Oh, lord. I'm going to need some extra help if I'm planning to teach Hope and care for two more babies," Mama says fanning her sweating face. "When are you due?"

Will doesn't reply. He stares at Regina's belly and rubs it softly. "We are having twins."

"Yay," Hope yells hugging them. "Can they sleep in my room?"

"We'll see," Regina replies.

Mama walks away and into the kitchen. I hug her from behind and whisper in her ear. "Thank you for letting Emmit stay."

"Next time, could you please ask before you offer, Libby?"

"Of course, Mama."

Fabby appears from the hallway. "May I introduce our new maintenance man and gardener, Emmit."

Emmit enters the kitchen a different man. Fabby trimmed his hair, shaved the sides, and shaped his once unruly grey beard into a neat and clean goatee. A tiny square of toilet paper with a red dot sticks to the side of his cheek.

Mama pulls a chair away from the table. "Welcome to the family, Emmit."

Karma nudges Fabby's leg, and she rotates the ball on his horn. "I'm sorry. I know you miss him. I do too. But death is a part of life, and you'll see him again someday."

Emmit chokes on his words as he takes a seat and folds his hands before him. "I am so sorry about your goat. I've never known such kindness in all my years. If I were you, I may not have been so forgiving. Thank you for trusting me with your family and home, despite what I did."

"You were just trying to survive," I say sitting beside him.

He looks down at his clothes and changes the subject. "I wish my wife could have seen me in this get-up," Emmit says straightening the dress pants and cream button-up Papa lent him.

"She sees you," I say staring behind him, as I place a plate of food between his arms.

"Is she here?" he asks me.

"She is."

"What is she wearing?"

"A white, short-sleeved dress that stops just passed her knees with tiny…"

"Pink roses," Emmit says finishing my sentence.

I nod and sit beside him. "I love her red lipstick."

"Miriam loved her Avon lipsticks," he smiles as he closes his eyes.

"Emmit, she says her father left her a trust account."

"What account?"

"If your wife had any unclaimed money when she died, it would go to the state," Papa says taking his phone out of his pocket and searching the Ohio website for unclaimed funds. "Here, type in her information, as much as you can, and if there is anything out there, this will tell you."

Emmit punches the screen with his pointer then hits search. There are two accounts listed. One of them was the insurance company that refused to pay.

"I don't understand. They said they wouldn't pay for her policy. Why does it say there are unclaimed funds from life insurance?"

"Well, Emmit, either they told you that so you wouldn't pursue it, or they realized they made a mistake and could not contact you to fix it. Now all you have to do is call them and supply a death certificate and they'll turn anything over to you. This other one appears to be a trust account, like your wife said," Papa says. "Tomorrow, I can help you gather what you need, and we can find out together."

"I don't know how to thank you. You have no idea how much this means to me."

"Don't thank us. Thank Miriam," I smile.

"Can she hear me?"

"Of course."

"Miriam, I'm sorry I wasn't there for you when you passed. I just couldn't take seeing you suffer. I love you."

"She said, no you don't," I laugh.

"That was a joke we would always say. I would tell her I love her, and she'd always say, 'No you don't,' and we'd laugh and laugh. Oh, how I miss her smile."

"You'll see her again, someday," I say resting my hand on his, "But for now, she wants you to eat. She says you're too skinny."

Emmit chuckles as he places his fabric napkin on his lap. "Well, I guess we better get to it. I don't want to disobey the old lady, do I? Mind if I say grace?"

"We'd like that," Mama says interlacing her fingers.

Everyone closes their eyes except for me and Papa. He glances at everyone at the table, then sets his eyes on me and winks.

I wink back, close my eyes, and pray with Emmit.

Chapter Thirty-Nine
Windfall

Papa helped Emmit gather all the necessary paperwork to claim his wife's insurance policy and her trust account. After Emmit sent copies of her death certificate and his driver's license to them, the insurance company released the funds electronically to his newly opened bank account.

To Emmit's surprise, his wife's policy payout comes to over one hundred thousand dollars. When he requested more information about the trust, they told him an attorney would meet him in person to deliver a cashier's check. Either way, Emmit has enough to buy a small house for himself. Papa is taking him to check out a few today. He's waiving his commission to keep more money in Emmit's pocket.

I drop the galvanized buckets on the ground outside the barn, but Karma just doesn't come out. He stands in the doorway with his head down.

"He's depressed. It may be a few days before he eats," Fabby says stepping off the porch. "Better clean them muddy shoes off before you get in the car. I just shampooed my carpets."

"I will. Do you think Kensie told everyone what my name means?" I ask as I hose off the bottom of my shoes.

"Who cares, Libby. It's just a name."

I scruff the top of Karma's head when he approaches me, pick up my bag, and slide inside the car. We both wiggle our noses and glance at the fresh goat poop on my soles.

"Out!" Fabby shouts.

I roll my eyes and jog back into the house. Emmit raises his coffee mug to me and smiles at my shoeless feet. "Stepped in poo?"

"Yes."

"I've done that a time or two," he chuckles to himself.

The only other shoes I have are my white canvas sneakers and they won't go with the sweater I am wearing or my leggings. I quickly remove my clothes, toss them in the hamper, and pull on army-green skinny jeans, a white V-neck t-shirt, and my sneakers.

I look in the mirror and grimace. My bright pink bra shows through the material of my top, so I take the top off again, change my bra for a cream sports bra, and pull my t-shirt on a second time.

My morning sucks.

I speed down the front steps, steer around Karma's poop pile I stepped in earlier, and flop back into the car beside Fabby.

"We are so going to be late."

"I'm sorry, Fabby."

"It is what it is," she sighs and peers over the seat as she backs up.

Adam loiters in the parking lot when we arrive.

"I think he likes you," Fabby smiles as she turns off her headlights.

"He wants to be a pastor."

"And he's wholesome? Good for you Libby."

"Fabby, stop. We just met."

"No. He just met you. You know everything about him thanks to your superpowers."

"Knowing everything about someone and knowing them are two different things."

"Yeah, yeah. Come on. Let's get this day over with. Mama and Papa said we could go to the mall tomorrow after school."

"Really? So, they are ungrounding us?"

"Not exactly. A client of Papa's gave him four tickets, and there is a movie they want to see."

"Well, at least we get to get out of the house," I say as I pull myself out of the car, and wave at Adam.

He takes long strides to reach us faster and sticks his arms out palms up. "Here, let me carry your books for you."

"That's okay. I can manage."

Adam puts his head down and starts walking beside me.

"So, how much trouble did you two get in for yesterday?"

"The principal just gave us detention for one day after school," Fabby grins.

Her face pales, then turns red, when she picks up the flyer of me off the ground. My face replaces the skull of skull and crossbones. Across the top, in bold, black letters reads, '*Beware: death has come to our school.*' She crumples it up and launches it aside.

They're everywhere. Two teachers are removing them and throwing them in the trash by a pillar holding up the school's overhang. This had to have taken all night. Off to the side, Kensie, and Kayla giggle with two other girls while

Janette and Anna rip the images down and ball them up in their fists.

When Fabby's two loyal remaining friends walk up to us, they tell us it's worse than we thought.

"They're inside too," Janette murmurs. "I'm sorry, Libby."

My heart pounds inside my head, as my ears start to ring. Fabby talks to me, but I don't understand what she's saying. Someone's hand touches my arm, and images of the school blowing off its foundation storm through my head as I scream. "Libby, don't," Adam says shaking me.

"Don't what?" Anna asks.

"Look at me," Adam whispers as he puts his face in my line of sight, blocking the front of the school.

The breeze picks up strength, gusts across my back, and blows all the fliers off the walls, and into Kensie and Kayla's faces, cutting them with their edges. Blood seeps between their fingers as they shield their heads and I move closer. Another hand joins Adam's as Fabby pleads with me to stop. "Libby, let it go."

I continue moving forward. I can't stop. It's happening again.

Fabby wraps her arms around me and squeezes me tight. "I love you Libby, but what you are doing is wrong. Please, I beg you. Stop before you do something God can't forgive."

The ringing in my ears subsides, and so does the wind. They're talking to me, but I can no longer decipher what they are saying. My muscles twitch in unison as my body starts vibrating.

"Libby!" Fabby shouts as I land hard on the pavement and shake violently.

I see them. The reaper, angel, and demon I destroyed by accident. They reach for me, and I turn away from them as Fabby shifts me to my side and speaks in my ear.

I'm hallucinating.

The blacktop cracks beneath me as I fight to bring myself back to the present and away from this hell I'm trapped in.

Adam covers the crack with his backpack and sticks his jacket under my head. "Libby, it's okay to be afraid," Adam whispers. "You did nothing wrong."

Is fear what causes my seizures?

I need to feel something else. I shift my eyes to Fabby. Tears flood her face as Adam's forehead touches hers, and they pray for me.

Why won't it stop? Am I so angry that I can't let it go?

Kensie's face appears crowding out Adam and Fabby. "Libby, I'm so sorry. Please forgive me. I went too far. Please don't die. I didn't mean it. I made a mistake," she cries.

A droplet of her tears mixed with blood falls in slow motion into my open eye burning it with its salt. Whispers echo inside my head and repeat the same word over and over.

Forgive.

My lips quiver together as I try and speak. Kensie leans down to listen.

"I forgive you."

"Thank…you." She chokes on her words, and pants heavily as she seizes my face with both hands. "I'm sorry I hurt you."

The principal disperses the crowd as an ambulance rolls towards us with their lights and sirens blaring. My jeans are wet when Kensie helps me sit up, but her jacket hides it.

"Three minutes, and forty-five seconds, Libby. That's too long," Fabby sobs wiping the moisture from her face with the back of her sleeve. "I thought I was going to lose you."

"You'll never lose me," I say hugging her.

A paramedic pulls Fabby back, shifting her out of the way. He wraps a blood pressure cuff around my bicep, while another medic drops a rolling stretcher out of the van.

"I don't need to go to the hospital."

He moves the coat away from my lower half and sighs. "Yes, you do."

"No, I don't," I insist.

The paramedic glances at Fabby who shakes her head.

"Okay. I can't force you to come, but I think you should call your parents and have them take you home."

"I will," I say as he puts his hand out to help me up, but I get up on my own. "Thank you."

"You're welcome."

Kensie ties her jacket around my waist. "I have extra sweatpants in my locker. Go through that door and meet me in the bathroom."

"I'm sorry about your face," I say to her.

"It's not your fault I look like I got in a fight with a feral cat. It's mine."

"Where's Kayla?" Fabby asks Kensie.

"She's removing the rest of the fliers from the hallways. I made a mistake, and I'm sorry, Fabby. Can you forgive me too?"

"If Libby can, so can I," Fabby says hugging her.

After changing into the navy blue sweatpants Kensie brought me, I walked down to the office. Emmit puts his arm around me and pulls me to his side. "You okay, kiddo?"

"Yeah. Just a dumb seizure."

Papa exits the principal's office and shakes his hand. He stops at the counter and scratches a quick signature on the sign-out log.

"Come here," he says drawing me into him. "Fabby said this was a long one. Are you sure you don't want to see a neurologist?"

"No, Papa. I'll be fine."

"I have a few more places to show Emmit. I can drop you off at home, or you can come."

"I'll tag along."

"Good. I can't seem to get a read on any of these houses your father is showing me. If my Miriam were here, she'd tell me what to do," Emmit says.

"Perhaps if we find the right one, she will stop by and let us know," I smile at him.

"Wouldn't that be something?"

"Emmit, why don't you tell Libby the good news," Papa says opening the passenger side door for me.

"What news?"

"I met with Miriam's family attorney today and he gave me the trust account check."

"And?"

"And see for yourself," Emmit grins passing me an envelope.

I bend back the flap and slide out a cashier's check for three million four hundred and fifty thousand two hundred and twenty-five dollars.

"Wow."

"Wow, indeed," he chuckles. "More than I can spend in the time I have left."

"So, are you buying a bigger house?"

"No. All I need is enough room for me, and maybe a dog."

"Are you buying a dog?" I ask raising my eyebrows.

"Not buying. Adopting."

"That's sweet of you, Emmit. I am glad everything worked out for you."

"Well, young lady, it wouldn't have if it weren't for you showing me mercy. Thank you."

"No problem, Emmit."

Papa steers into the driveway of a one-level ranch, with a nice-sized fenced-in yard, surrounded by wildflowers, and a small, elevated garden. His face lights up when he walks around the side of the house. "There's an old hand pump well outback just like when I was a boy," he grins.

"I think this might be the one," I announce as I smile at his wife sitting on the porch steps watching him.

"Is it Miriam approved?" Emmit asks me.

"Yes, it is."

"Well then, it's sold. Hector, draw up the papers."

"Don't you want to look inside first?"

"No need. If my Miriam likes it, then so do I."

Papa and I exchange smiles as he removes a folder from between the seats, opens it on the hood, and passes Emmit a pen. "Well, Emmit, make your offer."

Chapter Forty
Rash

Despite buying a new house, and having plenty of money, Emmit continues working around the farm with Papa. Today they are repairing the hole in the fence by the woods.

After yesterday's ordeal, Mama thought it would be best that I stay home. I'm glad I listened. Something about today seems off. I don't want to talk, and I can't eat. When I'm like this, I'm not sure what to do with myself, so I go sit in the barn.

I tuck my robe tighter around me, lie down on a bale of hay, and stare at Karma. He refuses to eat. All he does is wander around the yard, making weird crying noises. Mud cakes the outer rim of my slippers, and the bottoms of my pajamas are wet. I close my eyes and listen to Papa and Emmit hammering in the distance.

Blood is everywhere. It drips down my hands when I raise them. I try and look beyond my bloody palms, but the more I try and focus, the more the background blurs. Heat warms my back as fire rages behind me. A horse nays at my side, and I climb on its pale back staining its mane with my soiled hands. It gallops through the woods and stops on a cliff. Down below, hundreds of people—men, women, and children scream as they fall into the pits of hell. I feel nothing for them as they claw the surface of the earth pleading for their lives. Something heavy pulls on my shoulders. I reach back and touch the wings of a massive bird. My horse turns, revealing our reflection in a mirror. It's no bird. I have wings, one white, and one gnarly, clawed, and black. In the mirror, a demon crawls from the cliff edge behind me with a flaming torch and lights my white wing on fire while I shriek.

'Libby!'

Someone's yelling my name, but I can't see them.

'Libby, wake up!'

My skin burns and a bright light singes my eyes while I scream.

"Libby, wake up!" Papa shouts jolting me hard.

Mama stands behind him with Emmit. I stare at them as I tremble, and pant heavily.

"It was just a bad dream, Libby," Papa insists.

"It's never just a dream, Papa," I sob as I clutch his shirt and fall into his arms. "Something bad is going to happen."

Emmit frowns and leaves the barn. Mama sits on the other side of me and holds my clammy hand. "Libby, as long as we are around, nothing will happen to you."

I remain silent. Telling them what I saw won't help anyone for it isn't me that is in danger, it's everyone else. I glance in the corner, where Karma lies motionless. "Karma?"

Mama leans away from me and stands over the goat. Her eyes water when she turns around and looks at me. "I'm sorry, Libby."

"Why when bad things happen do they always have to happen at once?" I ask wiping my face of tears.

Emmit returns to the barn carrying a twelve-gauge shotgun. He pumps it once and aims it at the ground. "If trouble's coming, I'll be ready."

"Thanks, Emmit, but it's not that kind of trouble." I hop off the hay and sink into the soil before him. "No one can stop what's coming."

I hold myself around the waist and trudge my way back to the house. Crying won't bring Karma and Asher back, so I suppress my emotions and turn off the waterworks. "No more crying today, Libby," I say to myself as I head to the bathroom.

Dirt swirls down the drain as I step into the shower with my clothes on and wash the filth from my frame. My sopping robe slides down my salty skin and lands on the tub floor. I kick it behind me and remove my tank top. The water strikes my back like shards of glass as I turn around. I flinch away and grab my shoulder.

Fluid-filled blisters cover my back like boils. I step out of the tub and wipe the foggy mirror with my palm. In the blurry reflection, two angry rashes bubble, and burst on my shoulder blades stinging me with their fluid.

I drop to my knees onto the cold floor tiles and search under the sink for a remedy for my rash.

"God, what am I?" I whisper as I sob.

The door cracks open and bumps my legs. I shift to the side, and Mama throws herself at my feet. "Libby, what's wrong?"

"Can't you see them?" I ask riffling through the cabinet.

"See what?"

"The blisters on my shoulders. The weeping rash. Can't you see it?" I ask pointing to my upper back.

"Libby, there is nothing there," she insists swiping my back with her palm.

It didn't hurt when she touched me. I stagger to a stand and hunch my back towards the mirror.

Nothing.

I continue holding my shoulder as I stare at her frowning face. "Mama, I think I'm hallucinating."

She reaches into the linen closet, removes an oversized towel, and wraps it around me. "Come on, Libby. Let's get you to your room."

The mattress drops as I sink into it, and watch Mama dig through my dresser for clothes. "How about you put these on...," she says setting grey sweatpants, with a matching sweatshirt, and undergarments on the comforter beside me, "...while I go make you breakfast."

"Mama, thank you but I'm not hungry."

Hope runs in, and dives onto the bed beside me. "Want me to make breakfast?"

Mama smiles at Hope's progress. After many, many cooking lessons, Hope can finally make a full meal without burning anything.

"That would be great, Hope," Mama smiles. "Let's go."

I scrub my disheveled wet hair with the towel, throw it in the direction of the hamper, and pull on my clothes. My pajamas and robe are no longer in the bathtub when I go back to retrieve them.

Hope drags a chair away from the table and slaps the seat. "Sit by me."

Mama calls Papa and Emmit inside for breakfast. I set a mat at the table for each of us and help Mama carry the dishes to the table. Hope scoops a heaping pile of eggs onto her plate.

"That's way too many eggs for you," I say pushing the scrambled protein out of her reach.

I remove some of the eggs from her plate and drop them on mine. She stabs two sausages with her fork, dips them in syrup, and sucks the sweet sauce from their surface. "Fine. I'll just eat extra sausage."

Emmit chuckles. "That's how I like my sausage too. Smothered in syrup." He picks one up, dispenses a line of syrup on its surface, and shoves the entire link in his mouth. "Mmm... That's good stuff."

Hope laughs and stuffs a whole one in her yap, and immediately starts coughing. I slap her back as she gasps for air, and gags. The meat shoots out of her throat, lands on Mama's white tablecloth, and rolls toward Emmit. Mama tosses her napkin over it and furrows her brow. "Hope, cut up your food like a lady."

"Sorry," Hope says wiping the tears from her lids and taking a drink of water.

I rub my skin, checking for the phantom rash, but it doesn't exist.

"Libby, what was your nightmare about?" Papa asks as he stabs a pancake with his fork and drops it on his plate.

"I was sitting on a horse by a cliff, with one white wing, and one black watching demons throw people—men, women, and children into the lake of fire. A demon crawls over a cliff and lights my white wing with a torch."

"Sounds like you're struggling with the good and bad within yourself," Emmit says taking a small bite of sausage and winking at Hope as she cuts hers with a fork.

"I am," I say as I scrape a stain on the tablecloth with my fingernail.

"Well, I can tell you who you are not," Mama says refilling my orange juice. "Evil. From the moment God brought you into our lives we have been nothing but blessed," she smiles.

"Then why would I be shown both sides?" I say glancing at everyone for an answer. "Why did God give me the ability to hurt anything, and everything? Why would He do that if there is no purpose for it?"

"Libby, everything God does is for a reason. He created you for something special, and it is only He who knows what that is," Papa says standing up. "Give Him time. He will come to you and give you the answers you're looking for when the time is right."

I leave the table and go to my room. Nothing anyone says brings me comfort. The pit in my stomach only grows the more I think about my nightmare.

God wasn't in it. It was only me and the demons of hell. Why would I watch people die, and not care? That's not who I am.

God's message changes from one book to the next, but its' meaning is the same. No matter what country, religion, or origin you come from, or what you believe, they all speak the same truth.

He is coming.

Chapter Forty-One
Lost

I wish I could stay home, but Papa thought if we all still went shopping and to the movies as planned, it would take my mind off things.

He was right of course. After hitting several stores, we took our bags to the car and sat in the food court eating bagel sandwiches. I peer over the second-floor balcony. It's busier than usual for a Friday on account of the mall-wide sidewalk sales.

A set of twin girls bump into me on their way to the arcade. I gaze at Fabby. We aren't twins or even blood relatives for that matter, but we may as well be. Our bond is closer than many siblings we've met over the years. Some sisters grow apart as they age, and try to be their unique selves, but not Fabby and me. She catches me staring at her, joins me at the overlook, and rests her hand on mine.

External sounds disappear, and my ears begin ringing. I thought for sure a seizure was imminent, but something's different.

Something's wrong.

I slide my fingers from under her grasp and move away from her.

"Libby?" Fabby whispers as she moves back closer. "What is it?"

Heavy footsteps echo like a heartbeat in slow motion. I glance over the glass partition to the center court down below. The sun reflects into my eye as a door leading inside pushes inward.

A masked man, wearing all black, and carrying an automatic weapon, strolls through the entrance. The sound in my head speeds up as he trains his gun on his first victim and pulls the trigger.

Patrons scatter as the man in dark sunglasses sprays bullets into a crowd of shoppers. I scoop Fabby around the waist, throw her to the ground, and dive on top of her.

Mama and Papa run for us, as a second gunman appears behind them, and cocks his handgun. I push off my sister and dart towards them. Blood splatters my face and Mama falls to the tile.

I stop.

I'm stuck.

Everything slows down.

This must be a dream.

A bullet grazes my arm, stinging my flesh.

This is real.

A man from the table next to us throws himself over me and tucks Fabby under his arm. Papa kneels distraught beside Mama, covering her holes. "Stay with me, Lola," he cries.

His body flies to the side as a bullet pierces his temple.

"Noooooooooo!" I scream.

The stranger struggles to keep me under his frame.

Multiple reapers fill the first and second floors and mill about as the gunfire continues. I break free from the hero when a projectile sails by his face, slices through his clavicle, and lands in his upper chest.

The same reaper who came to give me the news about Dark One condenses beside my parents. "I'm sorry," it says as it rests its smokey palms, one on Mama and one on Papa, and removes their souls.

A godly creature lights up the space above my mother and takes her apparition. I seize its wing, blackening it with my rage as I shriek. The angel thrashes about as I yank it, trying to force it to let Mama go.

The man who gave his life to save mine fights to stay on the surface as the demons pull him toward hell. Mama tilts her translucent head and nods.

I shake my head. "No, Mama. Don't go," I plead.

Heat warms my face as she strokes it with her hand. She wants me to let go.

I turn to Papa. "I can't be without her," he murmurs.

Tears plaster my face, cleansing the blood from my cheeks, as I stare at the smoke coming from the angel's feathers.

I release the feathered appendage, letting the only mother I've ever known go to heaven. Another angel takes my Papa and carries him through the ceiling and out of sight.

The man, who protected my sister and me, screams as he disappears into the black hole. He may not go to heaven, but he isn't going to hell either, not after he sacrificed himself for us. I dive over the edge and reach into the abyss to retrieve him. I grip the claws of the creature holding him under and shrill. "Let him go."

It hisses back and digs its black talons further into the man's spine while squinting its orbs.

"I said let go!" I holler and punch my fist through its slimy skull. Its body falls into the darkness as the man's ghost wanders about searching for his purpose.

I scour the area for the shooters. One is below and to the right on the first floor scanning for more victims. The other shoots someone in the distance near the movie theater concession stand.

"Libby," Fabby murmurs my name.

Blood drools from her mouth when I finally look at her. "Fabby!" I scream searching for her wound.

A crimson puddle pools under her. A bullet pierced her side, puncturing her lung. I press my hands over the opening. "Please don't leave me, Fabby," I cry as her lips turn blue and she gasps for air.

The reaper appears beside her, waiting to take her away. "No!" I holler at it.

Her eyes go empty as a single tear slides down her temple and drips into her ear.

A ring of light surrounds her, and I knew at that moment I lost them all.

My eyes turn dark, and my face reddens as I move toward the spiritual creatures. The reaper points to the gunman behind me, reminding me who is to blame.

Everything liquid boils inside me, and my skin prickles. The ground quakes beneath me as I seize my hair in my fists and shriek louder than a thousand sirens going at once.

Angels, demons, and reapers vaporize as the aura emanating from my body fires through the air like a shockwave wiping the mall of their existence. The gunmen freeze where they stand as I screech my wrath in their direction. They take their sidearms, point them at their heads, and pull the trigger.

I gaze at my red, shaking palms as red and blue lights flash through an exterior storefront below.

Everyone is dead.

Everyone except me.

Why was I spared? Was it to punish those responsible for this atrocity?

Despair overwhelms me as I tremble and weep uncontrollably.

I want to be with them.

I want to die.

I should have died.

My legs give way, and I collapse on the tile beside my sister. I grasp her motionless hand, shut my eyes, and pray for death.

Glass shatters downstairs as a SWAT team breaches the mall. I open my eyes, and my sister stares back at me. I reach over and close her lids. Footsteps move as one as the police work to clear the first floor. I pinch a lock of Fabby's hair away from her face and curl it behind her ear. The blood of my family soaks into my clothing as I turn onto my back and gaze at the blood moon shining through the skylight. My lip quivers as an officer's face appears in my field of vision.

"Come with me," he insists tucking his arm under me.

"Don't touch me," I sob.

"You can't stay here. It's not safe," he insists trying to lift me.

"They're dead," I say to him.

"I know, and I'm sorry, but we have to go," he says picking me up.

"No!" I shout and thrash in his arms until he lets me go.

I crawl to Mama and Papa and hug their warm bodies. "Why did this happen?"

"I don't know," he murmurs wiping a tear from his cheek. "We really have to go."

"I'm not leaving them," I insist.

"Okay," he says sitting down and grabbing his radio. "What's your name?"

"Libitina Alvarez," I whimper as I choke on my words. "They killed my whole family."

The officer shuffles on his knees to me, takes my face in his hands, and whispers. "I'm sorry."

I collapse, hyperventilating in his arms, soaking his Kevlar vest with my tears as the all-clear comes over the radio. My name echoes down below, but I make no motion to stand.

"Libby!" Will yells landing hard on the ground in front of me.

"They're dead."

"I know," he cries as he pulls me away from the other officer.

He lifts me from the floor, but my legs don't work. Exhaustion zaps my strength, and heartbreak crushes my spirit. He hoists me up into his arms and carries me to the stairs.

Bodies lie motionless everywhere. An emotionless woman with a bullet hole in her leg holds her dead infant son on her lap. A young girl lies sideways on the wall surrounding the fountain still holding her mint chip ice cream cone. The green cream melts down the stone and mixes with her blood.

Will swerves around the gunman as another officer removes the assailant's face covering and jumps back.

Black holes take the place of the man's eyes. The officer makes the sign of the cross and covers his body with a sheet.

"Don't look," Will says as we turn down the hall leading to the exit.

"I made them kill themselves," I whisper to him.

"Libby, you're going to be okay."

"I've sinned."

"You punished them."

"I'm a sinner."

"They deserved it."

"I'm going to hell."

"Not if I can help it."

He slides me into the back of a patrol car and climbs in beside me. "Hospital," Will says to the officer behind the wheel. He puts his arm around me. "Regina and Hope are meeting us there. Everything will be okay."

"No, Will. It won't."

Chapter Forty-Two
What I Am

He is here with me. We sit upon a cliff of an unknown place and gaze out at the ocean as waves crash to shore.

I can't look at Him. The bright light surrounding Him blinds me. His solemn words filter through my head and reveal why He created me.

I am His wrath, and my purpose is clear. The decision is mine. I am the only thing separating the people of this earth from annihilation. If they don't change and heed His warning, I can't stop what's coming.

God took my family, but He did so for a reason.

He needs me to be angry.

He needs me to want revenge.

What happened at the mall was a mere glimpse of the power He has bestowed upon me. With the warm touch of his hand on my scalp, He awakens all of it. Everything I need to punish and destroy anyone, and everyone burns through my veins.

He knew if I had someone to lose, I wouldn't let Him give this to me. I would leave it as is, and only punish the wicked.

I miss my family, so if this is what it takes to be with them again, I will do His bidding. He drops a heavy skeleton key into my palm and disappears. It burns through my flesh and

chars my hand. I curl my fingers as it vanishes inside me. This is
where it will stay until I make my decision.

The reaper who took my family sits beside me as I flutter
my wings, and gaze at my branding. We swing our legs
over the edge and sit in silence as the sun goes down.

"What does it open?" the reaper asks, turning to me.

"The gates," I say without looking at it.

"Heaven or Hell?"

"Both."

"Do you think they will change if they know what's
coming?"

I rest the side of my face on my bent knee, and sigh. "No.
But I have to try."

I dive off the cliff edge and soar into the last remaining
light of the sunset.

My eyes flicker open, and Hope's eyes light up. "She's
awake," she yells over her shoulder.
Regina and Will stand beside my bed. I stare at the PICC
line sticking out of my arm and glare at them.

"What's this?"

"You passed out in the car, and I couldn't wake you. The
doctors gave you fluids and took some blood," Regina says
resting her hand on my forehead.

A man sweeps into the room wearing a long white lab
coat. "Agh, sorry to interrupt. I'm the resident on staff. They
asked me to take another blood sample."

"Why? You took eight vials from her?" Regina asks.
"And why are you doing it instead of a nurse?"

"They think the sample somehow got contaminated, so
they want another."

"Which sample?" Will asks as the doctor pulls on gloves.

"All of them," he says, raising his brows.

"No," I say yanking the line out and ignoring the blood rushing from my arm.

"You can't leave, yet, Libby," Regina says holding gauze over the hole in my arm.

"Does Auntie Marie know?"

"We thought you should be the one to do the notification," Will sighs, sitting in the chair at the foot of the bed.

"No. I need you to take Hope, and go see her," I announce walking towards the door.

"Libby, where are you going?" Hope asks following me.

"I have something important to do."

I put my head down, head for the door, and walk straight into Pastor James.

"Libby, I came as soon as I heard."

He tries to hug me, and I flinch away. "Don't touch."

"I'm sorry about your family," he says dabbing his eyes with a pocket handkerchief. "If there is anything I can do for you, please don't hesitate to ask."

"Change people."

"Libby, all we can do in this life is guide people in the right direction. We can't force them to do what's right."

"Then everyone is doomed."

Tears race down my face as I turn my back on him. Cool air floats up my naked backside as I stand before the elevators and punch the down arrow. The doors clank open, and Sister Mary Beth exits. Her eyes lock on mine and turn to saucers.

She knows something. Perhaps God came to her too. It doesn't matter. She has her mission and I have mine. I press the button for the parking garage, and the doors begin closing.

A hand seizes the opening and wretches it aside. Sister Mary Beth wedges her body in between, keeping me from leaving.

"Move." I take a step towards her.

She does not waver. "I know your purpose."

"I said, move." I take another step.

"There must be something we can do to stop this."

I stand an inch from her face, and scream in an ungodly voice, "Deliver...His... message!"

The fluorescent bulbs lining the hallway burst simultaneously.

She shows no fear and stands her ground. "Sweet child, remember who you are. This may be what He wants, but it's your decision to make."

I shove her back, and she lands hard on the floor. Regina, Will, Hope, and Pastor James run towards us. "My family is dead. Those people in the mall—men, women, children, are dead," I yell as she crab walks away from me. "And you want me to be forgiving?"

"Please, Libby. Give them a chance," she pleads.

"Deliver His message."

"What message?"

I stand tall over her and point to the growing crowd in the hallway.

"...For if we sin willfully after that we have received the knowledge of the truth, there remaineth no more sacrifice for sins..." Hebrews 10:26-31

"What truth?" Pastor James asks approaching me.

I step over Sister Mary Beth and crank my neck at him. "If you wish to see the future, you must ask for me to show you."

His lip quivers as he glances at Sister Mary Beth who shakes her head. He swallows hard and wipes a tear from his cheek as I face him. "Show me."

I snatch his head in my hands and press my forehead to his. He tries pulling away as images flood his mind. Will grabs my arm. Now he sees what the pastor sees. Regina places her palm on Will's shoulder, and the effect is the same. Anyone who touches me, or anyone with their hands on those touching me, can see the truth.

Can see our future.

Can see our demise.

Pastor James pants heavily as I release him. I gaze over his bent-over frame at the massive chain of people behind him. Now they are aware of what's to come, and what they must do.

I fold myself over and whisper in his ear. "You are His witness, and so are they." I nod over his shoulder. "Deliver the message. Deliver His warning."

The elevator slams open behind me, and I back into it as Pastor James steps forward and reaches for me. In the reflection of his glasses, flames flicker and dim inside my eyes as the door slowly closes.

When I arrive in the lobby and step outside, reporters flood the sidewalk. I ignore them as they rush me, and flag down a cab.

A female reporter lunges her microphone in front of my lips as my hand grips the cab door. "Miss Alvarez, please tell us how it feels to survive the mall massacre."

I turn to her as the rage builds inside me and seize her head with both hands. "You want to know what it feels like to lose everyone you love? I'm going to show you."

Images of every member of her family barrel through her brain like a freight train. Bullets pierce their bodies, and I launch their souls into the lake of fire as I scream. Her mother's nails dig into a muddy embankment as a sharp, black claw seizes her by the hair. The demon plunges her head beneath the lava with a devilish grin on its face and points its smokey finger at the reporter. She turns to look behind her, where I wait with a smile of my own, and grip her neck. Her feet flutter high above a cliff as I dangle her over and release her into the abyss below.

She's dying, inside and out, so I let her go.

Her body drops to the pavement as she clutches her chest. I kneel before her and lift her chin. Her eyes meet mine, and I murmur. "Deliver His message, or what you see, will become the truth."

Her head drops as I take my hand away and turn to the cameras pointing at me.

"He's coming. Change now, or I will open the gates, and release the wrath of heaven and hell upon this planet, ridding it of its plague."

I tuck my head inside the cab and gaze at the driver's reflection. "Drive."

He nods his head and steers the yellow sedan through the vultures on the sidewalk. "Where to?"

"Somewhere, I can be alone to think."

I give the man instructions to my family's cabin, and he pulls the car to the curb. "Look, I don't mind driving you somewhere. But judging by your outfit, I don't think you can pay me what it will cost to drive that far."

I grip his shoulder and show him his future. It ends the same as all the rest, violently.

"If you don't take me somewhere, away from people, away from this city full of sinners, then I can't make a fair decision. It will be based on right now. How I am feeling at this very moment. Is that what you want?"

I let him go, and he grips the steering wheel with his trembling hands. "Whatever it takes to get you to change your mind. We aren't all bad you know?"

"So, I've heard, and so I've seen. But there aren't enough of us anymore. Our numbers are dwindling by the day and God has grown tired. He gave His only son, and there is no one left to sacrifice."

"Please, give us another chance. Everyone can change if given the time and opportunity."

"People divided long ago, and a house divided will not stand. The time to change is now, but I'm not hopeful."

"You need to have faith."

"I have faith, just not hope."

Chapter Forty-Three
Pick a Side

Being alone isn't so bad. There are no people, or demons here, not even reapers or angels. It's just me, struggling with an impossible decision.

Do I allow us to live on, and continue destroying ourselves in hopes that someday, we will find our faith, not only in God but in each other? Or do I open the gates and release the wrath of God on everyone for turning their backs on Him?

God chose me for a reason. Giving me the power to decide the fate of humanity isn't a gift.

It's a burden.

Are we worth saving? I know what my choices are, but I'm struggling. Everyone thought the apocalypse would be an event, but they were all wrong. I may be what some consider the fifth horseman according to scripture or folklore, but no other horseman came before me bringing war, famine, or death, it's already here. We did that to ourselves. I'm just the consequence.

My father, Thaddeus Reginald Yarrow, named me Libitina, and he wasn't wrong for doing so. For I am death, not only in name but in purpose. If I chose the unforgiving path, everyone would die, including me. I'm not afraid to go. It will give our planet a chance to start over. Perhaps the next round of organisms will do a better job taking care of it.

My family was my happiness. Victims of the senseless violence that plagues our world, why shouldn't I kill us all? I am nothing without them. They were my everything.

There are so few of us left who would help our fellow man without requiring something in return. People just stopped caring about one another. Consumed by greed, power, and control, none of us are free from sin, not anymore. We've all made mistakes, hurt those we love, and said things we didn't mean.

The question I'm left with is, if they see the truth of what's to come and decide to change for the better, what is to stop them from making the same mistake? I can't see the future, but I can prevent it from happening. Everything I remember up until now tells me we don't deserve to be here. None of us do.

I wish I didn't feel this way, but the actions of others sway me to the darkness that grips my soul and leaves my heart void of love.

The spirited ones all feel the wrath of my pain. It's been that way for years. But what they don't understand, what I have never told any of them, is I feel pain too. Every time someone sins, it is like shards of glass spinning in my brain like a blender, and I just want it to stop.

Even now, as I sit naked on decomposing leaves surrounded by dead trees, I can feel it slicing through my head. It's like Mother Earth herself wants to inform me that she too grows tired of our abuse, and unwillingness to care for God's gift of life on this dying planet. The earth will replenish in our absence. Perhaps not right away, but eventually, it will heal.

I turn my head and frown at our family cabin. It doesn't have much, but there is running water, and a portable cot, long forgotten, to sleep on. I used to love coming here when I was a little girl. We'd go for walks, talk to the forest, play in the creek, and gaze at the unobstructed stars.

Now it's ruined.

Trash litters the woods around the property from trespassing hunters, and Styrofoam cups float in the polluted creek. The pines along the waterway slowly die, and the night sky fills with smoke from the factory built nearby.

I force myself from the moist soil and stagger to the creaking stairs. The weathered rocker Mama used to sit in when she watched us, no longer holds weight.

Time rotted it, along with everything else.

The soft floor bends under my feet as I enter the bathroom, and swipe away a fresh cobweb. The pipes screech their objection as I turn on the faucet, and orange water sputters out. When it runs clear, I plug the tub and sink into it. Filth muddies the water as I cleanse my flesh with a worn bar of rose soap left behind long ago. My gnarled hair still holds the blood of my family. I hesitate, then plunge beneath the murky surface, and rinse myself of the last part of them that touched me. After I scrub away any sign of their existence that may remain, I unplug the stopper and watch as the rusty water swirls down the drain.

I could have gone to buy clothes before I came here, but what's the point? I came into this world with nothing, and so I shall leave it that way. I carry my hospital gown to the line and pinch open a clothespin. It snaps in half and drops bits of wood on my foot. An ant crawls over a large piece, then disappears into the dirt. How lucky is he to live beneath the surface?

The crumbs of the clothespin land soundless in the soot of our stone firepit. I stare at the scorched papers inside. My family only burned wood, so this is someone else's mess.

I'm exhausted. Physical activity would be less tiring than sorting out my thoughts. I could stay here forever and never decide either way, but it isn't what God wants.

By now, the truth is spreading across the globe. It will do one of two things, rip us apart, or bring us together to save us all. I'm guessing the former.

All catastrophes throughout history have come in waves—floods, wildfires, earthquakes, etc., spread out over time.

This will be different. There will be no time to recover, rebuild, or start over. Once it begins, wave after wave of destructive events will spread across our planet like the wind.

No one can escape His wrath once I unlock the gates. I can hide and save myself for a short time when it all begins, but I won't. We deserve what is coming to us.

When did our division even begin? Did it start as a disagreement between two friends, or over dinner at a family gathering? Perhaps it started long ago when the continents shifted, dividing the world into multiple pieces.

It doesn't matter now, does it? We had our chance, and we blew it. Too self-consumed with our own needs and wants, unwilling to sacrifice anything for anyone unless it benefits ourselves.

Look around.

Do it.

If you had the choice to save the person beside you, would you? Do they deserve it? More importantly, would they do the same for you?

I doubt it.

Too many of you would be too busy trying to save yourself.

And that is the problem.

That is why we ended up here.

Instead of working together to save our species, and buy us more time, we close off and guard ourselves like territorial animals.

For what?

Self-preservation.

Why would God give us such a thing? It pits us against each other.

It was a test, and we failed.

Like dominos we fell, one right after another, losing everything God gave us, even ourselves. Humanity was never meant to live here forever, but God knows that. We lease our time on this planet until it's time to find new tenants.

Well, the time is now, and I am here to evict you all.

None of us deserves to be here. Not even me. For me to do God's bidding, I too must sin. I don't want this job, but someone must do it. That's why He created me, saved me, and opened my eyes to the world around me.

Everywhere I glance, there are signs of our shortcomings. Not only did we fail as human beings, but we failed to be humane.

All the more reason He made it impossible for me to have children. He didn't want me to be weak at a time when I need great strength. Children are a blessing, but also can be a weakness. I need to see both sides, that's why He brought my family to me and showed me how wonderful, loving, and forgiving people can be.

Then He ripped it all away and showed me what the real world has become. Full of people who take pleasure in doing the most appalling, unthinkable, and unforgivable things. Not only here, but around the world. Every time I turn on the television, it's nothing but chaos. We are killing each other, stealing from our neighbors, injecting poison into our bodies, and starting wars for no other reason than power.

I feel it all now—love, loss, happiness, anger, having everything, and then nothing. It's all there, swirling around a big fat pile of disappointment, and despair.

Now I understand why God is so tired. Losing those you love every day, over and over again, would crush you. It takes your heart and turns it black with bitterness. We have the power to stop it, but we choose to continue and accept what's happening to our world as the new normal.

As time goes on, things will become much worse, and we will accept it then too. So, what's the point in delaying the inevitable?

Chapter Forty-Four
The Good, and the Bad

I sleep for twelve straight hours but don't dream. The dust-covered sleeping bag slides to the filthy cabin floor when I stand.

I sit on the toilet and stare out the window at the thick tree-lined path Fabby and I used to go for walks on. It's overgrown, and covered in debris, but it still supplies a narrow way through. I wonder where it leads now. It once ended at an old farmhouse with an outhouse beside it. Fabby and I peered inside once. All it held were two holes in a slab of wood—no toilet paper, no running water, no magazines, or books to read. Primitive, yet useful when there are no utilities inside your house.

I dab my privates with the last few squares of toilet paper and sigh. Unless I plan on drip drying for the rest of my stay, I'll have to leave to buy more toiletries. I glance at my hospital gown swaying on the line. Not quite the right amount of attire for grocery shopping. I should have gone home first, but at the time, I was using my heart and not my mind.

I'm afraid to leave. Afraid that things have gone awry since my abrupt departure and solemn warning to the world.

I step out onto the porch, and my foot drops into a soft spot in the wood. Blood oozes from the sharper edges, while the mushy pieces caress the rest of my ankle. It holds me in place like a finger trap, tightening as I pull. I sit my bottom down, grip the edges, and pull them aside, freeing myself. It could have been worse. My whole body could have lodged inside and held me captive, but I couldn't be so lucky. I hobble to the clothesline, yank my gown off, and tie it in the front. The creek isn't far, so I limp my way to it. It's not very sanitary, but it's better than nothing. I dip my bloody ankle in and scrub the bits of wood lodged inside the wound.

Twigs snap behind me as someone approaches. I tiptoe to the opposite side of the creek and turn around. Two young hunters, with rifles on their shoulders, gawk at me.

"Hi," I say with a soft wave and reddening cheeks.

"Are you okay?" the dirty blonde asks as he rests his weapon on the ground and wipes his pointy draining nose.

"Yes."

"I have a first aid kit in my bag. I can clean that properly and wrap it for you if you'll let me."

"It's okay. You don't have to do that."

"Look, I get it. I'm a stranger and touching you may be uncomfortable. How about I pass it over to you, and you can do it yourself?"

"Okay," I say without looking at him.

He removes his backpack, unzips it, and pulls out a small pouch. "Here you go," he says tossing it to me.

"Where are your clothes?" his friend asks, raising his thick black eyebrows.

"I left them at the hospital," I say as I apply ointment to the wound and wrap it several times with gauze.

"Left against medical advice, did you? Can't blame you there." He removes his pack and riffles through it. "These are probably way too big, but there's a drawstring on the pants at least," he says pulling out a long-sleeve t-shirt and a pair of sweatpants and holding them out to me.

"Oh, I couldn't take those."

"Of course, you can. We are just finishing up, and I didn't fall out of a tree stand and into a pond this time, so I won't need them. Here," he insists extending his arm over the waterway.

"Thank you."

In my mind, I wonder why they came here. Perhaps God led them to me so I can see people can still be decent despite what happened.

I pity them, for their kindness isn't enough to save us.

"Do you need anything else?" the blonde asks digging through his bag. "I have some granola bars, a couple of bottles of water, and even some toilet paper left."

My eyes light up at the thought of not having to go into town yet. I just need a few more days to think. Maybe that's their purpose. To give me more time.

"Tell you what, take the whole bag. It's old and I need to buy a new one anyway." He swings it over to me and it drops beside me.

"I can't pay you for this."

"And I'd never ask you to."

"Here," the dark-haired one says. "Take mine too."

It lands on the other side of me. "Thank you so much for your kindness. What are your names?"

"I'm Josh…," the blonde says then points to his friend. "…and this is Eric."

"I'm Libby."

"Nice to meet you. Well, we have to get home, dinner is waiting for us. You're more than welcome to join if you like. We live a few miles down the road."

"Thank you for your kindness, but I prefer to stay here."

"Suit yourself," Josh says, picking up his rifle and slinging it over his shoulder.

They stomp to the muddy path and disappear as I lift the shirt to my nose. Eric's cologne smells like what Papa used to wear. A lump develops in my throat, and I swallow hard as my emotions take over.

I smell it again.

I want this. I need this. I want to be close to them again. Memories rush over me as I pull the top over my head and sniff the sleeves. "Papa," I whimper.

I rush around the hole in the porch and grab Mama's soap from the tub ledge. I inhale its scent, drop to the floor, and close my eyes. "Mama."

They spring open, and I leap to my feet. Drawers fly from the dresser and doors snap off the cabinets as I desperately search for a piece of Fabby. I peek under the cot. Hiding in the shadows, in the way back corner, Fabby's stuffed goat Regina bought for her lies on its side. I yank it from its hiding place and hug it. It wreaks of mold, and dirt, with a slight scent of her remaining. "Fabby."

I lie down on the cot, rest Mama's soap on my pillow, cuddle up with the stuffed version of Asher, and cry myself to sleep.

Someone is in the room when I wake up. I sense their presence. I open my eyes slowly. The reaper hovers before me with his hand floating above my face.

"What are you doing here?" I ask.

"What happens to us when everyone dies?"

"You'll no longer serve a purpose."

"So, we will die too?"

"Technically, you're not alive."

"Aren't we?" it says cocking its hooded apparition. "If you can kill us, then we must be."

"I don't know," I say sitting up and rubbing my eyes.

"I like my job," it says taking a seat beside me. "I don't want to lose it."

"It's not up to me."

"Isn't it?"

"I haven't made a decision."

"When will you decide our fate?"

My elbows crack as I straighten them and stand. "Not today. So, please go. I need to think."

It has more to say, but it remains silent as it vanishes through the dilapidated walls. I hike up the oversized sweatpants, tighten the drawstring, and stare at myself in the distorted mirror. Time warped the framing and swelled its back cover bending my image around a wavy reflection like a funhouse mirror.

I pull my hair back and secure it with an old hair tie. It snaps and drops my hair back to my shoulders. "Of course," I say to myself.

"Libby," a familiar voice says behind me.

"Emmit, how did you find me?" I say turning around.

"Your father and I used to talk about coming up here and fixing the place up. Looks like it needs more than fixing though."

He gazes around the room, and his eyes stop on the stuffed animal and bar of soap. "Libby, I know you think you've lost everyone…"

"I have," I interrupt and walk around him.

"Now let me finish, young lady," he insists following me outside. "But you are forgetting who's left. Your Aunt Marie needs you right now. Hope, Regina, and Will, they do too, and so do I. I had nothing when you and I met, and if it weren't for you, I'd still have nothing."

"But you don't have your wife, and now I don't have my parents or my sister," I say wiping my frustrated tears.

"But you have us, and we have each other. I know it doesn't seem like it now, but things will get better with time."

"Maybe for us, but what about everyone else? What about what we the people have become."

"Punishing everyone, for the choice a few gunmen made when they took your family away is not justice, Libby. It's murder."

"No, Emmit!" I shout. "It's not about them. It's about everyone. Don't you see? God gave me the key to release His wrath."

I storm inside and pick up the bible from the floor. I flip through it and stop at Isaiah 26:21.

"For, behold, the Lord cometh out of His place to punish the inhabitants of the earth for their iniquity; the earth shall disclose her blood, and shall no more cover her slain," I holler the words at him then snap the book closed.

"The End Times? Is that what this is?"

"I'm sorry, Emmit."

"When?"

"Soon."

"So, I guess I should finish up my bucket list then," he chuckles as he strolls toward the door with his hands in his pockets.

"Where are you going."

"To find a good place to jump out of a plane."

"Skydiving?"

"Yep, my wife did it a few times and told me it was amazing, but I was too chicken every time. She made me swear to do it someday before I die. Might as well be today."

He shuts the door behind him still chuckling to himself. A smile creeps across my face as I picture Emmit's loose-skinned cheeks flapping in the wind as he barrels toward earth. Good for him. Going out in style. If only the rest of the world did the same.

I sit on the porch steps and contemplate my next move. The only problem is, I can't seem to think about anything, good or bad. It's like I'm teetering on the top of a wall, and my body hasn't decided which way it wants to fall.

The ground before me sinks, creating a large sinkhole. A demon crawls out and slithers beside me. I'm not dead and neither is anyone in the vicinity.

"What?" I ask abruptly.

It says nothing as it glares at me with a twisted smile. Instead, it rests its black, bony appendages on the soggy board of the step, and drums its nails. Another creature crawls from the hollow as its drumming intensifies.

I've heard this before.

In a movie Papa and I watched together, soldiers would use snare drums to signal each other and intimidate their enemies.

The demon turns its back on me as two more exit and join the ranks.

My eyes widen as a large number of reapers appear between the trees and float toward town. The devil's troops fall in behind them.

I peer above the canopy as rays of light breach the clouds in several locations. Angels descend and disappear beyond the fall foliage, as I come to a slow stand.

It's happening.

I have no more time.

Humanity has made its choice for me.

Chapter Forty-Five
Chaos

Buildings burn up and down Main Street, as I breach the trees. A television flickers in a shattered storefront as the President of the United States addresses the nation and calls for peace and unity.

At the bottom of the screen, a banner speaks of worldwide destruction as God's message spreads across the globe, triggering World War III. A man comes to a stop beside me, lights a Molotov cocktail, and smashes it into the president's face, distorting his image.

He turns to me and smiles. "What are you looking at?"

I gaze into his smug eyes, and utter, "A dead man."

His face pales, then turns dark as he seizes my sleeve, and yanks me towards the ground.

Rage floods through me, popping every vein I own out unnaturally. I tilt my head up, grab his coat, and scream in his face. He covers his ears as the burst of sound explodes through his canals rupturing his drums. My back lights on fire, turning my sweatshirt into ash as my wings rip through my flesh and cast a shadow over him. He drops to his knees and begs for his life.

"Too late," I hiss as the key God inserted under my skin rises to the surface.

I point it at the sidewalk under him, and shriek. The concrete cracks between his thighs, opens wide, and swallows him whole. Retrieving his soul is pointless, it's already in its rightful place.

A woman rushes towards me screaming as a mob chases her down. They catch her, rip the cross from her neck, and stab her several times. I fly over to them.

Their mouths drop as I hover above her, take her soul when it exits, and launch it over my head. The blade snaps in half as one of the men tries to kill me. I downstroke my one black wing and crush him flat into the ground. All that remains is a puddle of blood and a pile of skin. The others run, but it won't save them. I open their eyes to the spirit world.

A line of creatures stops their escape and turns them back to me. I open the blacktop before them, and one by one the demons dive on their backs and launch them into the lake of fire below.

Crying turns my attention to a baby still sitting in her car seat. Her mother lies just outside her van, with empty eyes, and a bullet hole blackening her temple. I reach inside and remove the child as a man approaches with his palms in the air. "Please, don't hurt her. My wife, she wasn't well, and when all this started…" he waves to destruction all around us. "…she called me and told me to come get her," he says pointing at the wailing infant. "So please, if this is the end of us, let me spend a little more time with her."

I cradle the child in my white wing and pass her to her father. He takes her from me and strokes my feathers softly. "Thank you," he cries and turns from my emotionless face.

A reaper and angel float solemnly behind them as a camouflage hummer crashes through the intersection killing them both. The teenage driver climbs out and feeds the hair on his head in between his inexperienced fingers. "I'm sorry," he sobs to their broken bodies putting his head down. "I just want to go home."

The boy squints in my direction, backs up, and runs into the alley as I take flight and head west.

The more I see as I soar over the streets heading for the interstate, the more I hate who we've become.

Once I reach I-80, I travel through fire, debris, and dead bodies for over two thousand miles. The police have given up, along with everyone else. I catch a glimpse of a few people holding hands as I cross an overpass.

It's too late to pray to Him now.

He's not here.

Watching the destruction of His world and His children is too much. That's why He created me to bear the weight of it all on His behalf. He couldn't stop me even if he changed His mind. I know now that is why I can hurt anyone and anything, including Him.

When I opened the gates, I sealed the fate of our species.

I arrive at the San Andreas Fault, fly straight up like a hummingbird, and hover above the buckled line. I take the key in my palm, snap it in half, and launch the pieces on either side of the tectonic plates. The Pacific and North American plates shift simultaneously. The shockwave crisscrosses through dozens of faults and rips California apart. Fires launch into the sky in the distance as the cities shake violently. The Santa Ana winds vibrate my back and ruffle the feathers of my wings as they carry dust from the desert into the cities and suck the air dry of moisture. I fly to the northwest corner of Wyoming and touch down at the edge of the Yellowstone Caldera. A demon, carrying a torch, crawls from the steaming center. It rips my white wing away from my spine, lights it ablaze, and tosses it inside the eye of the volcano. The eruption launches debris and lava high above us. All the surrounding states pile high with ash as it floats to earth, suffocating its residents and killing all the crops.

My spine boils as a new wing replaces the old one and matches the other side. I travel east across the continent. Ash coats my body, turning it gray.

People sit in a circle in a field wearing gas masks and holding hands. Their voices are inaudible, but I imagine they are saying their last rights before they die. I press on, weaving in and out of the rubble until I finally arrive on the eastern coast of Florida. I dip my toes in the warm water and swirl it in a circle. The ripples travel to the Gulf and Atlantic, creating multiple tropical waves, and spawning massive hurricanes. The water rises rapidly, dropping the lower third of Florida into the ocean. People flee for their lives, but you can't outrun water, no more than you can outrun death.

Chaos spreads across all continents as one disaster after another turns the world upside down. If nature doesn't kill everyone, people will do the rest on their own.

All I need to do now is return to the cabin and wait for the fires of the west and the floods and storms of the east to meet in the middle. Tornados will gather all who remain and suck us into the atmosphere.

I take my time returning to the cabin. The outcries of the suffering and condemned carry over the howling winds as I move solemnly northwest. Survivors erect crude crosses, built from the remnants of their communities, and downed timber. They join hands and pray aloud for forgiveness while battling the unstable atmosphere I have created.

It's not enough.

Where were they when it mattered the most? Cowering in their homes and doing nothing to spread the word and prevent the inevitable. This long line of worshipers extends for nearly a block—the most I've seen thus far.

I haven't eaten in days, yet hunger eludes me.

My heart is nothing but a black hole—void of feelings, void of forgiveness, void of love.

Suffering fuels me now, and I am content and full.

I can no longer see the stars—smoke, storm clouds, and dust obstruct the view. The irritants don't bother my eyes, for they are numb like the rest of me.

After a long and daunting journey, I arrive at the cabin. Winds have taken away part of its roof and tipped the structure to the right. I ascend the rotting steps, nonetheless, climb onto the cot waiting for me, and sigh. My wings fall to my sides, shifting the dust bunnies across the cracked floor. A ball of dirt makes it to the bathroom where the wind picks it up and swirls it around before letting it go.

The cabin rattles beneath me as the earth objects to the treachery I've unleashed upon it. I hum to myself and think about all the times Mama rocked me in her favorite chair on the porch. Air whistles between the glass and framing of the remaining windows. I sense the pressure right before they rupture and send shards into the room. A piece slices the side of my face. I swipe it with my thumb and suck the crimson from my appendage. A thirst for blood has always been present in my life. I never pictured myself as a killer, but one can only take so much disappointment in mankind.

We all die eventually. It may as well be for a good reason.

A horn blares repeatedly in the distance. I imagine people are racing to the center of the country, thinking they can outrun what's coming. They are merely circling the drain. A last-ditch effort to stay on the surface before the abyss sucks them inside.

It's louder now as the vehicle draws near. I push myself from my resting place and shuffle to the crooked door. A white van barrels towards the cabin at a high rate of speed. I take flight and hover above it as it comes to a screeching halt.

Leaves fall from trees like a waterfall obstructing my view of the ground below. I move closer, as a man climbs from the driver's seat, and shields his face from the battering winds.

"Libitina," Pastor James calls to me. "Please, stop. I need you to listen."

I shriek to the sky and rupture a black cloud above us. Torrential rains and hail pound his bare arms and head, piercing his pale skin. "I need you to see us."

See us?

Seeing anyone will make no difference, but he can certainly try. He casts the side door open and pulls Auntie Marie out into the open. Seeing her sparks something in me.

Hope.

I imagine how much courage it took for her to leave the sanctity of her home after so long.

But faith and hope are not enough.

I flap my wings, and blow off the remaining leaves from the trees, obstructing my view further.

Regina and Hope climb from the back. Will exits and wraps his arms around them to hold them steady. "Libby, please. You need to listen. You need to see," Hope yells over the howling winds.

Emmit stumbles from the van and grabs the mirror. "I said I wanted to skydive to earth, not have the earth skydive to me," he shouts as he chuckles.

A tiny smile creeps into the corner of my mouth. He has a point.

I swoop down, snatch him around the waist, and launch into the atmosphere high above the forest. "Is this what you want?" I ask holding his face in my hands.

"What I want young lady, is for you to open your eyes, and see. Not look, see. If you want to let me go afterwards that's fine. As long as you see."

"My eyes are open, Emmit, and I don't like what I see, haven't for a long time."

"That was the past. You need to see the future."

"I already have."

"Not like this," he insists as he takes my face in his hands and forces me to look down.

Below me, Pastor James, Regina, Will, and Hope pray in a circle up at us.

"It's too late for that."

"Keep watching," he says pushing my head back down.

A woman and child come from the woods and join hands with Regina, and Hope. The mother stretches her free hand, and another person, fighting the elements seizes it and squeezes hard.

The chain starts small but grows rapidly as more people take each other's hands and pray.

"Fly higher, Libby," Emmit insists.

"You'll die."

"It's worth it, for you to see the bigger picture," he smiles.

I swoop higher and higher into the sky.

"Libby, stop," Emmit pants as he loses his ability to breathe. "Look again," he whispers.

I gaze down at the entire state. Hundreds if not thousands of people create a human prayer chain.

"Higher," Emmit murmurs as he passes out.

As I move upward, Emmit's soul separates from his body, salutes me, and floats to heaven on his own.

Sacrifice.

I continue upward, unwilling to let his human frame fall to the ground below.

If the land extended to every continent, the chain could create a circle around the entire globe. The world has united for the sole purpose of changing my mind and proving they are worthy.

One massive display of unity and faith.

Something I would have never expected.

I dive to the ground, leave Emmit's body beside the grave of his wife, and fly parallel along the line of worshipers.

They are all praying—to their God, to my God, to our God.

All of them.

There are no enemies here. Just people unwilling to give up despite the current state of things.

Faith.

Hope.

Courage.

Sacrifice.

Unity.

Combined, they light a fire inside me.

I cast the black clouds aside and ride a ray of sun straight to heaven.

God says nothing as I approach His mountain and sit beside Him. He leans forward peering over the cliff at the line below. Prayers echo around us. He reaches behind my back and touches each wing, changing them both to white.

"Bringing them together comes at a price," His voice booms as He towers over me and drops the two halves of the broken key into each of my palms. "The choice is yours."

Chapter Forty-Six
As One

I curl my fingers around the two pieces and say a prayer of my own. The price of saving their lives will cost me mine.

Not everyone will survive what I am about to do. I hope that some of the people who care about me, and still love me, despite what I've done, will have the opportunity to live on.

I'm not asking for anyone's forgiveness, and this decision doesn't come lightly. I hope those who make it through stay on the righteous path, and remember this moment, and what could have been their last days on this planet.

I soar over the edge and circle my way down to the earth. Regina hovers over Will's body. A branch snapped in my absence striking him with a fatal blow. She wails to the heavens as I take the two halves of the key and slam them together.

The shockwave throws them to the ground as it travels outward and around the globe. The continents shift one last time, joining together like they once were long ago.

A large hole near its center fills with fresh water from the mountains surrounding its basin. A river takes the excess and washes it out to sea. The earth buckles, and the environment adjusts, and settles as the sun beams down on mankind's new home. Natural disasters will keep them humble and be a constant reminder of what happens when we lose ourselves, our faith, and our humanity.

Will this save them from extinction in the future?

Perhaps not.

But that decision will fall into the hands of another for I have made my choice, and I choose to forgive, and to save.

I ascend high and view my creation from above. The mountains along the cliffs surrounding them will supply a barrier from the raging sea, and Mother Earth's womb will protect them and supply them nourishment in its center. Fruit trees and edible vegetation line the hills and mountainsides. Wildlife weaves in and out of view as they gain their bearings and search for a new place to call home.

Balance takes time, and life won't be easy. There will be times of great tribulation, now and in the future, as people grieve their lost loved ones and adjust to starting over with nothing but the clothes on their backs.

I circle back to earth and stand at the water's edge.

Slowly people filter through the trees, taking in the awe and wonder of the beautiful place I have created for them. With a sky so blue, and water so clear how could they not believe in miracles?

As more arrive, they shake hands, hold each other, accept each other, and work together to aid the injured and inconsolable.

Their sadness weighs heavy on me.

I drop to my knees as my wings snap off and float away. They drift into the river and disappear into the canyon that leads to the ocean.

Strangers rush to me as I fall sideways into the grass. A man tips me onto my back and speaks to me, but I can't understand his muffled words. Burning rubber filters through my nostrils as my eyes roll back, and I shake violently. Wave after wave slams through my head, until finally all is still.

I float above them. My wings have returned. A woman pumps my chest up and down while the man breaths into my open mouth. I fly away from them and sit atop the mountain overlook. They can't save me, but it doesn't stop them from trying. After several minutes they sit back on their bottoms and hang their heads.

Papa sits beside me and rests his arm over my shoulders. I lean into him as Mama and Fabby join us on the mountain.

"I'm sorry I couldn't save you."

"Don't be. We are all together now," Papa says.

Fabby takes my hand, and we float to the other side of the ridge. She points down to the far side of the lake. Hope and Regina sit on the beach supporting each other with their frames. I soar off the cliff and place my feet in the water as I sit in the sand next to Regina.

"I know you're here, Libby," Regina says to the empty space beside her. "I want you to know, we forgive you. All of us do."

I kiss her cheek, chilling her skin. She smiles and touches her face. "We love you too, Libby."

I leave them and walk along the waterway.

People gather, build fires for warmth, and erect shelters to shield the sun's rays. They share what little food they have with each other.

Less than a million people remain once the dust settles. Are all of them faithful to God?

No.

But one thing they could all agree upon is the survival of the species. Unity saved their lives, and unity is all that matters now. Keeping the peace, putting differences aside, and working together as one will help them grow.

I'm back with my family. It's all I have wanted since those fame-seeking men took their lives on that fateful day. Sacrificing myself not only saved humanity, but it also saved me from a lifetime of loneliness. If things ended differently, there would be nothing left—no angels, reapers, people, or demons.

This is better.

It took millions of years for the continents to divide. I returned them to one in a day. It isn't the same as back then. I had to make a few adjustments to ensure the protection of the remaining few. There are still streams, other bodies of water, deserts, and mountain ranges. They just don't exist in the same places as before. It's just one more adjustment people will need to make as time goes on and the environment stabilizes. Seasons will be different, but they'll adapt.

A body of water surrounds our new continent. No other land masses exist. One day people may venture beyond our borders and circle the continent to explore. There will be no need to venture further than that for there is nothing to find.

Two little girls run through me and into the water. They laugh and dance around holding hands. Their parents smile despite their bloody faces, and battered bodies covered in filth. The sun shines through their black curly hair as three more children join them.

Inside we are all the same.

We bleed red.

We all live, and we all die. Perhaps not at the same time or in the same way, but it's an unavoidable part of life.

Accepting change will be difficult. But if they stick together, remember this moment, and appreciate this second chance, they will survive.

Emmit approaches me, holding his wife's hand. They swing their interlaced fingers back and forth, stopping before me. "This is my Miriam," Emmit says to me. "Miriam, this is Libby."

She shifts her white dress with flowers dotting its fabric and curtsies. "Pleasure to meet you," she smiles.

"Nice to meet you too."

He kisses the back of her transparent hand and steers her around me. A teenage boy freezes for a moment as they pass through his body and continue walking.

I stare at the bible in the teenager's hand and smile. I didn't recognize him at first. Ash coats Adam's hair and blood smears across his face. He stands before a group of people sitting around a fire and opens his book. Everyone bows their heads as Adam speaks of God's mercy.

God gave me the power to save him and now I know why. He will be their minister. Adam will teach the word of God to the unfamiliar and explain why this happened to the survivors who don't understand.

Adam stops praying and nods as I rest my invisible palm on his. "Don't worry, Libby. I'll take good care of them."

I kiss his face, chilling it with my touch. Adam swipes a tear from his right eye and continues reading.

I glance out at the reflection of the sun shimmering off the water then turn to the land and take off. I sit beside my family once more and watch people from above.

Scientists named this future continent Pangea Ultima years ago, but we don't call it that.

This is God's country.

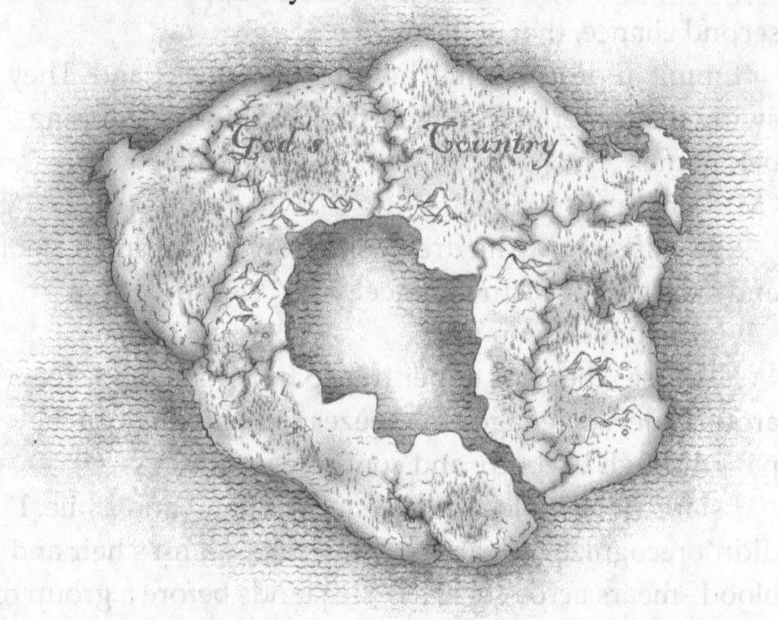

The End

If you enjoyed this book, please don't
forget to leave a review on Amazon.
Thanks for reading.

More books by this author.

No One Leaves
The Prickling
The Unnerving
Sidero: Book One
The Carpenter's Chameleon: Book Two of
Sidero

Dedication

I dedicate this book to my sister from another mister, my biggest supporter, and friend of too many years to count, Debrah Prettyman-Wright.
I love you. Thank you for always being there for me when I need you the most.